To dreams and those who continue to listen to you when you dream out loud.

One

"COME, MY BEAUTY, WE SHALL SEE IF WE CAN IMPRESS anyone tonight with our skill."

Brina patted the mare on the side of the neck, and the animal gave a toss of its silken mane. She smothered a laugh before it betrayed to those around just how much she was looking forward to riding out of her father's castle. She gained the back of the mare, and the animal let out a louder sound of excitement. Brina clasped the animal with her thighs and leaned low over its neck.

"I agree, my beauty. Standing still is very boring."

Brina kept her voice low and gave the mare its freedom. The animal made a path toward the gate, gaining speed rapidly.

Brina allowed her laughter to escape just as she and the mare crossed beneath the heavy iron gate that was still raised.

"Don't be out too long… Dusk is nearly fallen…" the Chattan retainer set to guarding the main entrance to Chattan Castle called after her, but Brina did not even turn her head to acknowledge the man.

Being promised to the church did have some advantages after all. Her undyed robe fluttered out behind her because the garment was simple and lacked any details that might flatter her figure. There were only two small tapes that buttoned toward the back of it in order to keep the fabric from being too cumbersome.

"Faster…"

The mare seemed to understand her and took to the rocky terrain with eagerness. The wind was crisp, almost too chilly for the autumn. Brina leaned down low and smiled as she moved in unison with the horse. The light was rapidly fading, but the approaching night didn't cause her a bit of worry.

She was a bride of Christ, the simple gown that she wore more powerful even than the fact that her father was laird of the Chattan. No one would trifle with her, even after day faded into night.

But that security came with a price, just as all things in life did. She straightened up as the mare neared the thicket, and she spied her father's man waiting on her.

Bran had served as a retainer for many years, and he was old enough to be her sire. He frowned at her as she slid from the back of the mare.

"Ye ride too fast."

Brina rubbed the neck of the horse for a moment, biting back the first words that came to her lips.

"What does it matter, Bran? I am promised to the church, not betrothed like my sisters. No one cares if I ride astride."

If she had been born first or second to Robert Chattan, there would be many who argued against her riding astride, because most midwives agreed that doing so would make a woman barren.

Bran grunted. "It's the speed that ye ride with that most would consider too spirited for a future nun."

Brina failed to mask her smile. "But I shall be a Highland nun, not one of those English ones who are frightened of their own shadows."

Her father's retainer grinned. "Aye, ye are that all right, and I pity those who forget it once ye are at the abbey and training to become the mother superior."

Bran turned and made his way into the thicket. Brina followed him while reaching around to pull her small bow over her head. The wood felt familiar in her grip. It was a satisfying feeling, one for which she might thank her impending future as well. Her sisters had not been taught to use any weapons. They were both promised to powerful men, and the skills of hunting would be something that those Highlanders might find offensive to their pride.

She snorted. Going to the church suited her well indeed, for she had no stomach for the nature of men. She could use the bow as well as any of them.

"At least I know that ye will nae go hungry." Bran studied the way she held the bow, and nodded with approval. "Those other nuns will likely follow ye even more devoutly because ye can put supper on the table along with saying yer prayers."

"I plan to do much more than pray."

Bran frowned and turned his attention to finding a good spot to hunt from. The burly retainer didn't believe her.

That thought sobered her. She would have to leave

soon, because the seasons were changing and the church was beginning to pressure her father for her. She didn't dread departing, beyond that it would be hard to leave her sisters, but she did detest the attitude from those around her that she was going to the abbey to do nothing but kneel in submission. Bran was correct about one thing, she would not be a mother superior who allowed the men who came to her church to act like savages the moment they received their absolution.

"Those rabbits will nae be waiting on ye."

Bran spoke up, his voice drifting on the wind from where he was perched in a tree. Despite the gray in his hair, he was still a strong man, and his legs with their knee-high boots were pressed against the bark of the tree to keep him solidly in position. His back was propped against a higher portion of the tree and his bow held steady while he looked back at her.

Brina smiled at the challenge in his voice. "I plan to fell one before ye do."

Bran chuckled and offered her a wink. "Ye sound like a lad."

"What does it matter if I am less than feminine? Better that I am practical, for that will bring me more comfort in my life with the church, and it will see more good done if I am not delicate but might face injustice with my shoulders set firmly."

Bran chuckled again. "For certain, it is a good thing that yer father has no' changed his mind about sending ye to the church, for ye have been raised too long with the knowledge that ye shall have no master upon earth."

"Now ye are teasing me, for I know the place that shall be mine. I simply plan to make the most of it."

"Aye, Brina lass, I can hear that ye do, and may God have mercy on those who try to cross ye, for ye will have none upon them."

Brina shook her head and swept her skirts away from her ankles so that she might climb up the trunk of another tree and perch very much in the same manner Bran was.

"I'd think that ye might be impressed with the fact that I intend to take to my place with such passion."

Bran didn't answer, but something entered his eyes that looked a bit like pity, and she forced her thoughts on to her arrow and lining it up correctly so that she might be able to ignore the emotions that threatened to send tears into her eyes.

She'd be a good mother superior. The best possible, because her father had given his word on the matter, and it was a poor daughter who shamed her father by refusing the place that he set for her.

Her sisters would wed their arranged matches, and she would be a bride of Christ. It was the way to maintaining peace and balance in the Highlands.

The light faded more, and the animals of the forest began to brave the semidarkness to seek out food. Brina didn't fear the night as so many did, but she kept that a closely guarded secret, for it was not something to share with those who did believe in witches and ghosts. It wasn't that she didn't believe in specters. It was just that she was not afraid of them.

An arrow sliced through the night air, and there was a thump as a rabbit fell. Brina bit her lip in reprimand, for her attention was wandering and now she had lost the advantage. Bran jumped down with a soft step, one he'd taught her to use while hunting. It was a skill that took practice and concentration, but he walked toward his prize, his feet avoiding the dry leaves on the ground so that no sound marked his path. He held the rabbit up, and even though she could not see his expression clearly in the deepening darkness, she knew that his face was split with a smile.

Well, he had earned his victory, but that did not mean she was going to return to Chattan Castle empty-handed. She focused her eyes on the shadows, seeking out any motion and listening for the tiniest sound. When she let her own arrow fly, it sailed true and straight toward the rabbit she had spied near the base of a tree.

She smiled before climbing down, remaining mindful of her every step so that she might be as silent as Bran had been. Her father didn't know that Bran had taught her such a skill, and she saw no reason to mention it. Such ability was considered essential for a boy who would grow into a Highlander. They were not the most feared fighters on the planet for no valid reason. Boys began training from the moment that they took their first steps. They practiced the art of blending in with the night so that their enemies might never know where they were until they struck.

Brina stopped halfway back to her tree and lifted her head. In the distance she could hear the faint sounds of a horse, its hooves beating against the earth at a fast pace. She climbed the tree nearest her and scanned the hillside until she saw the animal. A single woman rode it. A dark cloak fluttered in the breeze while she leaned low over the neck of her mount, but she had her hood secured on the top of her head to keep her features hidden.

"Who's that riding out?" Bran climbed a tree, but he only gained a view of the back of the horse and rider.

Who would be headed out from the castle at this time of day?

"Is she riding out to meet a lover?" Brina spoke the moment the thought crossed her mind.

Bran pulled in a quick breath. She'd shocked the man with her question, but she didn't lower her gaze in shame.

Bran grunted.

"There are things that no nun should be knowing about, because it will leave ye discontented in your maiden's bed."

Brina snorted. "What nonsense. I am not to know about lovers and their meetings, but as mother superior, I'll be expected to shelter those women sent to me when their husbands discover that they have fallen from grace."

Bran shook his head and refused her any further comment. Brina turned back to look at the path the rider had traveled.

So she was *riding out to seek a lover...*

The night was a perilous place filled with men who did not behave according to the rules that surrounded them during the day. Once you left the fortress behind, you submitted yourself to the mercy of whomever you met, and sometimes that was an ill fate.

"Enough hunting."

Brina frowned. "But we only have two rabbits."

Bran's expression was hard as he stared into the night, his bow hanging forgotten by one hand. "Aye, it will have to do. I need to return to the castle."

Suspicion filled her thoughts, but Bran didn't give her time to ask him any more questions. He was off to gather their horses before she reached the ground.

The woman must be insane.

Brina shook her head because she couldn't see how taking a lover might bring any true happiness. Lust was a deadly sin after all.

Insane, and no doubt about it.

❦

Brina returned to Chattan Castle with only the two rabbits, and the cook raised an eyebrow at her small offering.

"Are ye ailing?" The woman reached out to feel her forehead and frowned when she discovered that Brina was fit and solid with no hint of fever at all.

"My attention wandered."

The cook glowered at her. "And look what you have to show for all that lack of discipline. Only two rabbits, which will not go far."

The cook turned her back on Brina and mumbled while she took the game toward the long trestle tables that were used to prepare food. Even in the darkness, several women were standing at the table, using the flickering light from the great hearth to cut vegetables. Now that it was turning to autumn, the last of the harvest was being brought in, and there was an abundance of work for everyone if they did not want to suffer empty bellies once the snow buried the hillsides and streams.

"Do not worry, Sister. I believe it is the first time I have seen you return with so little to offer to the cook. She is simply surprised." Kaie Chattan, her sister, stood near the wall, while Brina hung up a cloak.

The cook heard and spun around with a snap from her fingers. "What's this bit of argument for ye? Did ye bring me anything for the table, Miss? Or do ye have blisters on yer hands to prove that ye have been of some use this day?"

"I brought ye some fish that I caught in a net while tending to the wash."

The cook made a scoffing sound beneath her breath. "Well, I still have no liking for yer tone, miss; 'twas full of pride, it was. I am yer elder, and my strict nature keeps every belly full during the winter. Recall that wisdom before questioning my methods of how I make sure there is plenty for all."

Kaie offered the cook a nod of respect. "Yes, I know, and I meant no disrespect but only sought to soothe my sister."

"She's to be a nun, and it is best she learns to make do without compliments." The cook came and took the basket of fish from Kaie. "I mean that kindly, young Brina, for I wish ye no hardship in yer future. It will bring good things to the Chattans to have one of the laird's daughters serving the church. I thank ye for doing yer duty to us all."

There were mutters of agreement from the women working at the table. Their knives never stopped moving, and the snap and pop of crisp vegetables filled the kitchen for a long moment while Brina felt the weight of too many stares on her. They were depending on her to take her place and please God so that blessings might continue to flow to the Chattans. She felt the weight of the responsibility pushing down on her while she suddenly thought of how it must feel to ride off into the night to please no one except herself.

The idea of doing only what she wanted shimmered like a dream, tantalizing her with the possibility of indulging her whims instead of listening to rules that she must obey.

Now you are the one thinking insane things…

Maybe it was time to ask her father to send her to the abbey, for she was rapidly becoming too ill at ease with the duty assigned to her. Perhaps if she left soon, there might be an end to her unease. All the women at the table had husbands and children; it was the babes who her thoughts lingered on the most.

"I'll say good night now."

Brina forced herself into action. She shook off her melancholy thoughts, determined to keep her chin up. She was Robert Chattan's daughter, and she was born of Highlander stock too. Her life would be good because she would make it so.

The hallways were dimly lit to conserve resources, but Brina discovered that she enjoyed the flickering of candlelight. There was something soothing about the shadows. She grinned, amused by her own thinking. She liked the dim light because no one might see her clearly enough to critique her.

There was a truth and a solid one.

She made her way through the winding stone

corridors that made up Chattan Castle. In spite of the way they all looked so similar, she knew them well from the years that she had been raised inside of them. What might strike a stranger as an endless series of hallways that all looked the same was something she knew how to navigate from recognizing a stone here and the chip in a door frame. Her own mother had spent two years needing help deciphering the passageways when she had come from the neighboring clan of Hay.

Her father liked his castle exactly the way it was, and made certain that any repairs to the interior maintained the same look, so that it would continue to be a labyrinth. He claimed that it would be their last defense if the stronghold were ever overrun. The inhabitants would have the advantage of knowing where the escape doors were hidden, while the invaders struggled to find their way.

Brina stopped when she entered her chamber, a soft gasp passing her lips and alerting the men inside to her presence. It wasn't fear that prompted the sound, but surprise, for the men were two of her father's most trusted captains, and her father stood with them. She could not recall the last time her father had entered the chamber that she shared with her sisters, Deirdre and Kaie.

"Come here, Brina."

"Yes, Father."

In spite of her recent thinking that it might be time to depart for her future, Brina suddenly felt her belly tighten as she moved across the floor toward her sire. It was very possible her father was there to tell her to go from her childhood home to assume the place that would be hers.

The day that had just passed suddenly felt too precious, but at the same time she was strangely excited by the prospect of going to devote herself to making sure that justice was carried out. As a laird's daughter, ambitious to become a mother superior, that position would give her the authority to right wrongs.

"Good evening, Father."

She stopped in front of him and lowered herself as she had been taught to do in the presence of her father and laird. There was a short grunt of approval, but she wasn't sure which man made it, because her eyes were cast toward the floor to complete her submission.

"Ye perform the acts of obedience so well, but yer tone is full of fire."

Brina raised herself and stared into her father's eyes. He was still a formidable man, even with his hair turning gray. The wrinkles near his eyes didn't make him look old, to her way of thinking, because her father kept pace with his Highlanders, never sitting down until they did. Even now he wore the same kilt and wool doublet as his captains, the three feathers in his knit bonnet the only difference, for they were pointed straight up with a brooch to keep them there. The captains had three feathers, but only one of them was positioned upright.

"I hear ye brought in two rabbits tonight. Tell me where ye were hunting." Her sire's voice was still strong and powerful too. It was also edged with authority and the expectation that his words would be obeyed quickly. What disturbed her was the hint of anger in his tone. Suspicion returned to needle her.

"Off in the north valley with Bran, in the trees there."

Her father cast a look back at the darkened corners. Brina could feel tension flowing through the air, and when her sire looked back at her, his face was a mask of disgruntlement.

"Did ye see anyone leaving the castle?"

Brina suddenly gasped, her mind connecting her sire's unexpected appearance and the serious nature of his questions. She should have thought to question how the woman she'd seen had been riding a horse. That fine animal was a mark of wealth, and so was the thick cloak that the woman had worn. Brina didn't need to see that the beds were empty to understand her sire's suspicion, but the idea stuck in her throat, for it meant that her sister Deirdre was turning her back on her clan, because Kaie had been in the kitchen.

"Sweet Christ, she's gone insane." The words went past her lips before she recalled that there were others in the room.

Her father made a low sound that left no doubt of his displeasure. Even though it was not directed toward her, Brina felt a ripple of apprehension travel across her skin.

"Ye have a temperament that would scare most men, Brina, but I suppose I should be thankful, for ye will tell me the straight facts."

"Well, of course I will. I do nae lie." Brina propped her hands onto her hips, and her father's lips twitched in spite of the darkness of his expression. "Nae, ye do nae, for ye fear no living soul because tradition demanded that I promise ye to the church."

There was a note of regret in her sire's voice.

Brina relaxed her stance, her heart aching to see him in such turmoil. "I will honor yer word, Father. I swear it."

"Ye swear too." Robert shook his head. "It's obvious that I did not force ye to learn to be meek and pleasing for a husband."

Brina felt her cheeks warm. "I should have said that I promise to make ye proud."

"Nay. Be who ye are, Brina. I let ye learn from Bran because ye needed more strength than yer sisters. Ye will have no husband to shoulder burdens for ye. I'm right proud of ye."

Shock held her silent for a moment.

Her father chuckled softly. "Did ye think that I would nae know that he was teaching ye to hunt with the bow?"

"I did think ye might be unaware of it." She raised her chin again. "But I swear… I assure ye that I meant no deception, only that it seemed rather unimportant compared to the tasks ye must deal with each day."

Her father growled, startling her with how much anger there was in that sound. She'd witnessed him yelling at other men, but he had always maintained his control with her and her sisters. That was a Highlander's way.

"Aye, there are pressing matters that I must face, ones I have no liking for, but I know now which of me daughters is set on deceiving me tonight." He pressed his lips into a hard line. "Did ye see her face?"

Brina shook her head, staring straight back into her father's eyes in spite of the rage she saw flickering there. "Nay, Father, I was too far away, and dusk fully fallen. She also wore a cloak with the hood raised over her head. It might nae be Deirdre."

There was a soft step near the doorway, and a figure appeared there, pausing in surprise just as Brina had. Kaie's eyes widened, and she raised a hand to cover her lips, but her trembling fingers betrayed her.

Their sire snorted. "Why so frightened, Daughter?"

Kaie's eyes shimmered with unshed tears, and she clutched the door frame tightly with fingers that had turned white. Robert didn't hold his temper in check tonight but let it fall on his second daughter.

"I've no stomach for a coward, and even less when that person is me own daughter. Stand ye firm in the face of my displeasure and tell me where yer sister is gone, for I see the guilt on yer face. Make yer choice, Daughter, for I'll nae be tolerating this behavior from me own children."

Brina had rarely seen her father so angry. He normally controlled his emotions and left one guessing as to his true opinion on matters. Once she had heard him telling her brothers to always mind their tongues, for as the sons of the laird, a hasty word might cause suffering when the other members of the clan followed those rashly spoken phrases.

Kaie shivered visibly, her delicate frame still in the doorway. Their father snarled softly.

"I told ye to step forward and face me, girl. Ye are born of Highlander stock, so stop shivering when ye should know full well that I am nae a man who is pleased when his word is broken. Yer sister is promised to Connor Lindsey, the banns cried years ago." Her father turned and pointed at the empty beds. "So tell me why she is no' sleeping in that bed and nae even beneath me own roof. Me men claim she is no' to be found."

"I pleaded with her nae to go…"

"Pleaded? Ye should have taken yerself to me, yer father, and told me of this sordid business! The Lindseys are nae a clan to be mocked, and I assure ye that Connor Lindsey will nae wear the horns of a cuckold gracefully! Are ye insane, girl? There might well be bloodshed over this insult to the entire Lindsey clan. I gave me word on the match, my solemn oath!"

"I told her that! I warned her that she would be found out, but she fancies herself in love, and I believe it to be true, for she is insane with it, unable to resist going to him." Kaie forced her quivering legs to carry her into the chamber. She drew in a stiff breath but managed to raise her chin in the face of their sire's displeasure. It gained her a grudging look of acceptance from their father, but fury still danced in his eyes. He pointed at her with a finger that carried the authority of the laird of the Chattans.

"Where is she?"

"I do nae know! I swear it on Mother's grave!"

Their father opened his hand, and Brina gasped. She stepped in front of her sister so quickly, her father didn't have time to realize her intention.

He delivered a sharp slap to her, but even in his anger, he controlled his much greater strength and used the flat of his palm to strike with. A blow from his closed fist would have sent her stumbling across the floor, possibly knocked her senseless too. Pain went through her jaw, and her head turned with the strike, but she jerked her face back toward him immediately.

"Kaie is too delicate for yer strength, Father."

"Ye are every bit the image of yer mother too, Brina." He pointed at her. "Step aside and allow yer sister to face what she has earned."

"She was torn between ye and Deirdre."

Her father was furious now, his face darkening, but Brina stood solidly in place.

"She has brought it to my feet with her silence on this matter! Step aside."

"I will nae."

A single sniffle got past Kaie's lips before she drew in a stiff breath and silenced herself. Laird Chattan propped his hands on his hips and glared at Brina.

"'Tis a fortunate thing that yer place at the abbey is already secure, Brina, for ye have a stubbornness that would offend any man I tried to wed ye to, and that is the truth."

He shook his head. "But it is also a fact that I admire yer spirit, for it reminds me of yer sweet mother."

Robert Chattan reached out and pushed her aside with a hand that was more controlled now. Brina moved, and her sister stiffened.

"Straighten yer spine, Kaie. Ye are promised to Roan McLeod, and he'll nae be thanking me for sending him a wife who trembles anytime he forgets to soften his words."

"I'm sorry, Father."

"Ye should be, for this is no light matter, but I

have to find yer sister before young Laird Lindsey gets wind of this affair. The man is a Highlander through and through and may just choke the life out of her for taking a lover who is his sworn enemy."

"Melor Douglas loves Deirdre; she told me that he said so."

"Is that a fact?" Their father's voice turned mocking. "Why, then, is the man no' at me table to ask for her? Are ye so naive as to think that a man will nae say many a thing when his cock is hard or when he is intent on shaming a man he considers his enemy? The Douglas hope to inherit the Lindsey land through Connor's sister, who everyone knows they intend to force to wed one of their own. I made an alliance with Connor Lindsey to keep those bloody Douglas on their own land and to make sure they gain no more territory, or we'll have them raiding us. Since I put my name on the parchments, the other clans have recognized Connor as the Lindsey laird, and there is balance once again. Without that, there will be blood spilled come spring, have no doubt of it, Daughter."

Kaie smothered a horrified gasp.

"Ye see there? That's why marriage is a matter for yer father to be negotiating, because there are details that come into play far beyond whether or no' a lass takes a fancy to a lad." Their father stopped for a moment and fixed Kaie with a hard look. "Are ye still pure?"

Kaie stiffened, her face tightening. "I most certainly am."

"Mind yer tone, Daughter. Those who allow scheming to happen without raising the alarm deserve to have their honor questioned. Ye will nae be escaping this with a few words tossed at me declaring how repentant ye are. This is more than just one girl shaming her father, because I am laird of the Chattan. Ye have been taught that since ye were old enough to leave yer nurse's arms—everything ye do has more weight because of who yer father is."

"I would happily remain pure forever, Father. I do nae want to wed."

Their sire made a disgusted sound and waved his hand in the air.

"Enough, I've a daughter to fetch back, and yer future is settled."

Kaie suddenly found her courage. "Please, Father, send me to the abbey. I want to be a bride of Christ."

"Has this castle been invaded by demons?" Robert sputtered because he was so frustrated. "Both ye and Deirdre seem to have gone mad with the desire to argue against the place that ye have known would be yers by my word."

"It is nae madness, Father. I have a true calling to serve the church." Kaie hit her chest with a tightly closed fist. "Allow me to go in Brina's place."

Brina felt her breath freeze in her chest.

"Enough, Daughter. I've shook hands with Roan McLeod, and that's the bond of every Chattan."

"Give him Brina," Kaie insisted.

"Nay." Their father made a slashing motion with his hand. "Yer sister has been raised to obey only God as her master; she'll take her position at the abbey."

Laird Chattan walked to the door, his stride taking him there quickly. He and his captains were gone almost in the same moment his words finished echoing between the stone walls. That left Brina and Kaie with nothing, save for the soft flicker of the candles that burned on the table.

"Do nae look at me like that, Brina. I meant it. I want to remain pure, not wed." Kaie snarled her words, turning so quickly that her skirts flared out from her ankles.

"Yer temper is misplaced, Kaie. I am a daughter too and made no choice on where either of us is intended to be sent."

Brina's voice was loud and bounced off the chamber walls. Her sister flinched, but Brina felt no remorse for her.

"How could ye keep silent? Men may well die over this."

Brina shivered, and it was not the chill in the air that caused her to do it; it was the possibility of revenge from the Lindsey clan.

"The Douglas clan would be a far-better alliance," Kaie snapped. "They are in love, and a Douglas would be a safer marriage in these times."

"The Douglas seek the crown, and everyone knows it. Deirdre may well stand beside her lover when he is run through because the rest of the clans do nae want the Douglas to hold so much power. We have a king."

Kaie shook her head. "A king who is naught but a boy. Who knows if he shall ever grow up? He would not be the first boy king who died before becoming a man and he has no brothers."

"You should nae say such things." Brina turned to look back at the chamber doorway. They had no door because they were maidens, and closed doors inspired rumors.

"And you should no' be so trusting…" Kaie's words trailed off, pity covering her features. "You have everything that I desire."

"But why have you never spoken until now, Kaie? Father could nae reward ye after the captains heard that ye did nae tell him about Deirdre."

Brina failed to mask her frustration. It bled into her tone, and she realized that she was becoming far too discontented with her lot. That was a poor choice to make for the only one who would suffer from her unhappiness would be her.

Her sister wrapped her arms around herself. "I'm sorry, Brina. Ye are correct, but I do nae have the same spirit that ye do. I long to go to the abbey, where I can commune with God."

Brina felt shock move through her. Kaie looked at her with eyes that were full of regret.

"I thought that maybe the feeling would pass, but it has done naught but grow and grow, until now, I feel as though I might burst with it."

Brina was tempted to go to their father in spite of the anger that she knew arguing with him would bring.

"I'll speak to Father for ye, Kaie."

Her sister blew out a soft whimper. "Ye were right when ye pointed out that my timing could nae have been worse. Father will nae allow either of us to disobey him. He cannae risk losing face with the other lairds because his daughters won't obey him."

Hopelessness invaded the chamber, and Brina felt it keenly.

As the daughters of the laird, they were expected to do their duty just as any boy born on Chattan land. Without remaining strong, the clan might be overrun by another one, and that would mean death for the men and slavery for the women.

She was expected to take her position as a nun, to please the church and God so that the harvest would be good and disease kept away. Brina shivered again, because part of her envied her sister Deirdre for the courage that had seen her embracing what she wished. It would not end well, or at least the chances of her lover becoming her husband were slim at best.

Brina lay down in her bed and offered a prayer of hope for a happy future. She and Kaie seemed destined to make the best of what their father wanted for them, but Deirdre was bold enough to challenge him.

Brina wished that she had more faith in having her prayer answered.

❧

If love was insanity, Deirdre was happy to commit herself to the illness. She hoped she never recovered. Melor Douglas cupped her head between his hands, holding it steady while he placed a kiss against her mouth. It was a demanding one that would leave her tender on the morrow. But for the moment she let passion turn the hard touch into something she enjoyed and returned. Melor pressed her down, moving his hands from her face to her chest, where he eagerly cupped the globes of her breasts through the fabric of her robes.

"Let us disrobe…" Deirdre threaded her fingers through his hair and whispered against his ear.

"Nay, I'm hard and needy of yer wet sheath. Hike yer skirts."

Deirdre frowned, a prickle of worry crossing her mind. Melor had abandoned the sweet touches that he had used to lure her into his embrace, almost in the same moment that she had yielded her purity to him.

"Melor... stop... I will nae be the entertainment for yer men." She smoothed a hand over the bulge of his biceps. "Send them away."

He growled at her, his hands grasping her hips with more strength than she liked. His hold bruised, and she gasped with discomfort.

"Ye'll do what I say, when I tell ye, woman, because I am yer master."

"Ye are nae yet, no' until ye see my father."

Fear was beginning to wind through her, and Deirdre tried to fend it off. Melor was her lover, the man she had braved the night to be with, but he had yet to make good on his word to see her father.

She would be his wife.

It wouldn't be the first time a Scot had married his mistress. Unlike the English, Scots often followed their passions such as she had. She was as much a Highlander as her brothers or Melor and the Douglas retainers who stood nearby to guard his back.

"I mean what I say, Melor Douglas. It is time for ye to keep yer word and ask my father for me."

"Is that a fact?" He chuckled, but it was not a kind sound. His hands released her hips, and she stepped away from him.

What she witnessed on his face turned her cold, for

there was no sign of the man who had seduced her with kind words and promises of a bright future.

"Ye need a lesson, Deirdre, one that will teach ye that I am yer master and what I want from ye, you will give without quarrel."

Arrogance twisted his features into a visage that wasn't nearly as pleasing as she had thought it to be. But she stood up to him, refusing to crumple at his feet.

"Ye promised me that we would wed." She raised her voice so that his men heard her clearly. "It is the only reason I gave ye my innocence."

He reached out and tapped her chin with the tip of one finger. "But ye cannae bargain with what ye do nae have any longer, Deirdre Chattan. Better learn that quick and maybe a few more things to keep me satisfied, or ye'll find yerself discarded like the slut ye are."

Slut…

The word burned across her mind. Deirdre leaned against the wall, too overwhelmed by the horror of seeing the man she loved sneering at her so gleefully while his men enjoyed the entertainment of watching her be shamed. She searched his face, seeking out any remaining hint of the man she had defied everything to be with. She found nothing but a savage looking back at her. Melor was only interested in what pleasure her flesh might provide him. Lust twisted his features as the tip of his tongue appeared and swept across his lower lip. The scent of whisky touched her nose.

"Ye'll get on yer knees now and suckle my cock like a mistress should know how to do…"

Her horror evaporated as her temper flared up. "Not until ye wed me as ye promised."

Melor reached out and struck her across her face. It was no light slap, but a harsh blow that sent pain through her head and neck. Deirdre jerked her head back around to face him with the aid of her temper.

"Ye promised on yer clan colors, Melor! Ye swore to me!"

He laughed at her. "But it does nae matter, Deirdre, because ye are nothing but a woman who disobeyed her father and laird. Ye will please me or begin praying that my seed does nae take root in yer womb and announce the fact that ye are a slut to one and all." He smirked and lifted his kilt to expose his cock.

"Come here, slut, and suckle my organ, or I swear I'll turn me back on ye and yer bastard." He reached down and handled his aroused flesh. "I have quite a few bastards, and I plan to plant some more of my seed good and deep inside ye before this night is finished."

Deirdre growled, her temper turning to rage. She lunged at the man she had fallen in love with and sent her knee toward the flesh that he was so determined to humiliate her with. Melor cried like a boy when she felt the sac beneath his cock crushing against her knee.

He jumped away from her, colliding with his men and toppling the chairs they had been sitting in. Their mugs of ale went crashing into the floor, while the room filled with the sounds of their profanity.

Deirdre didn't wait to see what Melor would say when he finally climbed back onto his feet. She raced across the chamber and tore the door open before anyone thought to try and stop her. There was a long hallway beyond the door that led to a steep set of stairs. At the bottom of those stairs was the main floor of the tavern where Melor had managed to convince her to meet him. It was half-full of men intent on drinking and playing games of chance while they enjoyed a bit of light from the proprietor's candles.

She left that light willingly behind, seeking out the darkness and her mare. Deirdre swung up and onto the back of the horse where it waited along the side of the building. She dug her heels into its sides to send the animal forward.

Tears streamed down her face, and she wiped them away with an angry hand.

She would never, never cry for a man again. All love between man and woman was false. Men were heartless creatures who understood only lust and power. She had been nothing but a tool for Melor to shame her father with. All the sweet words that Melor had murmured against her ear burned like a brand into her mind as the depth of his deception became clear. Lies she had believed, and worse yet, allowed to plant love in her heart. That affection withered now in the face of the sting still lingering on her face from his blow.

That was the truth of what men truly gave to women, pain and suffering. She embraced the hurt, forcing her thoughts to dwell on the memory of the look on his face after he had hit her.

She would never cry again.

❧

Deirdre didn't look at who was in the tavern, but heads turned in her direction when she left it. Behind the wool of their plaids that were drawn over their heads for warmth, several men watched from where they stood outside the walls of the establishment as she kicked her mare and charged off into the night.

"Well, it's true, even if I am nae happy to see myself proven right," Shawe Lindsey muttered beneath his breath and cast a glance at the mugs of ale being carried by in the hands of a serving lass. His throat was suddenly parched and dry beyond endurance, but he maintained his position next to his laird. Shawe waited to see what the man would do now that they had indeed discovered his bride-to-be a very long way from where she should be.

Shawe wasn't surprised by the silence of his laird. Connor Lindsey was a man who had been put in his place many a time while a lad, because he'd been born illegitimate to the way of thinking of many of the Lindsey clan. His childhood had been rough and full of fighting because the clan was in turmoil as it waited to see who would inherit the lairdship. The fact that his mother had wed his father, even if it was after his birth, had led to many who would have liked to see him die before becoming a man. Connor had learned to hold his tongue and keep his thoughts to himself well, something he was doing right at that moment while Shawe took another glance at the ale being served.

"Buy a round, Shawe."

Connor Lindsey didn't want to drink. He wanted to kill, and that was an honest fact. He produced a silver coin and sent it sailing through the air between him and Shawe with a flick of his thumb.

He also wanted to see whom Deirdre had been

meeting with even more, even if he suspected that he knew the answer well enough. There was one thing he always did, and that was never condemn anyone unless he saw the evidence with his own eyes. He stepped into the tavern and heard the slight ripple of whispers heralding his arrival. Men moved their gazes toward him, while keeping their faces on the companions they shared the rough trestle tables with. Long benches were jumbled about the tables, with only a few chairs at the far side of the tavern, where the high table was cleaned and waiting for a customer with the coin to spend on more grand accommodations.

The landlord looked at him, hope glittering in his eyes, but Connor swung his leg over a bench and straddled it. He wasn't there for wasting coin on having his ego pampered. The ale came from the same barrels, no matter if he was drinking it while on a bench or in a chair. Let the Douglas retainers he suspected were upstairs in the private suite squander their money.

Connor ground his teeth together. What was more correct to think was that Melor Douglas didn't think twice about spending the hard-earned silver of his people on his own comfort. The man held an interesting position in the clan, because while he wasn't in direct line to inherit any title, he still stood a good chance of gaining one, because so many of the Douglas were getting themselves killed. His fellow Douglas did everything they might to keep themselves in the man's good graces, because he just might inherit. Of course, that was a fine place for Melor to be. The man had all the money he wanted, but none of the responsibilities a title would press on him.

Connor had watched the man sidestep messy situations for years, but tonight he was going to connect the man to the deed of sullying Deirdre Chattan. A mug of ale landed in front of him, and Connor reached for it. He wanted to crush something, and his fingers wrapped around the drinking vessel with too much strength.

"We could just go up the stairs…" Shawe remarked.

"I'm waiting to see Melor Douglas."

Shawe raised an eyebrow, and Connor growled at him. The men around them were listening, and he watched one go up the stairs. Connor grinned, and Shawe chuckled in response.

"It does look like the fight will come to us soon enough. My purpose was to discover the truth of these rumors about Deirdre, and I intended to make sure I do nae jump too quickly and miss learning something that may be of use later."

Shawe lifted his own and drew off a long swallow of the amber liquid. "I've seen plenty already; 'tis a mess to be sure."

Connor stared at the ale but didn't lift the mug. He didn't trust himself to maintain control over his temper if he had even one spoonful of the intoxicating beverage inside him. Anger was flowing through him like a swollen spring river that had plenty of snow to feed it. But he'd learned to be patient and hold his thoughts deep inside until the time was right to strike out against those who tried to grind him beneath their boot heels. The Douglas had been trying to steal what was his for too many years.

That didn't mean he was going to allow Melor to ride back to Douglas land with a smirk on his lips.

"Maybe we should just take a ride on up to Chattan land and see what her father has to say." Shawe's voice was even, but his mug was empty, betraying how nervous he truly was.

"We'll be going up to Chattan land soon enough, but I'm going to deal with Melor Douglas first. I'm here to face the man and am nae leaving until I do."

Connor didn't care that a few heads turned in his direction.

Rage was flowing through his body, and it burned too brightly not to lend him strength, but Connor knew how to harness his temper.

No one was going to play him for a fool, not when his marriage was intended to restore faith in the Lindsey and his claim on the lairdship. Deirdre Chattan was going to discover that when he caught up with her, but the look on her face when she'd left told him that the true villain was Melor Douglas.

He was using the girl to try to grind Connor back into the dirt once again and smear the next generation with the same sordid rumors of the Lindsey laird not being the true heir. Since the Douglas still held Connor's sister, Vanora, that was something he could not tolerate.

Connor wasn't going to be so easy to crush now that he was laird, and he certainly wasn't going to allow his sons to come into the world with any rumors circulating about their legitimacy.

"Who's the man who claims he's looking for me?"

Melor was a bigger fool than Connor had believed. The man bellowed across the entire tavern from the middle of the stairs. There was a shuffle of benches and feet as men chose their positions on the argument about to break. Some tossed their silver toward the owner and made a hasty exit from the scene, while others moved to the side of the room where Melor was standing with his retainers. A small number remained where they were, unwilling to bow to the Douglas kilts that were clearly on display. There were McLeod, McLeren, and Monroe colors on the men still inside the tavern.

"Show yer face, unless ye're a coward and can only speak yer mind over a pint of ale like an old man."

Shawe drew in a stiff breath, but Connor pushed his plaid off his head and stood up. He heard Melor stepping up behind him and was amused by how heavy the man's steps were. For a Highlander, Melor wasn't very skilled, which left Connor respecting him even less.

"The Douglas dinna take kindly to men who say they are looking for them."

Connor turned to face Melor and had the satisfaction of watching the man stop abruptly. Connor lifted his foot over the bench so that his legs were able to branch evenly beneath him.

"If that's a fact, maybe ye Douglas shouldn't be toying with lasses who do nae belong to ye."

Melor snickered, his lips splitting into a wide smile. "Well now, young Laird Lindsey, as I see it, if ye can nae keep yer woman in her place, it is nae my responsibility to refuse to enjoy her when she comes to me."

There were chuckles from the Douglas retainers, and a few of them grinned openly. Shawe growled beneath his breath, but Connor maintained his grip on decorum. Melor's weakness was plain now; it was his arrogance.

"I suppose that I shouldna be surprised to hear that the Douglas have no respect for the church."

Every man wearing the Douglas plaid sobered instantly. They snarled, and their nostrils flared while Connor took the moment to grin.

Melor pointed a thick finger at him. "No man accuses me of such a thing, especially a bastard."

"Ye confessed it yerself, Melor Douglas, and I am nae the only man who heard ye bragging about having a woman whom banns have been read on. To seduce her was to disrespect the church, and there is no mistaking that. It's a simple fact."

There was a ripple of agreement from many of the men watching. Melor pressed his lips into a hard line as he heard it. Clearly the man wasn't accustomed to hearing men express their displeasure with him, for his skin darkened. He was too accustomed to people agreeing with him because of his blood.

"It does nae matter what ye say, young bastard Lindsey. I did have Deirdre Chattan." He snapped his fingers and grinned smugly once more. "I think ye should thank me for teaching her a thing or two about how to ride. I hear ye suffer from a lack of a good mistress and had planned to claim yer bride before winter. The fact that I showed her how to keep time when she's tending to a man's cock will surely come in handy when the snow flies."

Melor thrust his hips forward with his words, drawing chuckles from his men. He was still smiling when Connor lunged across the space between them, easily reaching him. The man was a sorry excuse for a Highlander, for he had misjudged just how fast Connor might move.

Connor sent his fist into the man's face twice before Melor even began to curse. Shawe followed with the other Lindsey retainers, and the tavern became a mass of profanity and flesh-on-flesh sounds. There were more Douglas retainers than Connor had with him, but the other men who had been watching joined in the fight. Tables broke into splinters as men were dropped onto them. Ale went splashing onto the floorboards, and the serving girls ran for the safety of the storeroom, while the tavern owner yelled at them all to take it beyond his door.

Connor was happy to do that.

He grabbed Melor by his doublet and threw the half-senseless man toward the door. Melor stumbled, the last few blows from Connor's fists having left the man searching for his wits.

"Ye try to insult me by bragging about what ye did with a lass who ye lied ta seduce, but the only one *that* brings shame on is yerself and yer clan, Melor!"

Connor grabbed the man once again and hurled him out into the night. Melor hit the dirt and spit out a curse that would see him locked in the stocks if anyone reported the man to his priest.

"Well, I had her Lindsey. I've fucked Deirdre Chattan!" Melor laughed. "There will be no stained sheet flying the morning after yer wedding. She'll likely birth my bastard and baptize it as yer heir!" Melor staggered to his feet, his men closing in to stand at his back. Melor grinned and wiped the blood leaking from his lip across the sleeve of his shirt before he spit.

"If we can nae inherit the Lindsey land one way, we'll find another, now won't we, young Lindsey?"

Connor felt his grip on himself slipping. "Better ride out while ye can, Melor Douglas. I am nae the only man here with no taste for the ambition of the Douglas. If ye have no honor with yer dealings with the Chattan or Lindsey, ye'll do the same to others once ye have what ye want from the Lindsey."

"Ye've got too much daring in ye to question my honor, Lindsey bastard pup."

Connor shrugged. "It is nae difficult when I see ye making war on me through a woman. I'm a Highlander, man, and I fight men face-to-face. That's Highlander honor, and what I see here is that ye do nae have it."

"But I've got cunning, Lindsey, for I didna have to force yer bride's skirts up. She embraced me of her own free will, just because I said I'd wed her. Better keep her under a watchful eye, for she is weak-minded." Melor smirked with victory.

There was a shuffling in the dirt as other men came forward. They were all Highlanders, and none of them cared for the fact that one clan was plotting to take over another.

Melor was still too arrogant, in spite of the way his eye was swelling shut or the fact that he and his men were grossly outnumbered. The man was too egotistical to realize that his clan colors weren't going to help him survive the next hour.

His men, on the other hand, weren't as impractical

as their master. They whistled for the boys holding their horses somewhere hidden in the darkness. There was the pounding of hooves against the ground as the lads came running in response to the summons. Melor looked as though he wanted to argue with his men.

Connor flexed his fingers, and the knuckles popped.

"By all means, Melor… stay. I've never been a man for putting off something that needs doing, and tearing ye apart is something I very much want to do."

"Ye would nae dare. I am heir to the Douglas title."

Melor's men didn't share their master's confidence in their position, for they unsheathed their swords and crowded in front of Melor to protect him, because they were honor bound to do so. Connor answered them with his own sword and heard the men behind him draw steel too.

"You are an heir, no' in the direct line for the earldom, and every man here knows it. Ye are vermin, and this world would be well rid of yer lying stench."

"Ye might think so, Connor Lindsey, but it was still my cock yer bride has been warming." He spread one hand out in front of him. "And every man here knows it."

"And 'tis my steel that I'd like ye to warm now, Melor Douglas, for ye need to be run through before ye decide to steal another bride with yer lies about wedding her. Every father in the Highlands will thank me for doing it, because we dinna need the trouble a man like ye brings with yer deceptions. Seducing a lass is fair enough, so long as ye do nae lie to gain her compliance. A man's word should be kept; that's

Highlander honor, and ye have tarnished it with this bit of foul play."

A grumble went through the men watching, and Melor took a step back, looking unsure for the first time.

"If she were any sort of good daughter, nothing I said would have drawn her out of her father's house."

Connor smiled. "Ah well, there we agree. No one should be taking the word of a Douglas."

Melor's eyes widened, and he lunged at Connor, making it past his men, who tried to keep him safe. Connor allowed the man to charge and let his sword drop away. Melor's eyes brightened with victory, but it was premature. Connor stooped and ducked beneath the swing of the large sword to come up in front of the man. Connor grasped a handful of Melor's doublet to hold him close while he pressed the tip of a small dirk against the soft underside of his chin.

"I'd like to kill ye, Melor, make no mistake, but I believe I will let ye live so that I might have the pleasure of watching ye be beaten by men who are just as ambitious as ye are."

The man whimpered, disgusting Connor. He shoved Melor toward his men and watched as they helped him mount his stallion. Once he gained the saddle, he turned a furious look toward Connor and the other men assembled there.

"I'll nae be forgetting this night! I swear it on the Virgin's tits!" He didn't wait for any response but kicked his stallion harder than any good horseman should. The creature jumped and started off into the night with a sharp snort of discomfort.

"Swine." Shawe spit on the ground and sheathed his sword. "Ye should have let me kill him if ye were nae going to do it."

"I'd rather watch his own kind eat him. With a lad on the throne, the Douglas are fighting each other for power."

Shawe shrugged. "Ah well, there is that bit of entertainment that we might look forward to, providing he does nae have us murdered before someone arranges his demise."

It was a possibility, but one Connor wasn't worried about. He turned and looked for the proprietor of the tavern. The man stood nearby, wearing the colors of the McLeod clan. Connor dug into his doublet and pulled a small leather pouch from a pocket inside the lining.

"For yer trouble, McLeod. The Lindsey do nae forget to even up with those they do business with."

The proprietor opened the pouch and peered inside. He nodded with satisfaction and offered his hand to Connor. They clasped forearms before the tavern owner tucked the silver inside his shirt.

"The Lindsey are welcome here, and I didna know about the girl or I'd have sent her on her way. I certainly knew nothing about the deception. I agree with ye that we do nae need that sort of thing, and I'll nae have it happening beneath me roof. Douglas colors or no'."

"The girl is my concern; forget her name. We all need to trust someone; it is a shame hers was placed in Melor Douglas."

Connor raised a hand, and his horses came with

nothing more than a silent signal. His lads were watchful. They might be young, but they were practicing the skills of Highlanders, and being alert was essential. Connor gained the back of his stallion, his thighs grasping the warm sides of the animal while he rubbed the neck of the beast in greeting. He looked toward Shawe and found his captain watching him, waiting on his next order.

"Now it's time to ride to Chattan land."

Two

"DID YE THINK THAT NO ONE WOULD SEE YE?"

Deirdre froze, recognizing her father's voice. She had somehow convinced herself that things could not become worse. Obviously she was mistaken.

"Or that of the hundreds of souls who seek shelter in this castle, no' a single one of them might flap their lips about the woman they saw riding out at dusk? On the back of a horse that I own and keep?"

Her father appeared from the shadows of the kitchen, and he was not alone. She had no reason to think that he might be by himself, but she realized that she had hoped for it. A laird who offered his unprotected back to the unknown was often repaid by a dagger being plunged into it. It was not even her father who ordered his Highlanders to keep close to him. They did it because they wanted the clan to remain strong. A murdered laird was a sure way to announce to every neighboring clan that the Chattan could not look after their own lands. That was a fine way to invite raids, for in the Highlands, if you couldn't hold what was yours, another clan would happily take it from you.

"Do nae dare stand there in silence when I'm giving ye a chance to speak, Daughter. Ye have shamed yer clan, and that is saying it gently."

"Ye are correct, Father."

Deirdre stepped all the way into the kitchen and felt the warmth of the hearth hit her chilled face. She hadn't noticed the cold so much, for the hurt inside her was a thousand times worse.

Her father snorted, his frustration clear as the church bell at dawn. "Fetch yer sisters to me chambers. It is time for me to look at ye all and make firm decisions."

Deirdre lowered herself and heard another gruff sound from her father. She didn't linger to allow him time to berate her for her respectful motion. Her future marriage to Connor Lindsey would have made a strong alliance for the Chattan. That she had thought to have an even better one with the Douglas was of little worth now.

Melor had used her to destroy her father's hard work in arranging the match with the Lindsey. Kaie might even suffer for it, because the McLeod might think that all three sisters were lightskirts.

She pressed her lips into a hard line and felt bitterness rise up to choke her. She welcomed it, embracing the hatred that sprouted from it.

Twin tears stung her eyes as she contemplated how it was possible that a few short hours had changed her outlook on the future so dramatically. What had seemed so full of hope and happiness was now a bleak and barren wasteland where the only thing she had was shame.

The word "barren" stuck in her mind. She hesitated

in the hallway, looking toward the chamber where her sisters slept and the dark passageway that would take her to the kitchen stockroom. The air was musty inside the stillroom but she knew her way well.

She reached for the herbs she wanted and muttered a soft prayer of thanks for the fact that they were not completely dry, else they would have been locked away, because they were potent plants that could do as much harm as good. She turned to look at the back of the room, but the two maids who slept there were curled up and facing away from the doorway.

Good, at least something was in her favor tonight. Or perhaps she should say morning, for the horizon was beginning to lighten. Moving to the hearth, she picked up a large iron hook and used it to pull the kettle that was left near the back of the huge fireplace. An entire sow could fit into the fireplace, but now that winter was looming, only a single pot simmered for the morning porridge and a kettle to have hot water on hand.

Deirdre poured a measure of the liquid into her mug and smiled at the steam that rose from it. She carefully recited the Lord's Prayer twice to time how long it needed to steep before lifting the mug to her lips.

Maybe saying the Lord's Prayer would be considered blasphemy when she knew that the potion would ensure that her monthly courses came, but Deirdre didn't know any other way to judge the time needed. Twice through for steeping herbs and three times to hard-boil an egg.

She refused to care about it and drained the mug.

The taste was bitter, making her nose wrinkle, but she smiled when she finished, because while Melor might have enjoyed laughing at her tonight, she was going to have the final word on the matter of whether she conceived his child. Yes, she had been a fool to believe his affection sincere, but she had never been so naive as not to drink a bitter dose of herbs every time she returned from meeting her lover. Men were so prideful that they never bothered to think that the women surrounding them might be every bit as clever as they were.

Pigs.

She tossed the wilted leaves and berries in the slop pail before wiping the mug and setting it back with the others. She hurried off to fetch her sisters. Tension tingled along her back, but she welcomed it, because at least she was free of the constant waiting for Melor to make good on his word. He never would, but she would not wallow in her grief. He wasn't worth that.

No man was. Not now or ever.

Deirdre held that truth close to her heart.

❧

Brina had never noticed that her father was aging.

His face looked more wrinkled, and his eyes lacked the sparkle she seemed to recall so vividly. The fire in his chamber was built up, the red and orange flames flickering through the darkness that had yet to be broken by dawn. A faint pink glow was beginning to tease the horizon, but darkness and shadows still reigned supreme.

Which made her suspicious, for the dark hours

were the time when evil was strongest. The night had already been full of tension as she waited on her sister's return. Deirdre was quiet and her face tight, while Kaie looked nervous.

"I suppose I'm to blame for no' wanting to lose ye." Laird Chattan nodded and turned to face them fully. He was a large man, with shoulders that were wide and a stance that was steady. His kilt was pleated and belted about a waist that was still trim because he was not prone to sitting about and drinking ale while those who called him laird toiled to produce that ale.

He was a true Highlander, one who stood shoulder to shoulder with his men and expected to sweat just as often as they did.

"I'm wounded by the way the pair of ye have repaid my leniency in this matter, Kaie and Deirdre."

Her father pointed toward her sisters.

"The pair of ye will regret this business, for the privacy I blessed ye with will be no more. Ye'll be watched now as befits those who betray me trust. Get ye gone, for I've no' the stomach to see ye any longer this night. Ye shall wait on my word as to what will happen to ye. Be sure that there will be action taken for this betrayal."

Kaie smothered a soft cry behind one of her delicate hands.

"And ye shall ask me for nothing, Daughter, for ye have earned only my scorn."

Kaie lowered herself and left the chamber. Two husky women who had been standing against the back wall followed her. Both were midwives and women of knowledge. Her sisters would not find it simple to dupe them. Deirdre cast Brina a look that was full of regret.

"Get ye gone, Deirdre. I am finished with ye until yer new nurses bring me proof that ye are no' breeding."

"He swore he would wed me, Father."

Their father turned on her like an enraged stallion. "Are ye daft? Did ye somehow miss the fact that young Lindsey came to our table and declared his intentions before one and all like an honorable man should? How ignorant do ye have to be no' to question any man who whispers to ye during a spring festival and then expects yer maidenhead without the church's blessing?"

"He was Melor Douglas."

There was a snort from the captains, but their father cursed. Viciously and long.

"A Douglas? I'd call ye simple, but I know full well that ye have good wits in that head. The Douglas clan is planning to rule Scotland, girl, and they wanted the Lindsey land bad enough to raid it. How could ye betray my word with a man who killed the family of the husband I betrothed ye to? Melor Douglas used ye for revenge against Connor Lindsey. Now get out of me sight before I forget that ye are at least young enough to be expected to be foolish when it comes to matters of yer heart." Robert Chattan shook one finger at his eldest daughter. "Better pray for yer mother's sweet soul, for I should have ye lashed, but ye are her daughter with all yer passion. So I find that I cannae order yer blood spilled."

Robert Chattan suddenly closed his eyes as a ripple of emotion went across his face. He drew in a deep breath before lifting his eyelids once more. His voice was quieter now, a hint of a ghost from years lost to the passage of time in his tone.

"Go on, Deirdre, for all that I treasured yer mother's love for me, I cannae forget that yer recklessness might well have brought disaster to us all. The Lindsey are nae a clan to be insulted, and that's a solid fact."

Deirdre went, her face white but her chin level. Brina heard her father mutter in the suddenly silent chamber. The wind howled beyond the window shutters, making them rattle a tiny amount.

"I want to thank ye, Brina, for no' shaming me."

"Ye should nae have to; it is my place."

Her father walked toward a long table that sat near the wall. He picked up a wooden mug and drew a long drink from it. Wind blew through the shutters, bringing the scent of the fermented beverage drifting on the air to her.

"Aye, and it is that place that I must speak with ye about. It is time that I let ye go, Daughter, in spite of the fact that it pains me to say it."

Her father's knuckles were white where his fingers wrapped around the mug. Brina stared at the telltale evidence of his regret, allowing that to combine with the hurt that flooded her heart and dilute it so that it was bearable.

"I'll ride once daylight is fully broken. I need to look Connor Lindsey in the eye when I reveal what yer sister has been about. We will take ye to the abbey along the way."

Brina nodded. "Kaie wants to go with me."

Her father stiffened, but she did not let that keep

her silent. "She does nae want to argue with ye, Father, but she longs to serve the church too."

His lips twitched up into a grin. "I am going to miss ye something terrible, Brina, for ye are a fine daughter." He shook his head. "Either one of yer sisters would have pleaded with me to take Kaie in her place."

"I do nae wish to marry." The words were past her lips before she thought of how disrespectful they would sound to the captains standing nearby.

Her father snorted with amusement. "Of course ye do nae. I've allowed ye to be raised up knowing that I would never present ye to any man who would tell ye that you were his."

Her father's voice trailed off as he realized that he was agreeing with her. She could see the resistance in his eyes.

"Please reconsider, Father. Kaie—"

"Enough, Brina. Ye know well that the place of a laird's daughter is to do what is best for the clan. The Chattan need the alliance with the McLeod."

Brina ground her teeth with frustration.

"If that is the way it must be, then I will wed Roan McLeod, and Kaie can follow her calling."

"The man would label ye a hellcat, for ye are no' meek enough for marriage, even to a Highlander."

The captains behind her father both grinned, and she felt her temper heat.

"I've been taught manners. I know how to be respectful, and I will nae shame ye."

Her father chuckled. "Ye'd try; I know that."

He drew a long sip from his mug.

"I might have been able to do that before Deirdre went and disgraced herself. Now my word will have to stand with the McLeod and the church, because if I go changing it on all three of ye, no one will accept it for anything."

She knew the tone of voice that her father was using. It was solid and unbendable. It was the laird of the Chattan declaring what would be, and no one argued with the laird.

He was trying to maintain peace.

Brina lowered herself before quitting the room. She struggled to hide the discontentment brewing inside her.

She would not give him a reason to label her a hellcat again. There had been few times that she disliked her sire, but she detested what he'd called her.

She was not a hellcat. Having the courage to speak her mind was not something to regret or place unsavory titles on.

She didn't return to the chamber that had been hers for as long as she could recall. She walked toward the stairs and climbed up into one of the towers that allowed the Chattan to see anyone approaching. Dawn was now creeping across the land, illuminating the shadows and revealing that there was nothing sinister there at all.

Brina looked over the fields stacked with drying bundles of barley and wheat. Pumpkins and squashes lay between the drying vines that they had grown on. There was still greenery where carrots and beets had yet to be harvested and taken down to the cellars. She lingered over the most common, thatch-roofed homes and the smoke rising gently from their chimneys. She drank it all in, trying to memorize every detail, for the next time she saw Chattan land, it would be from over her shoulder as she looked back on it.

But she would not look back. Her future was bright, and she felt an eagerness rising inside her to take charge of the duties that would be hers. She smiled, feeling the warmth of the rising sun on her cheeks. Soon enough every man who met her would dip his head with respect toward her. She was going to enjoy watching them rein in their pride, and that was the truth.

Call her a hellcat if they would, but she would not be bending to any man's whim.

❧

Laird Chattan rode from his castle with a full two dozen retainers. Brina traveled between the twin columns that they formed. She held her chin high, excitement sparkling in her eyes. Many of the inhabitants of the castle stopped their labors to watch her go. They leaned out of windows on every floor of the towers and quickly climbed the stairs to gain the curtain-wall walkways. Children waved, and someone began to ring the small church bell.

Once away from the fortress, she denied herself a last look at her childhood home. Only a slim splinter of doubt bothered her, and she was determined to pluck it before it festered. She focused her mind on the lessons she had taken to help ensure that she served the abbey smoothly in times of good harvest and poor. The sun rose, but it seemed to lack the warmth that should have still been upon them. Instead the wind whipped at the hem of her overgown, and she shivered when it grazed her knees above her boots.

Winter was coming early this year. The fields that they passed were busy. Everyone could feel the bitter chill in the air, and they hurried to bring in the last of the autumn harvest. Much of it was not ripe, but the sky began to darken, hinting at snow. Anything that froze would be lost, and the bundles of grain needed to be taken away before ice knocked the seeds from the stocks.

The horses didn't care for the weather. They kept to a brisk pace, eager to carry their riders to their destinations as fast as possible. The daylight faded quickly, and the sound of the wind became forlorn.

It also carried the sound of riders when they entered a narrow valley. The hills rose up on both sides of the road, making the sound echo. Brina suddenly felt unease prickling across her skin. Her father's men frowned and looked toward the road in front of them. Her father raised his arm to stop them.

Once the Chattan retainers obeyed, the sound of approaching horses tripled. Brina looked up and felt her eyes widen at the sight of the steep terrain they were in. There was only one road here that led down to the midlands where the large abbey was. The deepening dusk masked the colors of the men who rode toward them, making it impossible to identify them until they were too close to avoid.

"Hold."

Brina flinched, that single word echoing inside her head, for it was spoken in a voice that carried authority.

"Bad news always does travel faster than anything else." One of her father's captains spoke next to her and nodded toward the men coming up the road.

"There's young Lindsey himself, and the man is riding hard."

Connor Lindsey rode without a saddle. His stallion was a huge coal-black beast. Only a blanket was secured around the middle of its back, and Connor sat confidently atop it.

More than confidently actually. He looked pleased and was leaning over the neck of the animal to help it move faster. The man appeared half-wild, and his gaze swept over them with a quickness that drove home just how used to assessing others he was.

"I guess I should no' be surprised to see ye here so soon." Robert Chattan spoke slowly while Connor straightened up.

Brina gasped, the sound an impulse that rose from her chest instantly. It became clear why Connor Lindsey rode such a large stallion. The man was huge. He had golden hair and blue eyes that glittered like ice when they landed on her father.

"I was intent on riding toward Lindsey land—"

"Ye're going the wrong direction." Connor's tone was hard, and her father drew in a short breath.

Robert Chattan held up one thick finger. "After I saw my third daughter settled at the abbey, for it seems that I've kept me daughters beneath my roof a bit too long."

Connor's men waited on their laird, silently watching him to see what he would make of her father's words. Tension filled the air, and Brina shivered. There were more Lindsey retainers, twice as many as her father's, and their laird glared at her father with eyes full of anger. Her fingers tightened on the leather of the reins, her gaze moving from side to side in an effort to determine the best escape route.

"We needs discuss Deirdre," her father announced.

Connor snorted, and his captains mumbled beneath their breath. But the younger laird held up his hand again, and his men fell silent.

"Agreed." But the man didn't leave the back of his stallion, and that action declared to one and all just how little trust he had for the Chattans.

The rest of the retainers sat on top of their horses, their expressions forbidding. If the conversation turned ugly, there might be blood on the ground very soon. Their swords were still resting in the sheaths that were tied along their backs, but that could change very quickly.

"Laird Lindsey, be very sure that it was never my intention to keep this matter from ye."

Connor's eyes narrowed.

"Do ye expect me to believe that ye would have told me that yer daughter was meeting a lover?"

"I do." Robert Chattan sent the two words toward the younger laird without a hint of hesitation. "If ye do nae believe that, we have no reason to be talking any business henceforth, but I'd be sad to hear it."

Connor Lindsey snorted again. "I'm a fair bit more than sad at the moment."

"But ye are here, and make no mistake, man, I am very happy to see ye riding toward my land to try to talk the matter through."

Connor's attention shifted to her, and she felt his blue eyes cutting into hers.

"This is yer third daughter?"

Sensation rippled down her back and sent her heart beating faster. Men in her own age group did not look directly at her, at least not for longer than it took them to avert their eyes. Her undyed overgown reminded them instantly that she was promised to Christ. She couldn't recall the last time a man had truly looked at her for longer than a brief moment.

There was no mistaking the anger in his blue eyes, but there was something else there too. Brina stared at him, refusing to lower her eyes, because she felt compelled to show him that she was not timid. It was a reckless urge, but one that she failed to control. A hint of approval flickered in Connor Lindsey's eyes.

"Maybe we still have business to discuss." Connor looked back toward her father. "I still desire an alliance with the Chattan."

"I see the way yer thinking is heading, and I'll tell ye straight that the shame my eldest daughter has brought on me is enough. I will nae be open to telling the church that they will no' be getting the daughter I promised them."

Connor returned his stare to her, and if she were any judge of a man, he was doing his best to intimidate her now. She refused to lower her eyes, and something entered his that sent heat into her cheeks.

"Send Deirdre to the church."

Brina felt her belly tighten. It was a twisting sensation that did what his bold stare had failed to—she lowered her eyes because she could not master her own emotions and did not want him to witness them.

"I cannae do that, man. Deirdre is no longer... pure."

Her father growled the last word, his wounded pride obvious in his tone. Brina raised her eyes to find her father watching her with longing in his gaze. He nodded at her, regret thick in his expression.

"Ye've a good eye, Lindsey, for Brina is a fine daughter, but I cannae offend the Lord by sending him a child who I failed to raise with proper respect. Brina goes to the church as I swore she would. If ye will nae have Deirdre, I will release ye from our agreement."

Connor frowned. "I need a wife who does nae come with rumors. Yer eldest might do well at the abbey, where there are nae men to whisper in her ear."

Brina felt every set of Lindsey eyes turn toward her. She shifted beneath the weight of those stares, while her breath became lodged in her throat. Her father could change his mind. A shiver went down her spine as she looked back at Connor. With a few sentences, her father could send her to this man's bed.

Her father grunted. "I've said my piece concerning Brina, Lindsey. Take yer eyes off a bride of Christ."

Connor Lindsey looked back at her, and there was something in his expression that promised her that he was neither pleased nor content with her father's words.

"But I've no' said mine. Ye promised me one of yer daughters. Yer second is set to wed Roan McLeod, which leaves only yer youngest who is suitable for me." Connor nodded toward her. "I'll take her now."

"Ye will do no such thing." Brina spoke up without thinking about it. Surprise crossed the faces of the Lindsey men watching her, but their laird remained focused.

"I promise ye, lass, that I mean what I say."

Brina failed to understand the rising unrest inside her, but she growled softly. The man was clearly insane with his anger over Deirdre's betrayal, for no one challenged the church.

"So do I."

Her father scoffed. "Brina has nae been raised to accept a husband. Ye would find her neither meek nor obedient, Lindsey."

The corners of Connor's lips twitched. "Aren't nuns expected to obey the church?"

"Do nae attempt to compare the respect I have for God to something that might be given to a man."

His lips parted into a smile that flashed his teeth at her. "I see what ye mean, Chattan. She does have a fiery spirit."

"Mind yer words, Lindsey. She's promised to the church."

"And she would no' be the first third daughter who was exchanged for one of her older siblings when they dishonored their marriage contracts."

Connor's amusement vanished in the blink of an eye. Once again he was deadly serious, his eyes icy. But her father shook his head.

"I cannae agree to that."

"You mean that ye will nae, Chattan, and I'm disappointed to hear that, for it dishonors the agreement we shook hands on."

Her father stiffened, but Connor made a slashing motion with his hand.

"Enough. There's a hint of snow in the air, and I am going to gain the Highlands before moonrise. Clear the way, man."

Her father's men began to move before their laird ordered them to. There were far too many Lindsey retainers for them to want the confrontation to continue.

"We're nae finished, Lindsey."

Connor was already riding past Robert Chattan as he spoke. His men surged forward, the sound of leather and hooves against the rocky soil rising around her. Brina had been pushed back by the retainers until she was near the end of the Chattan men. Her mare tossed its head, the press of so many stallions near it making the animal skittish. She leaned down, sliding her open hands along the neck of the animal.

"There now. 'Tis well and good... They will soon pass..."

A hard jerk sent her falling against the mare. Brina closed her arms around the animal's neck as Connor Lindsey pulled her reins along with him. The mare let out a startled cry but turned and followed the surge of Lindsey retainers.

"Connor Lindsey! Unhand me daughter at once."

Connor turned his stallion with a skill that was impressive. It was also slightly sickening, because he was a master of the beast, and he turned to face her father after leaving her behind him. His men reached for her reins and moved her behind them. She slapped at their hands, but they continued to move her until she was in back of every single Lindsey man.

"Give me yer blessing, Chattan."

"I will nae!" Her father was furious, his voice

booming through the bodies that stood between them. "Send her back here at once, Lindsey. Brina is promised to the church!"

Connor's men began to push her even farther up the trail, four of them using their horses to herd her away from her clansmen. But it was the sound of steel being drawn that drew a gasp from her. She turned her head to see that the Lindsey retainers were pointing their swords at her father, Connor Lindsey sitting solidly in the first row of men blocking her kin from reaching her.

"I am more concerned with the promise ye made to me, Chattan. She goes with me now. When ye swallow some of that pride, ye know where to find me, but I swear I'll defend what I consider my own if ye ride on me tonight."

"Stop—Brina is nae yers…"

Connor Lindsey didn't give her father any more time to argue. He turned his stallion once again, and the beast was galloping up the trail before she finished gasping with surprise. He reached over as he passed, and grabbed the reins from her shocked fingers. Her mare began running alongside his stallion. She grabbed the mane of the horse, the pace too brisk to risk sliding off the back of the animal. She'd surely break an ankle or even a leg, maybe her neck if fate was in the mood to be cruel today.

She snorted. Fate was most certainly of the mind to be unkind. She tightened her thighs around the mare, instinct making her want to stay firmly in the saddle. Her temper flared, but dying in a broken heap on the rocky road seemed an even worse fate.

The Lindsey retainers were urging her forward. She could feel the press of the horses and men behind her. Her heart accelerated, making her breathing raspy. She looked toward the ground again as desperation began to pound inside her head.

Maybe she could roll when she hit the ground…

A hard arm clamped around her waist. She shrieked because it felt like she was going to fall between the horses when Connor dragged her onto the back of his stallion. The lack of a saddle made it easy for him to place her in front of him, sitting sideways across the wide back of the animal. He released her mare and imprisoned her within his embrace.

For a moment she was stunned into stillness. Her breath was frozen in her throat, and it felt like her heart stopped.

He was so warm against her…

Her eyes widened with the shock of feeling her body leaning against his. She could even feel the beat of his heart against her shoulder. They were riding into the wind, but her cheeks burned with a blush. It was so hot she struggled to escape from the contact that was causing it. She turned on him and gained a warning flash from his blue eyes before she shoved her hand into his chin. She couldn't think beyond the need to gain enough space between them to restore order to her thoughts.

"Release me…"

Connor grunted as her palm smacked into his jaw.

"Ye'll end up trampled, lass." His arms tightened around her.

"Then let it be so."

Brina kicked, and Connor made another sound that was low and full of frustration. He leaned down, pressing her against the neck of the horse. She had to turn her face to avoid having it pressed against the stallion's mane. Her cheek still ended up resting on the velvet hide of the animal, the sound of its breathing filling her ear because Connor looped the reins around his fists and used his body to hold her against the animal.

She lay trapped beneath him, unable to do anything more than growl with her temper.

"Being wed to me will nae be worse than having fifty sharp hooves puncturing yer flesh and breaking yer bones."

He whispered against her ear, and the sound shocked her again because it was deep and husky. Part of her wanted to smile in response, and that fanned the flames of her temper.

"I could nae disagree with ye more." She strained against him, snarling when he didn't move even a tiny amount. "Get off of me."

"I meant what I said about considering ye mine, Brina Chattan. If ye will nae behave, I will keep ye secure so that ye do nae fall."

She felt his leg near her feet and kicked at it. The only thing she gained from him was a soft grunt.

"I can see that yer father was no' jesting about the fact that ye are nae meek." There was a hint of enjoyment in his voice that kept her cheeks burning brightly.

"What I am is obedient to his promise that I serve the church. Ye should respect that. This is madness."

"It is done, lass, and ye may sit up only if ye do nae hit me again."

"Or ye shall lie on top of me like a brute?" Maybe it was unwise to offer him a suggestion of how to control her, but she couldn't resist the urge to bicker with him.

His chest shook as he chuckled. "Well now, if ye act like a hellcat, I will treat ye like one."

She sputtered with her outrage and strained against him once more. "I am no such thing!"

She could still hear him laughing, and it made her furious, but she was helpless against his strength.

"I think ye just might be, Brina, and I find that a pleasing idea."

He sat up, pulling her along with him. His hand gently wrapped around her face to keep her ear turned toward him. It was a gentle yet firm hold that shocked her again with warmth and something like pleasure.

"Struggle, and I swear I will lie on ye until after moonrise." His words were muttered in a husky tone edged in steel that sent a shiver down her back.

But his words weren't what disturbed her the most. It was suddenly abundantly clear why girls promised to the church wore only undyed robes. The garment kept men from getting too close. She shivered, a ripple of awareness traveling along her skin. She couldn't seem to stop it, only experience it, since she was still bound against Connor Lindsey. She couldn't recall the last time a man of any age had embraced her; even her father had stopped hugging her once she had passed her tenth winter. She felt oddly agitated, as though sitting still were beyond her self-control.

Was that how the insanity began?

Perhaps she had judged Deirdre too harshly for succumbing to Melor.

Dusk fell, and she faced the deepening darkness with a growing sense of dread. Connor never eased his pace. The man seemed to know his way, even as the last of the light faded and the moon hid behind dark clouds. Once the sun was gone, the temperature dropped dramatically. Brina couldn't see the snow flurries, but she could feel the icy flakes hitting her face. She shivered once more and reached for the hood of her cloak, which was lying down her back.

Connor lifted it and dropped it into place for her.

"I can take care of myself."

One of his hands rubbed down the length of her arm, sending a fresh wave of sensation through her. She enjoyed it and couldn't ignore that fact.

But that was wrong, so very wrong.

"Ye'll learn, Brina Chattan, that accepting a bit of care from my hand will be something that ye anticipate."

"Nay, I will nae."

He turned his head, and she felt his breath brush her cheek.

"I promise ye, lass, ye will."

❦

Connor pulled his horse to a halt hours later. The darkness made it hard to judge the amount of time that had passed since he'd stolen her away from her father. He allowed her to slide off the horse, and pain erupted in her feet the moment when she was forced to support her weight. She stomped at the ground to restore her circulation.

"Ye can take yer ease, but we are only stopping long enough for me men to do the same."

He pointed at an outcropping of rocks that were dark shapes in the darkness. Brina went toward them because the need to escape was still pressing down on her. She was moving too fast and stepped on a stone that rolled. A sharp sound escaped her lips as her ankle twisted painfully, but she hopped and made it around the rocks to the privacy that her body needed.

Relief flooded her. She found herself leaning against the rocks while the tension between her shoulders eased. She was suddenly caught up in the urge to weep. Tears stung her eyes, but she refused to allow them to fall.

There was no time for crying. She needed to think.

What it was time for was escape, and the clouds above her would help her achieve her goal.

❧

"Now that was a right interesting bit of work to watch." Shawe spoke softly, but there was no missing the question in the man's tone. "Are ye looking to get locked in the stocks, then? The church does nae like anyone trifling with its nuns, especially when they come with a good dowry and are the daughters of powerful lairds."

Connor nodded because he didn't trust his voice. The church would indeed have him bent over in the stocks and possibly whipped if they caught him near Brina Chattan without an agreement from her father that one of her sisters would be taking her place at the abbey. She was not just another bride intended for

Christ and lifelong servitude to the church. She was the daughter of a laird, and that meant the church could expect her father to send her with a sizable dowry, as well as look to the Chattan for protection should invaders come by sea to pillage the gold-laden abbey where young Brina was expected to make her home.

He smiled slightly, the corners of his mouth twitching upward, because he just couldn't help but be amused by her temper. The lass had spirit, and that was something that he was drawn to. The aunt who had taken over raising his sister when their father was killed had always berated his sister for having any spark of defiance in her. Connor felt his amusement vanish, because thinking of Vanora always did that.

Vanora was held by the Douglas, and the clan made sure that she remained inside one of their strongholds. She was younger than he and had been born after his parents had married. The Douglas had tried to take the Lindsey land through her, claiming that his parentage was in question, even though his father had sworn on the church steps that Connor was his son. With a child on the throne, there was no one to force them to release Vanora, and he did not have the men to challenge the Douglas clan. His own arrangement with Deirdre Chattan was a move to reinforce his borders against another attempt by the Douglas to kill him and claim the Lindsey land.

He'd sworn that he would not see that happen.

But taking Deirdre to wife wasn't a wise move. Not now that she had been exposed as Melor's mistress. Any son she gave him would always be under suspicion. The gossips would cheerfully point out that if she loved the man enough to defy her father and the church to go to him, being married wouldn't stop her from falling from grace again. The older women would point at Connor's children with Deirdre and compare their features against his and Melor's.

Connor drew in a stiff breath and looked toward the direction Brina had gone. The wind went still long enough to hear a distant crunch from dried fallen leaves, but there wasn't a second. He pushed his feet into the rocky soil to give chase, because along with not raising his daughter to obey men, Robert Chattan had also taught her how to move silently through the night.

Connor would admire it, just as soon as he caught her.

❧

"Ye didna listen to my instructions, lass."

Connor spoke from the shadows, too close for her to do anything but recognize that her escape had been foiled.

"Why would you expect that I would? You are nae my laird, nor the man my father has promised me to."

Brina tried to force her voice to be firm, but it quivered a tiny amount, betraying her unease. She found herself unsure how to deal with anyone who didn't give her plain robe deference. Connor Lindsey emerged from the shadows and looked straight at her. She was keenly aware of the fact that he was intent on treating her like a woman who might be spoken to, flirted with, or even touched. That fact was as tantalizing as it was forbidden. The clouds broke, allowing the moonlight through, and it washed over Connor Lindsey. Her entire body responded to his nearness in ways that she had never realized were possible. Little prickles of sensation ran along her arms and down her body. Her breathing was no longer even, and her heart rate accelerated too. She shook her head, but her body refused to behave normally.

Connor frowned.

"Yer father promised me one of his daughters for my wife, Brina Chattan, and I plan to hold him to his word. Ye heard me say that plain enough."

He reached out, and she gave a soft cry, but that did not stop him from latching onto her forearm. "Just as ye understood that I didna want ye moving beyond the privacy of those rocks."

Brina drew in a stiff breath and opened the front of her cloak so that the undyed wool of her robes was illuminated by the moonlight. She turned a ghostly gray due to the moonlight, the same as the rocks that lay scattered on the landscape.

"Look at me, Connor Lindsey. I was promised to the church on the day of my birth. I am sorry about my sister's lack of respect for her impending union with ye, but I cannae refuse to honor a promise made to God. Look at my robes. I belong at the abbey; I always have."

He did as she said, his gaze traveling down her body, all the way to where her new boots peeked out at the hem and then back up, until he was looking at her face once more.

What she witnessed in his eyes made her shiver. Determination shone there so intensely, she felt the heat of it crossing the distance between them. Such a thing was impossible, and yet she would have sworn that it was true.

"Many called me bastard because my mother refused to wed my father for two years after I was born. Even when she did marry him, there were plenty who claimed she had refused him because of her shame in knowing that I was nae his son." He raked her with his eyes once more. "Look at me, Brina, and see a man who is laird against all the rumors and swearing of many men. I will have the Chattan wife I spent so much effort negotiating for. One who is honorable and still pure, so that my own son will nae have to hear whispers about his blood."

For a brief moment she felt compassion for his plight. She shook her head to dispel the feeling.

"I must honor my father's word to the church. If I fail to do that, how could anyone have any faith in me? Any daughter who doesn't obey her father is one who will fail to honor a husband." It was a solid fact that had been drilled into her since she was a baby. Honor was not something that could be sidestepped upon occasion.

"I cannae fall from grace, even if yer cause is a just one, Laird Lindsey. My place is waiting for me at the abbey."

"Ye have honor, Brina Chattan. I don't doubt it." There was a rich timbre in his voice that sounded like approval. Compliments were another thing that she had not had many of, for she was expected to be humble when it came to pleasing those on earth.

"But that is only another reason why I will nae change me mind. The church can make do with yer sister."

He spoke with a solid authority that reminded her

of the way her father set down his orders to his men. Connor Lindsey truly was a laird and was used to being in command of all those around him. Her pride refused to relent. He was not her laird.

"I will nae wed ye, and that's my final word on it, Laird Lindsey."

Her emotions spun out of control in an instant. She lifted her arm and flung off his distracted hold. Her action gained immediate response. He lunged at her, flinging her back against him and clamping his arms all the way around her body. Her arms became trapped against her sides, and he lifted her right off her feet with his greater strength.

"Now, lass, ye have nae given me a chance to prove how much ye might enjoy being my wife."

"I have no intentions of allowing ye to touch me. Unhand me this instant!"

He chuckled, his chest vibrating against her back. She felt his breath brush the side of her neck, and sensation rippled across the skin. She shivered, but it had nothing to do with the temperature.

"We do nae seem to making much progress with words, lass. Maybe we should try a bit of action."

A kiss landed on her neck, his lips pressing gently against the same spot that had registered his warm breath. She jerked, straining away from him.

"Ah… ye are nae so unaffected, now are ye, Brina? There is naught but a cold bed waiting for ye at the abbey." His lips returned to her nape, this time lingering longer on the spot. He trailed several more kisses down the length of her throat, until he reached the neckline of her gown.

"In my bed, there will nae be any clothing to interfere with my kissing yer sweet flesh…"

Her imagination exploded with images of him stripping away her gowns and continuing to press hot kisses against her body. All the way down until he reached her breasts. Heat coursed through her, threatening to drown her in sensation that she could not deny that she found pleasurable.

But it was the same thing that had seen Deirdre fall to ruin.

She kicked and twisted, trying to regain some distance so that she might think.

"Ye cannae do this! Ye would shame me the same way that Melor did to my sister."

The arms around her suddenly tightened. She could feel the change, and she heard the stiff intake of breath that revealed his displeasure.

"Do nae compare me to a Douglas, Brina. Those bastards have raided Lindsey land and stolen my sister."

"But ye are stealing me. If ye detest them so much for doing that, ye must set me free."

"What I need to do is take ye to Birch Stone, where I can experiment with just where ye enjoy being kissed without worrying that yer father is going to ride upon us at any moment."

She tried to shove her elbow back into his belly. "I will nae go with ye!" He avoided her blow, but she swung her balled fist down into his groin and felt her hand connect with his soft flesh.

"Christ Almighty, ye're nae suited to the life of a nun at all." His arms opened for a moment as he bent over. Brina made it one long step before a hand hooked into her loose overgown and yanked her back. She stumbled and lost her balance, falling backward.

Connor rolled onto his back, taking her along with him, and then up rolled up and over her so that her back was against the ground. He lowered enough of his weight to pin her and still her struggles completely. In one short moment, he made her his captive with his greater strength. It was horrifying and terrorizing, because never before had she ever felt so helpless.

Except for today, when he took her away from her father.

"Please…"

"That will nae work tonight, lass, but I am sorry to hear the fear in yer voice. I swear I will keep my word about treating ye gently. I will nae force myself on ye, but I will take ye to my land, where I'll have the time to court ye."

He'd lowered his voice and muttered his promise against her ear. She shivered, but Brina wasn't sure if it was the words or the deep timbre of his voice that made her do so. The scent from his skin surrounded her, filling her senses every time she inhaled, and she realized she liked it.

How could she?

She muttered a soft cry and renewed her struggles. There wasn't much she might do, because she was pinned beneath his greater weight, so she sent her hands toward his face, her fingers curled like talons. She felt her nails sink into his skin. He snarled and arched his neck to escape her attack.

"I already thought ye had the makings of a hellcat; now I know for sure."

Connor pushed up and away from her, but he flipped her over onto her belly and leaned against her back to control her once again. Brina strained against him, welcoming the bite of his harder grip because it drove her enjoyment of his body away.

"I am nae a… a…" She was gasping for breath, the effort of trying to shove him away from her making her pant.

"Not a hellcat?" She felt his chest vibrate with his amusement. "Well, ye scratch and hit like one, and that's a fact."

Brina strained again. "Ye're horrible to call me such a name simply because I will nae crumple at yer feet and weep with defeat." Her hands were pressed to the ground, and she felt a sizable rock beneath her palm. It sent pain through her hand, but she grasped it and pushed back against Connor with all her might. Her effort gained her a few inches because he wasn't expecting it. She lifted the rock, then brought it smashing down onto his shin. The soft leather of his knee-high boots did little to shield him from her attack, and he jumped with a low growl.

"Give me that rope, Shawe." Connor looped a hard arm across her waist and sent her onto her back once more.

"I was nae going to tie ye up, Brina, but ye are too much of a hellcat to leave with yer hands free to inflict pain on me."

"I'm trying to escape, ye daft man! It is the only decent thing to do. That does nae make me a hellcat."

"I can understand how ye think that, lass, but it only makes me surer that what I'm doing is the right course of action to follow. I've no taste for a timid woman, and ye have nae the amount of meekness a nun will need to last a lifetime serving the church."

"That is my father's choice, nae yers, Connor Lindsey!"

She still held the rock, and she sent it toward one of the hands that held her down. He yelped and grabbed her wrist, his strength drawing a startled gasp from her lips, because he had obviously tempered it until now. The rock dropped from her fingers as pain bit into her. The moment she released her weapon, the torment ended, and he leaned down over her until she felt his breath against her lips. She turned her face away, but that allowed him to press a light kiss against the side of her neck. Sensation rippled down her body from that touch, surprising her with how much pleasure her skin might feel.

"Nay, lass, it is my choice now, because I've caught ye, and Highlanders keep the women they manage to steal."

She snarled and heard a soft sound that was far too close to a chuckle come from one of his men. Obviously they had company now, and her face flamed to think that her shame was being witnessed. She heard the rope hit the ground near her head before Connor released one of her arms to reach for it. She swung her closed fist toward his head and hissed when it connected. Pain snaked down her arm and into her shoulder, but the grunt she heard from him was worth it.

"Get yer hands off of me, Connor Lindsey!"

He threw his leg over her instead and clamped her body between his thighs. She growled as he grabbed one of her wrists, and she felt the rope looping around it. She gritted her teeth, waiting for pain to bite into her when he tightened that binding.

It never came. Connor controlled the knot in spite of her struggles, securing both her wrists together in front of her before he released his legs, and she rolled over in a huffing tangle of cloak and robes.

"Ye have too much spirit to make a good nun, Brina, but I would nae expect ye to know that."

"That is an unholy thing to say!"

He reached down and lifted her to her feet with an ease that humiliated her. It shouldn't have been right for him to be able to capture her so simply.

"No, it isn't. The church will no' be pleased, I understand that well enough, but yer father made an agreement with me, and I plan to keep it. Yer father will be the one making peace with the church."

He leaned over, and a moment later she was hanging over his shoulder like a fallen deer. He clamped a hand over the backs of her thighs, sending heat into her face because she was suddenly acutely aware of how close his hand was to her bottom.

"I will nae go with ye."

She straightened up but shrieked when he landed a hard slap directly on one side of her rear end, and collapsed back over his shoulder.

"Ye're going, one way or another, lass." He kept his hand on her bottom, his fingers gently rubbing the spot he'd spanked.

"Move yer hand away…"

She was reduced to pleading once again, because her body was quivering in response to his touch. It made no sense, but she could not seem to control her responses, and she was more aware of her sex than she ever had been.

"Only if ye behave, lass."

His hand moved, and she shuddered. Relief crossed her mind, but it did not banish the odd awareness completely. She couldn't hear his feet hitting the ground, but he was moving through the trees, taking her away just as he had said he would.

It was madness. The sort that would see them both condemned by the church. But he kept walking, and she heard the soft sound of horses. Connor set her down on her feet, and she drew in a soothing breath as her belly complained about being forced to lie over his hard shoulder. There seemed to be nothing soft about the man at all.

Especially when it came to what he decided was the right course of action.

Connor gained the back of his stallion without any further hesitation. His men were all mounting their horses, none of them looking as if they might have misgivings about what their laird was doing.

She wasn't the first woman who had been taken to satisfy honor...

That thought sent a chill down her back, for it promised her a future that included being nothing more than a possession to a man who had reason to seek vengeance against her.

He'd promised not to force himself on her, but there would be no one to stop him should he change his mind.

She trembled and fought against the rope binding her.

"I'll give ye a toss-up, lass."

One of Connor's burly retainers grasped her waist and lifted her up behind his laird.

"Lift yer arms, Brina, and loop them over my head."

Now she understood why he had tied her wrists in front of her body. There was even a small amount of rope between her hands so that he could keep her wrapped around his body while they rode.

"I'll hold on to yer belt."

He turned his head to look at her. "Ye'll lose yer grip and fall once yer strength diminishes."

"I'll take that risk, or better yet, place me back on my mare."

She heard him make a soft sound of frustration beneath his breath.

"I will nae. So ye can lift yer arms, or I will have Shawe do it for ye."

Brina hissed at him. "Ye're a brute to do such a thing. I've never placed my arms around a man, except my father when I was little."

He rotated his entire body, so that he almost facing her. "Are ye telling me that ye are too timid to touch me, lass?"

"I am nae timid, simply dutiful to my sire's word and the place that he has said is mine."

The words were out of her mouth before her wisdom warned her that challenging him wasn't the best idea. If the man thought her timid, escape might be so much more possible.

"Then place yer hands over my head and prove that the idea of pressing yer body against mine does nae disturb ye, little Brina."

Disturb her? It did far more than that, but her pride

refused to allow her admit it. Saying it would only stroke the man's ego.

"Ye are acting like a barbarian to want to have me tied about ye like some prize ye took during a raid."

His eyes darkened. "But I do consider ye a prize worthy of stealing, lass. I wouldn't be taking ye if I didna think that way."

His tone had deepened, and he was mocking her, but at the same time tossing a challenge at her that her pride was quick to rise to. She lifted her arms before thinking about it but came to her senses with her hands raised between them. She hesitated, berating herself for so quickly taking the bait he dangled in front of her nose. If she planned to escape from him, it would only be by thinking before she acted.

Connor took advantage of her raised hands and put his hands through hers before she finished thinking. She caught a quick glance at a mocking grin on his lips before he raised his arms up and ducked his head beneath the circle of her bound arms. She had no choice but to rise up off the back of the horse for a moment when he straightened up. He caught her wrists inside his warm hands and pushed them down his body to his waist. She was pulled against his back; her only choice was which on side of his back she wished to place her chin.

She snorted with frustration. That was no true choice, for the scabbard encasing his sword was strapped to his back so that the pommel rose above his left shoulder. She might place her face against that leather, but it was sure to give her bruises and possibly cuts, because the leather was well waxed to keep the sword from rusting in the Scottish weather.

That left her the option of leaning against his right shoulder. His waist was trim, but her arms barely reached around him, and the amount of rope that he'd allowed between her wrists didn't afford her the ability to keep a few inches between them. Her senses were filled with the scent of his skin and she felt an odd quiver in her belly. Connor urged the stallion forward at almost the same instant.

She heard an owl's cry, and his belly tightened beneath her hands as he made the noise. Many clans had a cry that was uniquely their own. The clouds were closing over the moon again. By using the owl's cry, it would be very hard for her father's men to track them. Connor knew the ground they traveled over well. He guided his horse through the trees, leaving the known roads well behind them.

The motion of the horse bounced her, and she gasped when she landed hard on the most tender part of her body. Connor frowned.

"Hug me tight and move yer hips with the motion of the horse, lass. I've seen ye riding astride, so I ken ye can do it well."

Brina found herself grateful for the darkness, because her cheeks flared with a blush. She was bounced twice more before Connor made a sound of disgust and reached over her back to cup one side of her bottom. She jumped forward before he got the chance to move her to where he pleased. A soft moan issued from her lips, because she was now pressed against him, with nothing save for a few layers of clothing to separate their skin.

"Ye've a stubborn nature, Brina."

"If ye are going to complain about me, sir, I suggest ye return me to my father's men, for I never promised to be an obedient wife—not to you, that is for certain."

"A fact that makes me more sure that I'm going to enjoy having ye, lass. Ye'll not find the Lindseys to be men who force their daughters to be meek. We leave that to the English, since it appears they are no' men enough to stomach a little spirit in their lasses."

"Ye are insane."

"Nay, lass, I'm happily anticipating the next time we wrestle. Hopefully we'll be alone so that I may spend a little more time investigating yer sweet blushes and what my kisses do to ye."

She snarled at him. His belly vibrated in response, and she knew that he was chuckling, even if she couldn't hear the sound because he was looking forward once again. Her fingers curled into talons when she felt it, for her temper was rising again. There was something about the man that brought out anger in her. She was forcing herself to maintain some manner of civility and not dig her hands into his midsection. But the desire was there, and it shocked her with how hot it burned.

There was a softer target just a bit lower…

That thought sprang up in her mind, and it brought a renewed surge of heat to her face.

Oh, she knew full well what was beneath the man's kilt.

Brina bit her lower lip and chastised herself. She didn't know well. Not in detail, that was to say. But there had been a few times that she had spied what males had and women didn't.

It was called a cock.

She'd heard that a time or two, and she also knew that a woman could drive her knee into it if she needed to wound a man.

Her lips twitched up. Her hand had done a fair amount of damage when she had connected with that spot.

Brina flattened her hands again and felt the ridges of muscle hidden behind Connor's doublet. She frowned when she realized that his name rose so easily into her thoughts. She should be able to think of him in some derogatory manner, such as labeling him her captor or considering him a barbarian. Instead his name paraded so easily into the center of her thoughts.

Yet that was not the only thing she was aware of. Pressed so close against him, she drew the scent of his skin in with each breath she took. It was different than anything else she had ever encountered, because for some reason, she enjoyed it. No matter how much she might try to tell herself that it was wrong to notice that she liked it, she could not change the fact that she did.

He smelled male, and part of her was stirring in response to it, that part she had always been forbidden to listen to. She had hidden it deep beneath her plans for a future where she was a mother superior, and ignored it, but now, lying against his back, she could not stop her mind from noticing all the pleasures that came with the contact. Just as she had enjoyed the kisses he'd pressed against her neck.

To think that her skin was so sensitive...

She understood now why those promised to the church were dressed in undyed wool from birth. It kept them from discovering how good another human felt while clasped in their arms, because everyone kept away from her when they saw her wearing the garments of a nun. Her plain wool skirts were bunched up around her legs now, the knee-high boots that she wore protecting her lower legs from the night chill. They were sturdy boots—a gift from her father because he knew that they would most likely be the last new pair she ever wore. In many abbeys, the newest girls went barefoot to prove their dedication to serve no matter how humble the conditions they would have to endure. Even though she would eventually become a mother superior, she would begin as a novice, just as every other girl did.

As Connor's wife, she wouldn't have to suffer those hardships. There would be those who would consider her fortunate, but she couldn't ignore the fact that she would have to dishonor her father to embrace being wed to Connor Lindsey. Her word was the only thing that she truly owned. Men so often thought their honor was more important than a woman's.

Of course, the church would tell her that her place was lower than a man's. She knew that well enough.

She couldn't wed him, not without her father's blessing. But there seemed no way to prevent the man from taking her where he would. Even with the night being so black, he guided his horse with an experienced hand. Neither the men following them nor their horses hesitated. They continued on, the clip from the animals' hooves the only sound they made. She thought of screaming, but the rope binding her wrists was a rather blunt reminder of the fact that Connor was stealing her, and she doubted that he'd hesitate about gagging her too.

The plaid lying across his back kept her nose from becoming chilled when she turned her face into it, but the rest of her body was drawing warmth from his flesh too. He was far warmer than she might have thought a man would be, and her female body clung to his as the horse continued to cover ground. She shivered, the new emotions shaking her down to the foundations of her beliefs.

Every year that she had grown and taken instruction on what was right or wrong was being challenged. Her pride ached because she did not seem to have enough discipline to ignore what she liked about Connor Lindsey. Deep inside her mind, dark whispers were stirring like snakes, slithering and winding through the lessons she had been given on keeping her body pure because it belonged to Christ.

"Release me, Connor. This will bring trouble to both our houses."

She knew that he heard her, she felt his muscles tighten beneath her cheek and hands, but he never pulled the stallion up, not even to slow its progress. The night still surrounded them, growing colder almost as if evil were rising from the ground in celebration of what he was doing. Her eyes strained to see, but the night was darkening even more. The first snow of the season began to drift down onto her unprotected back. The snow did not melt, and it was a full month early. It was falling too quickly too, covering their tracks in a foot of fluffy ice that would give her father no way to know where they had gone.

Despair finally won the battle to wrap around her. It smothered her confidence, leaving her without hope.

Three

DAWN WAS GRAY AND MISERABLE. THEY STOPPED TO rest the horses, and Brina pulled her frozen fingers to her mouth to blow her breath on them. Her fingers pained her because she had not been able to turn her hands about to protect them from the frigid air.

Her heavy wool cloak was soaking wet down the length of her back, where the snow had melted against her body heat. But at least the wool continued to keep her warm. She stomped her feet to regain feeling in them, while the men began to rub the legs and ankles of their mounts. They untied the small fabric bags of feed that had been secured to the backs of the younger lads who weren't carrying full swords yet. Connor had stopped them near water, and the men waited to feed the horses until the beasts had dipped their noses into the stream for a long drink. After that the men tied the sacks around the horses' heads and left them to eat while they might.

"I didna think of yer hands, lass."

Connor captured one before she realized he had finished tending to his stallion. He pulled a small dirk from the inside of his doublet sleeve, surprising her. Highlanders did like their weapons, but not every man had his clothing sewn to accommodate more weapons. That spoke of a harsh life, one where Connor needed to watch his back and be prepared for treachery.

He sliced the rope in the center so that her hands might separate; her arms were stiff from being in the same position so long. A tiny moan of relief escaped her, but she stepped away from him when he reached for the loop of rope still knotted about her wrists. His lips pressed into a hard line in response.

"I can see to my own comfort."

Brina took over the task of soothing her skin where the bindings had bruised her, while she lifted her chin in defiance of his attempts to do it. He frowned, his eyes narrowing.

"Go on and see to yer needs, and do nae make me chase ye down, Brina, for I swear that I will no' be in a kind mood if ye put me to that trouble in this chill. I hope ye know now that I will do whatever I must to take ye with us."

"Ye should notice that God is no' pleased with what ye have done."

One of his eyebrows rose. "Ye think this chill is heavenly wrath, lass?"

She tossed her head and worked on one of the knots at her wrist, but he had tied it tight, and her fingertips ached as she tried to dig at the rough rope.

"It would not be the first time God sent punishment to those who displeased him. It is too early for snow."

"There have been other years when the snow fell early." He tilted his head to the side, and his lips twitched. "Maybe God is making sure we have a good reason to stay beneath the covers of a warm bed."

Her eyes widened, and so did his grin.

"But I can see that I will have to take better care of ye. I would nae want yer fingers to be too sore."

Connor reached for her wrist once more. Brina jerked against his hold, but his fingers remained solidly in place. All she managed was to make her own shoulder ache.

"It is only my hand against yers, Brina. Stop acting so skittish over so simple a touch."

She felt her jaw drop open with stunned shock, but she pressed her lips together as her temper flared. "You are quite the fiend, sir. I have never allowed even simple touches, for to do so would have been misplaced when my future was to serve the church. I do not know how it is on yer land, but my ankles were switched for forgetting that my body was for God's service and no other's touch. Yer frustration with my reactions is yet another reason why ye should abandon this insanity. I was raised to be a bride of Christ; I know nothing else."

Her words shocked him, or maybe it was her tone that made him frown at her so furiously. She felt her throat constrict, because she was daring quite a bit to raise her voice in reprimand to a laird while others might hear, even if he had stolen her.

The fact that she was correct wouldn't change the reality that he would set the conditions of her life where they were going. It was foolish to anger him, for she would be the only one who suffered if she offended him.

"I admit that I didna think of that and that ye are correct; girls bound for the church are nae allowed to flirt on Lindsey land either." His expression softened, as did the grip on her wrist, his thumb beginning to rub gently along the delicate skin. "I believe that I am going to enjoy courting ye, Brina."

"This is nae courtship; it is—"

"It is done."

The fingers holding her wrist tightened, so that her arm was held immobile. She felt the cool kiss of the dirk's blade against her skin as he slid it carefully beneath the rope and jerked it quickly through the rough binding. The severed loop of rope fell away. He released her wrist and reached for her other one.

Knowing that he was reaching for her hand sent a tingle of anticipation along her arm. She realized it was absurd to jerk away from him when she couldn't remove the rope herself, but she still flinched. The involuntary motion made her mad, only this time with herself. She should be able to master her own body.

Connor didn't finish reaching for her wrist. He stopped in midair, waiting for her to stand steady.

Waiting for her to find her courage.

In spite of all the teaching in her childhood about meekness and humbleness that would be expected of her, Brina had never understood her lessons to mean that she should behave like a coward. It stung even to question whether she was doing so now.

She was still a Chattan after all. Born of Highlander

stock, even if she was a female. Brina lifted her chin and held her arm steady.

"Go on, then, unless ye'd care to hand me that dirk so that I might do the task myself."

Her words didn't fool him, but she noticed a flare of something in his eyes that looked very much like respect.

"I believe it wise to keep ye unarmed for the moment; ye did enough damage with that rock." He cupped her wrist, gently this time, and held her limb with only a fraction of the pressure he'd applied before. The moment felt longer than normal, as though she were poised inside of it, lingering there between breaths, while she noticed every tiny detail, such as how his attention focused on the task of sliding the knife between the rope and her skin. As soon as he had jerked through it, she drew a quick breath and pulled her hand free of his grasp.

His soft chuckle drew her lips into a frown.

"We make a better pair than ye know, Brina, for I was called bastard as a boy and spent many a night sleeping in the stable while my uncle was doing his best to ensure that I didna inherit the Lindsey title."

"Why were ye called bastard?" Such was a harsh thing for a child to bear, and she discovered herself feeling remorse for the little boy who'd had to face that reality. It seemed cruel, because illegitimacy was the result of his parent's sin, not his own.

"My father stole my mother, and she refused to wed him until her father agreed to give him her dowry."

She gasped, her temper flaring up. "And ye would do the same to yer own sons?"

His lips rose into a confident smirk. "I admit that the idea of producing babes with ye is to my liking."

Brina turned and grasped a handful of her skirts so that she might climb up the embankment to the privacy he'd mentioned might be hers. She could feel him watching her, but she kept her eyes on where she was going. The man was too pleasing to look upon by far, and the idea of yielding to his whim was too enticing when she considered how many years she had trained to ignore such things. His amusement stoked her temper, tempting her to try her nails out on him once more. That urge shamed her because of how intense it was. Turning her back on him was the only thing she could think to do, but she swore that she was going to be the embodiment of the hellcat he called her if the arrogant Highlander placed even one finger on her because she'd given him her back.

Nuns weren't supposed to swear, but she meant it.

❧

Connor watched Brina until she was behind a large outcropping of rocks. He listened to her steps and heard her stop. That was a relief, for he wasn't in the mood to chase her.

No, he was feeling shamed by her words, no mistake about it.

"Are ye sure ye want to keep her?"

Shawe spoke softly, and Connor heard a measure of the same discomfort he was feeling in the man's voice. He should have recalled that women raised to become brides of Christ were expected to shun all contact from men. Brina had more courage than he'd given her credit for, because the lightest contact between them must have been jarring for her to endure.

"Ye know my reasons, Shawe." Connor turned to face his men because he was not a man who expected to be followed just because of who his father had been. He looked each of them straight in the eye before continuing to speak.

"We need the alliance with the Chattans. If I wed Deirdre, there will be talk from the Douglas that my children are nae Lindsey, but Melor's bastards, even if I chained her to the tower-room wall for the next ten years."

There were several nods of agreement.

"But I would nae care to do something like that to the lass. The Lindseys need a mistress who can run Birch Stone and do her part in making sure life is good for every member of the clan. I want no wife who needs guarding every day of her life."

Now there were a few muttered "ayes" from his retainers.

"Robert Chattan promised me one of his daughters, and the middle one is betrothed to McLeod's son, so I cannae be taking her without causing trouble with the McLeod. That leaves Brina, or we go home without an alliance with the Chattans and the McLeods when her sister weds."

His men didn't care for that idea. They'd been on the trail for close to a month now chasing down the rumors of Deirdre and her lover. The men in front of him wanted their wives and families, but they were willing to follow him in the cause of bringing home a wife for the laird who would bring good fortune to them all.

Some lairds took English or French wives because they came with silver and gold, but in the unstable country, a wife who was related to a strong clan was worth more than money. If he took a French girl to his bed, he might find his castle besieged for the gold she had come with. A dead man didn't get the chance to enjoy his coin.

"What of the church?"

It was Kurtus who spoke up, displaying a frown of disapproval.

Connor tilted his head. "I say the church can have Deirdre, for she needs their strict guidance more than Brina. As the elder sister, her dowry will be greater, and that should appease the church. By keeping Brina, we shall have a Chattan lass who conducts herself with honor. If ye do nae agree, speak yer mind while we are within riding distance of the abbey, but I say, if we take Brina there, we shall have little to show for all our time on the road and a difficult future without an alliance while the clans around us make strong ones."

That sealed his men's opinions. Connor watched them weigh the idea of their neighbors making alliances while they failed to do so. That would mean a dark future for the Lindseys, and no mistake about it. His men nodded, none of them stepping forward to protest. That didn't mean they were completely content with the matter of taking a bride of Christ away from the church, but there was one thing that a Highlander might agree upon, and that was a fair exchange. The Chattans would be the ones adjusting their thinking, since it was their woman who had upset the agreement.

It wasn't perfect, not by far, but Connor was relieved to see his men turning to prepare to ride on without any further discussion. They would take Brina with them without any protest and do their duty in making sure their laird's future wife remained with the clan.

Connor didn't bother to worry about the fact that some lairds wouldn't have allowed their men to protest their actions. He was the laird, and he would lead the Lindsey the only way he knew how, through fairness. He'd never order a man to do a task that he wouldn't complete himself, and he'd never refuse to hear any of his men speak their mind if they thought it was best for the clan.

That was what drove him, the need to do the best for the clan. He'd spent a good part of his youth never expecting to marry at all because he was bastard born and worse yet, a bastard of the laird that had no legitimate sons. No family would want to risk their daughter wedding him because there might be fighting over who was to become laird and killing him would be a good way to end the argument. Any wife he had would die along with him. But fate had decreed that he would be laird. Now he'd wed, but for the gain it would bring his kin and the stability it would offer when his wife gave him a legitimate son to end all doubt about who was laird of the Lindsey.

The days of his being at the mercy of his greedy uncle were past.

That thought burned inside of him so brightly, it

had kept him warm on nights that had killed other youths. In the corner of a stable, where his guardian had left him to survive by whatever means he might, he had held tight to his honor, because it was the only thing that was truly his.

The church wouldn't like what he'd done, but he'd suffer their displeasure to prove to his clan that he was strong enough to place their welfare before his own. Just as his mother had held her head high and not wed because her own father was being so stubborn. It had cost her dearly, but in the end she had secured her dowry for the Lindseys, making sure that the clan grew stronger in spite of the shame being directed toward her. He would not fail to be just as determined. Building a better future for his children was more important than any hard feelings Robert Chattan might harbor toward him at the moment. He'd stand firmly in place, and the Chattan laird would relent after enough time had passed with Brina secured at Birch Stone.

❧

She was tempted to run.

Brina looked toward the trees that grew halfway down the valley on the other side of the boulders behind which she had taken her privacy. They looked closer than they were, she knew that from her hunting lessons, but still she gazed at them and felt the longing to run grow stronger. The fresh blanket of snow also made her frown, for it would show her tracks clearly.

Connor would run her down easily with that

stallion of his. The creature was huge and strong
from traveling the uneven paths of the Highlands.
Frustration bit into her, but she forced herself to be
practical. The time was not right now, but if she could
employ enough patience, she might yet find a chance
to escape.

She would also need to be clever.

Connor Lindsey was no fool, and slipping past him
would take some thinking on her part. She drew a
deep breath and banished her temper so that she might
use all her mental abilities in plotting a solution.

She had to escape. It was the only honorable thing
to do. The promise that her father had made to the
church bound her to try and take her place at the
abbey. There was also the example that her sister
Deirdre had just experienced with Melor. Men were
not to be trusted and she'd be wise to remember it.
They used women for their own gains, and that was
a hard fact. Connor Lindsey might claim his intention was to wed her, but there was no contract to
bind him to that. The man could very well ruin her
and abandon her in order to shame her father for the
dishonor Deirdre had painted him with.

It would not be the first time a woman had been
used in such a way. Much of Scotland's history was
written in feuds that lasted for generations.

She bit her lower lip, feeling the flicker of something inside her that interfered with her logic. It
was a sense that Connor was not the fiend she had
called him, a belief that was growing from the lack of
brutality in her abduction. The man might easily have
used his greater strength to break her, and she doubted

anyone would have thought ill of him for it. Her sister had done a grave thing to him, one that the man's clan would seek retaliation for.

Was that her fate, then? She sat down on a rock and faced the trees while she considered the lack of pain in her body. Her thighs were sore, but no more so than when she hunted. Her face was not bruised, but her fist hurt from when she had struck Connor.

He hadn't hit her in return.

Well, that wasn't completely true. She felt her cheeks heating with humiliation as she recalled in perfect clarity the feeling of his hand connecting with her bottom.

"Are ye hoping that sitting there will delay us long enough for yer father's men to catch up with us?"

Brina jumped, but she landed balanced and evenly as she turned to discover Connor standing a few paces behind her. Satisfaction flickered in his eyes, and she felt her temper flare again for the amusement she seemed to provide him.

"That would be ridiculous, considering we rode all night and the snow would have covered our tracks..." She shook her head, disgusted by the fact that she was so quick to allow her thoughts to spill from her lips. The man was her captor, and if escape was truly her goal, helping him to know that she had the ability to reason was not in her best interest.

She gasped and turned around to cover her mouth with her hand. Of course! She was such a trusting fool not to see the way of it before. She needed to play upon his ignorance of her and her skills. If he believed her tamed, slipping past him would be simple.

"Are ye truly that upset no' to be on yer way to the abbey, lass?"

Brina turned to look at him. "Of course I am. What manner of daughter do ye believe me to be? If ye think me so easily knocked from the path of being obedient to my father's will, I cannae understand why ye might wish to take me to wife."

His lips curled up into a grin, and she realized she had made yet another error. He took two long steps and closed the distance between them. Sensation prickled along her skin, a feeling that she might have expected because of the icy chill in the air, but she knew it came from him being close. Her belly tightened, just as it had when he had touched her.

"Which is exactly why ye are here, Brina, because ye understand honor, and that is what I need in a wife."

"There is no honor in this abduction. I am nae just another daughter of Robert Chattan; I am promised to the church." She opened her hands and tried to appeal to his sense of integrity. "I know that Deirdre stung yer pride, and for that I am sorry, but taking me is against everything righteous."

"I disagree, lass. There is righteousness in a man keeping his word, and when that man is a laird, there is even more so. Yer father made me a promise, and I plan to make sure he keeps it."

"He promised ye Deirdre."

Connor shook his head. "He promised me an alliance that would be sealed with marriage to one of his daughters."

"Which ye know full well was to be my sister

Deirdre. Everyone knows that. It is the only reason
Melor Douglas sought her out."

He closed another step, judging her reaction to his
nearness. Brina ordered herself to stand firmly in place,
confident in her position because that was something
he would understand. Quivering or pleading would
only allow him to see her as bendable to his will, so
she kept her chin level.

Connor slowly smiled when she held firmly in
her stance. She had to tip her head up maintain eye
contact because he was now so close.

"I do believe, sweet Brina, that ye would have done
better if Melor had tried his hand at seducing ye."

She scoffed at him, and he chuckled when he
heard the distinctly unfeminine sound. "No man has
ever tried such a thing, because I am *promised* to the
church." She threw her hands into the air. "Ye are daft
even to make such a comparison."

He laughed at her temper, his eyes sparkling
with enjoyment.

"Now that is my point exactly, Brina. Ye are an
interesting combination of feminine wiles and prac-
ticality. Ye are nae so concerned with me becoming
angry because ye speak to me so directly, because ye
are accustomed to being direct in everything ye do."
His grin faded, and his expression became serious. "Ye
do nae know how to employ deception."

She frowned, realizing that her outspokenness was
going to undermine her attempt to escape from him.
If the man respected her, he wouldn't lower his guard.

"Yet that is another reason for ye to give me my
mare and allow me to depart. Our marriage bed will

be a cold one, for I am too old to be taught new ways now."

His eyes narrowed, but not in anger as she had witnessed before. This time there was an unmistakable sensuality about his expression. Brina stared because it fascinated her to see a man looking at her like that. A warning was ringing in the back of her mind but couldn't seem to break through the spell of her fixation.

"Well now, lass, that is a matter of opinion, and no' one that ye may argue with, for a man does nae choose what he likes. He is just as powerless against it as ye are. I assure ye that I am up to the challenge of enticing ye to learn new ways."

Alarm raced through her, and she jerked her gaze away from his face. "That was nae meant to be a challenge but to make ye see reason."

Turning her attention away from him was unnerving. She felt a tingle on the back of her neck. She looked back at him to discover that he had taken advantage of the opportunity she'd afforded him and was standing right in front of her now, his hand hovering over her cheek, where her blush stained the skin scarlet.

She jumped away, only to find that he'd grasped a handful of her skirts, and the hold kept her in place while his fingers gently brushed the side of her face. He did it slowly, his eyes glittering as he watched his hand traveling along the side of her jaw.

"Ye say ye do nae like me, and yet ye blush, Brina. That is something that cannae be ignored. It is the woman in ye, the one who ye have tried to suppress, but now ye do nae need to any longer. I promise that

I will show ye how to enjoy every moment of being in our marriage bed."

She shivered, the stroke of his fingers sending a ripple of awareness through her that shocked her with its intensity. His fingertips continued across her face until they touched her lower lip, and she gasped, never having guessed that her mouth might be so sensitive.

"I will nae dishonor my father's word, nae for any amount of pleasure."

She swatted the hand holding her skirts, but all that gained her was a smarting palm, because the man never moved. His fingers remained locked in the fabric of her garments, his grasp pulling down slightly so that she was pinned in place. He stepped closer, and her nipples tingled just because she could feel him so near.

His hand was no longer on her lips, so there was no true contact between them, but she could smell him and hear his every breath as he kept her in place with the grip on her skirts. The hems of both robes covered his feet, and she discovered it an intimate thing for him to be so near her.

"We are nae getting any closer to agreeing by discussing it, lass."

"On that, I concur."

His hand cupped her cheek again. "Ah… we agree. Now that is exactly what I was hoping to hear from ye." He slid his hand toward the back of her head to curl around her nape beneath the single plait of her hair. He leaned over, and she felt the brush of his breath against the skin that his fingers had traveled over. She arched her neck, seeking distance, but the hand clasping her nape held her in place.

"So perhaps we should try something a bit different and see what sort of reaction we gain from one another." He kissed her cheek and then trailed light touches of his lips along the entire length of her blush. Pleasure went racing through her, and she was powerless to prevent a soft sound from escaping her lips.

"Ah... more agreement..."

Confusion clouded her thinking for moment. He angled his head and bent down so that he might kiss her. The first touch of his lips was soul shattering. She jerked, her hands coming up to plant solidly against his chest and push with every ounce of strength she had. She twisted her face away from his, escaping from the kiss for a moment.

"No one has ever kissed me!" she shrieked, unable to remain composed. She struck out at him, her nails trying to find something soft to dig into.

"A fact that needs changing."

In spite of her temper, his voice was controlled and husky. He leaned down and placed another soft kiss against her cheek. "Admit that ye enjoy it, Brina. I swear I do as well, for yer lips are as sweet as honey."

She shivered, the dark promise in his voice threatening to lure her away like a fairy song from legend.

"But... it's... sinful..."

The fingers on the back of her neck tightened, pulling forward a small amount so that her face tipped back up and presented her mouth to his once again. He hovered over her mouth for a moment, and she saw that he was holding back, tempering his desire.

"I swear that I will wed ye, Brina. There will be no shame, only pleasure."

He kissed her again, this time following her when she turned away from the contact. It wasn't a hard kiss. Connor controlled himself, and she shuddered because she knew that he was employing effort on her behalf. That knowledge overwhelmed her with how tender it was, and she lost the battle to resist. Her mouth moved beneath his, trying to mimic his motions.

"That's the way, lass..." The hand on her nape began to guide her instead of binding her.

She liked his kiss. It was a hard certainty that filled her mind as his lips slid along hers, teasing and gently tasting, while she shivered in the grip of not knowing what to do. Even if she had been instructed at some point on how to kiss, Brina doubted she could have recalled what the lesson entailed. She was too over-whelmed by sensation to think. It flooded her and took her down into a moment where there was nothing except the way his mouth moved against her own.

He surrounded her, and her body felt as though it was made to melt against his harder one. Her breasts pressed against his chest, and she wanted to sigh with the enjoyment she gained from it. Her nipples tingled and drew into hard buttons when his lips became bolder against her own.

His kiss lost its innocent touch, becoming harder by degrees as his hand guided her head into the position he wanted. The tip of his tongue glided across her lower lip, shocking her again, only this time she eagerly embraced that shock. She wanted to be closer to it, to him, and she tried to move her lips in unison with his. Excitement was growing inside her, and she became eager to discover what his next touch might be.

He growled softly, but the tone was almost wicked. Her eyes sprang open as she recognized the sound in some deep part of her mind that harbored every thought that had been labeled forbidden.

"Enough, Connor."

She pushed against his chest, and his hold slackened. She never would have escaped by trying to back away from him, so she ducked beneath his arm and hiked up her skirts so that she might move faster.

"Damn it all... Brina..."

She didn't wait to hear what else he planned to say to soothe her. Brina made it past the rocks that had granted her privacy from his men, and stumbled down the few steps to where the horses were getting a last pat from their riders. A soft cry crossed her lips when she spied her mare. A younger lad held the reins, but she took them from him quickly and wrapped them around her fingers.

A hard hand clamped down on top of the strips of leather. It wasn't a hard grip, but it was firm enough to trap her.

Connor placed his other hand on the side of the mare, pinning Brina between his arms. He wasn't actually touching her, only caging her with his arms and body, but she quivered, too aware of him by far. Sensation was coursing through her veins like whisky. Somehow she'd failed to notice that he was so much larger than she. It was a fact that she encountered daily with Bran and her father's retainers, but Connor was different. She noticed his strength for reasons that were dark mysteries inside her mind, and feelings arose from those shadows while she became increasingly aware of the way his body might shelter hers.

"Easy, Brina…"

"I am at ease," she snapped. "I want to ride my own horse; that's all."

She heard him draw in a stiff breath, the fingers wrapped around her own gently massaging.

"Can I trust ye on yer own horse?"

Her eyes widened. She had never told a lie. Brina stared at the velvet-covered side of her mare and debated how to answer him. "I… um…"

"That is what I thought, lass."

He scooped her off her feet in the next moment and tossed her up and over his shoulder again. Her robes became a tangled mess around her legs, and her braid swung around her neck. But the thing that she found intolerable was the unmistakable sound of male amusement rising up around her. Connor's men were enjoying the sight of their laird carrying her right well, and her temper sizzled with the knowledge.

He tossed her over the back of his stallion this time and mounted before she could lift her head.

"I've a mind to sleep in a warm bed tonight, men."

His men sent up a sound of approval. Brina was hanging across the horse like a bag of grain, with her face pressed against its smooth coat. Her long braid went trailing toward the ground, while she flattened her hands against the side of the animal so that she might sit up.

Connor kneed his mount, and the animal surged forward, as eager as its master to find a warm place to spend the coming night. The motion sent her bouncing against the side of the beast, while the forward momentum made her slide back against Connor's thighs.

She growled, low and viciously, while she wished with all her soul that she knew how to curse. But she didn't know a single word of profanity, because her stupid undyed wool robes had always kept the men around her from muttering anything profane in her hearing. The only insulting words she knew came from the scriptures.

"Fiend!" She snarled the word and lamented it, because the man was worse than just a demon. He was a brute and a savage, and she wanted to call him something terrible that she would feel remorse for later, damn it all.

But she liked his kiss… and his touch.

Her cheeks flamed bright when she heard him chuckle. Brina felt his horse climbing up the steep trail that led toward the coast. She bounced with every step, until finally nausea became a more pressing concern than her temper. Blood had rushed to her head, threatening to send her into oblivion, and part of her was defeated enough to consider just allowing oblivion to claim her. The night of no sleep was beginning to wear on her now, but another hard bounce and her belly refused to allow her to escape the pain.

"Connor, let me up, please."

She detested how pitiful she sounded, but her head was spinning, and any moment she was going to lose the meager contents of her belly.

A hard arm hooked beneath her belly and lifted

her up. Relief flowed through her even as her skirts
and cloak went flying around her with the aid of
the horse's motion. The fabric blew back, exposing
her legs, while she tried to shove it down enough to
keep her thighs from being seen. She struggled with
the cloak and her pair of gowns, while the stallion
continued to move. Connor lifted her up and sat her
facing forward. She would have liked to take offense,
but the honest truth was that by lifting her, he made
it possible for her to jerk her clothing into order.
When he set her down, she was straddling the horse
with his arms around either side of her to control the
reins. The motion of the animal sent her back against
his body.

"Are ye going to behave?"

He muttered his question next to her ear, sending
a new jolt of sensation down her length. She instantly
recalled how his lips had felt against her own.

"Nae in the manner that ye believe I should. Ye are
not my father, nor my laird."

He chuckled a moment, and she fought the urge to
jab him with one of her elbows.

"That was not meant to please ye."

He angled his head so that he might speak directly
next to her ear. She was struck by how intimate their
positions were. Something she had never thought
to feel, much less deal with. Her sisters were more
accomplished than she had given them credit for,
because controlling her own responses was proving a
herculean task.

"And why no', lass? Pleasure has its place in life. I
believe ye enjoyed learning that a kiss might bring such."

"I didn't…" Her words trailed off, because she had enjoyed it, and she didn't know how to lie either.

"It was but a small sample of the sort of true enjoyment a couple might seek in each other's embrace."

Her fingers clenched into a fist, and she sent her elbow back toward his belly. He clamped his arms around her before she gained her target. Her arms were squeezed tight against her sides, and she felt his breath against the exposed skin of her neck.

"Stop toying with me." She sounded as grumpy as a child who had not taken its afternoon nap.

"Now why would I do that, lass? We have a unique reaction to one another, and no mistake about it. I'm looking forward to teaching ye how to kiss me back when ye're in my arms."

Brina stiffened in his trapping embrace. "Do ye enjoy humiliating me, Connor Lindsey? Is that it, then? Ye want to repay my family by shaming my father?"

He stopped chuckling and became silent for a long moment. "It is nae a shame to enjoy a kiss, lass. 'Tis a natural thing between a man and woman." His hands began rubbing gently along the length of her shoulders and arms, sending little ripples of pleasure through her.

"No' for a nun, it is nae."

His arms tightened, only for an instant before she heard him blow out a hard breath. She was surprised to hear that her words could draw a reaction from him. His strength was so much superior to her own that he seemed removed from her ability to affect him. Yet she had.

"Ye are no' going to be a bride of Christ, Brina. I've no intention of being cruel to ye, but I give ye my solemn word that what I say is my bond. The Lindseys need the alliance with yer father, and I cannae have any woman the gossips might claim is no' birthing my children."

"But—"

He reached up and placed his hand over her lips. Surprise widened her eyes as he pulled her head back to rest against his chest.

"No more argument from ye now, Brina. Be very sure that I am laird where we are headed, and my word will be obeyed. If ye want to fight with me, ye can do it behind the closed door of our bedchamber, no' in the sight of me men. My word must be respected, just as yer father's is on Chattan land."

She tried to protest, but her words emerged as nothing but smothered sounds.

"One more word, lass, and I'll take ye off somewhere private now where ye can say what is on yer mind, and I will be happy to show ye again how much ye enjoy my kiss."

She drew in a harsh gasp. Heat filled her cheeks, because she had to admit that part of her liked his idea. Her lips began tingling with recollection and longing for another opportunity to have his mouth on them.

"But if we do that, lass, I believe we shall nae make Birch Stone this day, and that would mean that I would have to keep ye warm tonight with naught but my plaid and body."

He placed a soft kiss against her neck, and she shuddered while she drew a rocky breath. His hand moved from her lips to slowly stroke across her chin and beneath it, before smoothing along the skin that he had just kissed.

"But I believe I like that idea a bit too much, and I need to think of my men passing the night without their wives if we end up lingering and wasting the daylight." He turned her head so that their eyes met, and she forgot to draw breath when she witnessed what was flickering in his eyes.

A hard promise was there, one that hinted at a man who was being pushed to the limits of his control. She was strangely attracted to the battle in his eyes, because he was resisting the urge to have her.

As shameful as it was, she discovered that she found it complimentary.

"So let me ride my mare if ye truly do want to cover more ground." Being held so close to him made her tremble. Escaping from it seemed more important than slowing their progress.

"I'll put ye on yer mare, lass, but with the promise that if ye make me chase ye down, we'll be settling the matter of our future the moment that I get me hands on ye."

"Ye claimed that ye would nae be cruel."

But then most men didn't think rape a cruelty, but more something women should bear. Some men even claimed there were women who enjoyed being forced to yield to their lust. She turned her face forward because she refused to allow him to see that she feared such a thing.

She should have expected it the moment he arrived and took her.

Gentle fingers cupped her chin and turned her face back toward his.

"I will nae rape ye, Brina."

"Is that so? Isna that the way yer father brought ye into this world?"

His eyes narrowed. "Nae, it isna."

"Then why wouldn't yer mother wed yer father?"

She didn't expect him to smile. Her words were insulting, questioning his word, which would have angered most men. Connor flashed a grin at her instead.

"Because she didna want my father to be denied her dowry, so she refused to wed, and the church went after her father because there was a babe they didna want to suffer being illegitimate. Her father relented."

"Well… do nae be thinking there will be the same between us. My father never changes his mind."

"Neither do I, Brina Chattan."

❧

She pressed her lips together so tightly, they turned white.

Connor felt his temper straining against his determination to remain on the trail home, because he wanted to take her over the ridge, where he might wipe the rejection from her eyes. She didn't trust him. It was only fair, something he should expect, considering their situation, but it still burned into his mind until he found it hard to think of anything else. She enjoyed his touch, and part of him was very impatient to show her just how much she would like being his wife.

"I suppose I'll have to wait until ye have reason to trust me."

She blinked, uncertainty appearing in her eyes before she turned to look forward. The scent of her skin rose up to tease him with how feminine

she smelled. Women were indeed amazing creatures, for they were endowed with a form that was
pleasing to men from the tops of their heads down
to their toes. There were plenty of men who made
the mistake of only taking when it came to their
female partners, but he had been lucky to live in the
stables, where he'd met a man who taught him how
to worship a woman.

Connor grinned when he thought of Old Sawson.
The man had served the stables since he was a lad
and been ignored by the mistress of the estate when
it came time for promotions among the household
staff. That fact had never kept Sawson from enjoying
life. The man had taught Connor by example that
true happiness came from inside a man first, and if
that man were wise, he learned to take the time to
seduce a woman before he took her. A slow stroke of
the hands and careful placement of the lips were the
only keys to unlocking passion inside a lass, which
was something that no man could force. He found
his thoughts returning to the kiss he'd stolen from
Brina. It was the truth that he'd taken it, but she had
returned it sweetly when he didn't bruise her lips in
some quest to prove he was her master. He felt his
cock twitch beneath his kilt but held the chuckle that
wanted to escape his lips.

There were much better ways to master his newly
claimed bride. In fact, he was beginning to see the
early onslaught of winter as a happy event, because
it would grant them long days of being allowed to
do nothing save explore the delights that they could
experience together. He was going to enjoy taking a

wife, even more so because of the memory of his aunt telling him that he'd never have a union blessed by the church. Never hold a woman in any embrace that wasn't labeled sinful.

Connor frowned as he considered his aunt Mildred. She had been a hard woman who enjoyed her greed and made no excuses for the fact that she considered herself better than any other Lindsey because her mother had been noble-blooded. She had enjoyed the years his uncle had been laird and given her freedom to do whatever she pleased. Connor had often wondered why his aunt didn't kill him, since she had made it plain that she wanted him to lie in his grave before his uncle did.

Vanora had taken more abuse from Mildred than he had, though. His sister had been kept carefully in the castle, where Mildred had overseen her education and behavior. The little girl had been broken and taught to obey without the slightest protest, so that Mildred might select the girl's husband and maintain control of the Lindsey clan through her.

But that plot had failed. Connor didn't feel any remorse for the death his aunt had suffered. In his eyes, being run through with a sword was a kinder fate than she deserved. He smiled as he considered the fact that by sending him to the stables, Mildred had made it possible for him to escape the Douglas raiders who intended to take control of the Lindsey clan by stealing his sister and killing the last of their grandfather's blood. The Douglas ran both Connor's uncle and aunt through before quitting the castle and taking Vanora with them. They planned to inherit through his sister, once she was old enough to wed and breed. Her offspring would be raised to be loyal to the Douglas and their interests.

A clever plan, but one that had been taunted by his presence. Even born a bastard, he had been acknowledged on the day of his birth by his father, and there was no way to ignore that his mother's eventual marriage had made him the heir to the Lindsey lairdship. It had taken years in court to prove it, and Connor had other lairds to thank for seeing the matter settled. McLeren, Cameron, and McLeod had all agreed that the Douglas would not be adding another large territory to their holding, and they had made sure that Connor inherited.

It had certainly been an interesting twist of fate to leave the stable and lay his head in the largest chamber in Birch Stone.

Brina shivered, and he reached down to pluck up her hood from where it was hanging between their bodies and raised it up to cover her head. His touch startled her again, but she was becoming more accustomed to it. He felt her quiver and attempt to lean forward to keep their torsos from rubbing together. The undyed wool of her skirts fluttered in the wind and covered his knees while they rode.

Your fate is changing, little Brina… Just as drastically as mine did…

She was not going to become a bride of Christ, in spite of the lifetime she had been preparing for it. Connor allowed his lips to rise into a smile, because he was finally looking forward to sleeping in that chamber that had once belonged to Mildred. It was a fine room, to be sure, but one he had considered useless until now.

Now he had a bride to take to it, and that pleased him. Greatly.

. ❧

The sky never cleared but became darker as the clouds began to press down on them. It seemed like the horizon was falling, the space between heaven and earth decreasing because the clouds were so thick. Snow fluttered down in soft flakes for half the day, but sometime near sunset it began to pelt them unmercifully.

Brina huddled beneath the hood of her cloak, shivering as the air became frigid. Her knee-high boots no longer kept her feet and calves warm. The speed of the stallion kept her gowns fluttering, which prevented them from holding any heat against her legs. Her single comfort was warmth coming from the man behind her.

It was amazing how much heat radiated from his body. As the daylight bled away into darkness, she discovered herself grateful for his insistence that she ride with him. The horse never slowed its pace, and it seemed to have no difficulty with the rocky terrain they rode across. There was a sense of eagerness that increased as darkness began to wrap around them once again. Exhaustion raked its claws along her body. Each motion of the horse began to grind her joints. She moved her hips in unison with the beast and the man behind her, because to do anything else was to invite torment along the insides of her thighs and her sex.

Brina was certain she had never been so tired in her entire life. Her eyes burned in spite of the chilly air, and her neck muscles felt as though they were too weak to hold her head up any longer. If she had slipped off the horse to the ground, she would have slept where she landed, because she didn't think that she could do anything more than collapse.

"Look there, lass... That's Birch Stone, our destination."

"Ye are pleased to be home." She was too tired to think about what was wise to say or not. Ahead of them, lights twinkled, looking warm and inviting.

"Aye, I am, lass. Birch Stone is a strong castle. Ye can see the sea from the top of the towers, and that allows the salt air to blow through the towers. It is a fine place to make yer home."

He was proud of it too. She couldn't miss the pride that edged his words, but it was not the sort she had learned to dislike. There was the pride that a man truly earned, and then there was the sort that was nothing but empty greed for respect that those men didn't want to go to the trouble of earning.

Brina looked at the towers rising up against the night sky. They looked cold, and a chill traveled down her spine in response. She wasn't sure why she thought they looked cold, for she had been raised inside a fortress very similar. Birch Stone had five towers rising to different heights. A curtain wall was built between them, and she could see that there were two sections to the castle, one upper area that had three towers and another curtain wall that sloped down from those to protect it further from land assault. The farthest towers were imposing, and her heart sank as she contemplated trying to escape from them. Not only would she have to make it out of the towers and through the inner yard, there would be another yard with overlooking towers to cross before freedom might be hers. High cliffs rose on either side of the walls at a midpoint too, making the castle look like an extension of the mountains.

"There will be a warm hearth and something to sup on, I promise ye that, lass."

Brina felt guilty for the bitterness that rose from her in response to his words. Every soul had the right to be happy when they returned home, but she felt nothing except scorn for the welcome Connor spoke of. Exhaustion nipped at every inch of her body and even felt as though it were soaked into her bones, but still she cast a look behind her, searching for some sign of an escape from the fortress looming in front of her.

"Ye have quite a number of promises for me, but I wonder why ye expect me to trust in yer word when ye will make good on it only after I have broken my promise to my father and kin. Calling me names does no' change that, Connor Lindsey."

She heard Connor make a low sound beneath his breath. "Do ye really long for the life of a nun so much?"

"That is too personal a thing to ask. Ye have no right to ask me such a question."

"No right? I am going to be yer husband." His tone was rich with determination. "If ye will but let go of some of yer stubbornness, love might grow in yer heart for our union."

He was trying to tempt her again, his voice deep and husky. Part of her admired his dedication, but it was not enough to drown out the years of being taught to obey her father.

"The church brings order to Scotland. If I turn my back on my place there, how can any of us expect others to serve? There would be nothing but war without the church to keep peace."

"Becoming my wife will place alliances between the Chattan, McLeod, and Lindsey. Those three clans will make the Douglas think twice about raiding any of us and trying to absorb more territory."

"That is something that ye crave, but the church is bigger than any single clan; that is why they are able to keep peace."

One day Connor would be old, and if no one respected that he was laird, he might be run through so that another could take his place. Any children she gave him would be thrown from the towers she looked at because of their blood. When monarchs fell, the land was often full of anarchy.

"And ye are one daughter, Brina. Changing yer destiny will nae unravel the fabric of Scotland."

"Ye insult me be saying that."

He blew out a hard breath. "Not so, Brina, for the very fact that ye are virtuous is why I took ye. Keeping ye is a compliment, and that's a fact, for ye are worthy."

"What I am is yer revenge against Melor Douglas."

She muttered the words as her heart began to sink into despair. Her mind was full of dark tidings, and she didn't have any strength left to push them aside.

They had reached the entrance to the gate between the front two towers. Up on the curtain walls, fires were set to illuminate anyone approaching the fortress. There would also be archers up there, with their arrows notched and ready to let loose if the captain of the watch gave the order. With darkness fully fallen, anyone riding up to the gate would be considered suspicious. Such was a healthy attitude for any fortress on the coast as well as so far north.

"Ye have one fact correct, lass. I do have what I sought, and I plan to keep ye. If it must be against yer will, so be it, for I will have my Chattan bride." He slid a hard arm around her body, binding her against him while he pulled his stallion up so that they might be identified. He let out another owl's screech, long and loud, while his men held their horses steady behind him.

A faint ringing sounded from atop one of the towers, and it was answered by another bell down on the curtain wall. The ringing began to spread along the wall until a steady chiming filled the air. A heavy groan sounded from the curtain wall. Brina heard it as much as she felt it vibrating through the air. The thick chains that raised and lowered the iron gate began to wind, filling the air with the loud sound of metal colliding with metal. The arm around her waist held her against a body that was just as solid as the gate rising up in front of her. Connor didn't wait for the way to be completely cleared. He leaned down, pressing her against the neck of his horse so that they could ride beneath the gate that was still only half-risen. His men sent up a cheer, both from outside and from within the fortress. She heard it echoing along the curtain wall and from the arrow slits high up in the towers too.

The sound terrified her because it magnified just how helpless she was now that she was surrounded by Lindsey retainers who so clearly approved of their laird's bringing her into their castle.

Combined with the hard body pressing her down, she felt more like a prisoner than she ever had. Panic tore at her, making it impossible to remain still. She struggled against everything because she felt as though she could not breathe. The sound of the horse's hooves against the packed dirt of the outer yard was too much for her to bear, and she couldn't remain poised and collected.

Connor snorted next to her ear, his arm tightening as he sat up straight again. There wasn't even an inch allowed between them, and she strained to break away from his body.

"I cannae breathe!"

The second gate was already rising to welcome the laird home, and Connor rode through it without hesitation. He dropped the reins and used his second arm to clamp around her, because she was tearing at his forearm in her quest for space between them.

"I should have left ye tied."

His voice was low and full of irritation, but that did not deter her from struggling to gain freedom from his embrace.

"All the better to force me to yer will... is that it?"

The stallion came to a stop in the inner courtyard, and Connor snorted with what sounded like rising temper. Brina tossed her head and shoved at his arms again, her own demeanor anything but sedate.

"What are ye saying, Brina? That ye have a

preference for rope biting into yer flesh? Somehow I doubt it."

"Do nae, for it is the truth. I swear I like it more than yer arms about me."

And she meant every word at that moment. One of his men approached them, lifting his hands to help her off the stallion. Connor unlocked his imprisoning arms at long last, and she took instant advantage of the freedom. She slipped down the side of the animal, delighted not to have a saddle to contend with, which made it simple to push herself off the top of the beast. Her own body weight took her the rest of the way to the ground in a quick motion that startled the horse.

It wasn't the wisest thing she might have done while in the midst of so many full stallions. Her skirts flipped up, causing many of the animals to toss their heads and pull against those holding their reins.

"Are ye mad, woman?"

Connor jumped down and grabbed her arm in a grip that stung for the first time. He propelled her out of the way of the horses with a hold that allowed her no choice. That gained him a hiss from her as her temper flared up. Brina didn't bother to quell her mood, because she feared that the only other thing she might do was collapse into a weeping mound at his feet. It was fight or complete surrender, and it felt as though there were nothing in between.

"Mad? Ye dare to ask if I am insane. Ye are the one stealing from the church! That is madness, sir! It is—"

"It is done!" Connor made a slashing motion with his hand as his voice echoed off the stone walls of the fortress. He released her to do it, and Brina discovered herself standing firm in the face of his displeasure. She kept her chin held high as she snarled back in response to his words.

"No, it is nae!"

Brina could feel the eyes of his men on them, but she refused to care. Let him be repulsed by her defiance and lack of respect for his position and gender.

"Send me to the abbey, for I will nae obey ye, Connor Lindsey."

She had never spoken so brazenly before, and a surge of power burned through the exhaustion that had been threatening to buckle her knees.

Connor suddenly chuckled, and the sound was not a kind one.

"We'll be seeing about that, lass."

He moved faster than she recalled him being able to. Maybe it was the darkness, but one moment he was staring down at her from his greater height, and the next he had lunged across the space between them and clamped his hands about her waist. She gasped and dug her feet into the dirt to move away from him, but he tossed her up and over his shoulder with a single powerful motion of his arms.

No human should find it so easy to carry another.

"I'll bid ye all good night, for I have a need to settle my bride inside, lads!"

A cheer rose up around them, making her sputter with fury. She hung over his shoulder like a sack of grain, but Brina had no intention of remaining so docile. She flattened her hands against his broad back and pushed herself up so that she was straight. There were several chuckles in response to her rebellion, and more of the men in the yard turned to see what was amusing their comrades.

The smiles that appeared on their faces sent such heat into hers that she would not have been surprised to feel her skin sizzling because it flamed so hot. The three feathers standing up on the side of Connor's bonnet suddenly caught her eye, and she grabbed it off his head before he reacted to the fact that she wasn't going easily over his shoulder.

Brina sent it flying a second before Connor bounced her, and she tumbled down with a gasp, her belly tightening as she anticipated hitting the stone steps he had begun carrying her up.

"Ye're a true hellcat beneath that nun's robe, Brina. I cannae wait to bare ye."

He captured her in his arms as she fell, cradling her across his body while crushing her at the same time so that she couldn't continue her fight with him.

"I believe I am going to enjoy taming ye."

"Ye will nae."

He carried her beneath the wide double doors that led into the first tower that belonged to the second portion of the fortress.

"I will nae tame ye, or I will no' enjoy doing it?"

There was a hint of wicked enjoyment in his tone that sent her straining against him once again.

"Neither!"

He laughed at her while she heard his boots hitting solid stone floor.

"But I will tame ye, Brina. Ye many depend upon it."

There was a scurry in front of them, doors opening, and then he suddenly released her feet. She had been straining against him so hard that her legs went flying up into the air before they fell back down. Their knees knocked against each other, and she discovered herself grateful for the fact that he had bound her against his body with one solid arm. If he hadn't, she would have landed on her backside, but that didn't keep her from shoving her fists against his chest once she regained her footing.

"Release me."

"I think no', Brina. If ye are going to act like a hellcat, ye will have to take what comes with behaving so wildly."

"This is unholy…"

There was a scuff against the floor behind them, and he stiffened before releasing her.

"It seems that we disagree again, lass, because I see nothing unholy in enjoying one another when we shall soon be wed."

The firm belief in his voice agitated her, and she flipped the edges of her cloak open to reveal her gown. She gripped a handful of the undyed fabric and felt her fingers ache because she had tightened her fist so much.

"Look at me, Connor Lindsey. I cannae wed ye."

He reached down and grasped the two straps at her waist that buttoned toward the back of the overgown to keep the fabric from billowing loose while maintaining a nonflattering shape. He yanked hard enough to pop the buttons off, and she gasped as she heard them scatter onto the floor.

"What I see is a dress that ye do nae need to wear ever again."

He pulled the loosened gown upward, and her arms were caught up as he stripped the garment completely over her head and away from her body. Connor held the overdress like a trophy, lifting it high in one hand while she crossed her arms over her body. Clad only in her undergown, she felt exposed and on display.

"Taking my clothing changes nothing."

"Neither will wearing it, for I've made my choice, and ye are here."

He turned and threw her overgown into the hearth. Brina gasped and lunged toward it, but Connor caught her, his arms jerking her to a halt even as the fabric caught fire. Light flickered brightly across the chamber as the gown burned quickly, and then just as fast as it had ignited, it died back down into the glowing bed of embers. Her undyed gown was naught but glowing ash among the logs that still burned.

"Now be finished with yer ideas of serving the church, Brina. Ye will be my wife, not a bride of Christ." He released her, and she looked up to discover him watching her with an expression that was impossible to read.

"Burning my gown does nae remove the promise I made to my father."

A muscle along his jaw began to twitch.

"Be very sure that I intend to enjoy having ye, Brina. We shall have a warm marriage. That is my promise to ye, and yer father isna here, so it will be my word that ye must deal with."

She snarled and cast a quick look about. A small pile of smooth stones near the hearth that were there to catch the heat and prevent it from escaping up the chimney. She bent down and picked one up.

"I won't be the only one dealing with what is here, Connor Lindsey."

There were several gasps from behind him, but the man laughed loudly enough to drown everything out. He threw back his head and let his amusement bounce off the ceiling. She was tempted to hit him again, the urge so strong, she must have moved her hand in some small way, because he suddenly jerked his head back down to where he might watch her. There was a challenge flickering in his eyes, one that dared her to try what she would.

Brina felt her teeth grind, and she threw the stone at him with a huff. He caught it, with a sure hand and an arrogant smirk.

"I look forward to our next encounter… *hellcat.*"

Four

CONNOR TURNED AND LEFT. BRINA STARED AT THE longer pleats of his plaid swaying slightly with his stride. His sword was still strapped to his back, and she had to bite back a scathing response. His bonnet was still missing, allowing her an unobstructed view of his hair. He kept it just shoulder length, and a section of it was pulled back in a small plait to keep it from falling into his eyes. It was a sandy-blond color, lighter than her own, and hinted at Norse blood flowing through his veins.

Aye, that made sense sure enough; the man was a Viking, completely without respect for any rules save for what he desired. The fact that he had the strength to do what he pleased only renewed the surge of temper that had seen her fighting with him in front of his men.

Well, she was not sorry. She wasn't some bride who needed to take her position with grace and good cheer.

Brina turned away from the large hearth and allowed it to warm her back. Without her overgown, she found the night air chilly, but the fire was radiating vast heat that felt good on her meagerly clad body.

She swallowed roughly when she faced the fact that she was not alone. She recalled hearing those women gasp now but had somehow forgotten while Connor was there to agitate her so completely.

She cringed inside but kept her chin steady. Let them see that she was not impressed with their laird. Maybe one of them would show her a secret way out of the castle while the rest considered themselves well rid of a temperamental mistress.

Four women stood near the doorway, all of them watching her silently. Each wore the Lindsey plaid with its yellow and lavender threads. The plaid was worn as an arisaid, with the length of it going down their backs with only one corner visible over their right shoulders. Each woman wore a belt that kept the plaid secure against her waist, and the portion that draped across her back might be raised to shield her head from the rain. A long moment stretched out while they stared at one another.

"Well now. What's all this standing about for?"

An older woman entered the room and paused for a moment to look between the four women and Brina. Her hair was streaked with gray, and a large ring of keys hung from her belt, announcing the fact that she was a woman of position at Birch Stone.

"The laird burned her church robe," one of the women answered, but in a soft voice that betrayed just how uncertain she was of her laird's actions. The other women waited to see what the woman with the keys would make of Connor's actions.

"Well, I'll say that's a fine idea, for ye have no' the temperament for a nun. I had to brush the mud out of the laird's bonnet, and ye broke one of the feathers too." The older woman clicked her tongue and snapped her fingers at the women. They instantly began to move, each of them apparently knowing what she was expected to do. "Ye are nae meek enough to be a bride of Christ at all. We all saw that clear as daylight."

The girl who had spoken looked toward the older woman. "She threatened the laird with a stone too, threw it at him right in front of us all."

Brina felt her cheeks heat, and the older woman was quick to notice. She smiled, and wrinkles appeared at the edges of her eyes. She propped her hands on her hips and surveyed Brina from head to toe with a gaze that was keen and sharp.

"I am called Maura, and the laird has set me as the head of the house here. I do hope that I can trust that ye will keep yer temper for the laird, since I'd hate to have to have men in here while ye're bathing."

Brina lowered herself without hesitation, bending her knees with one foot tucked in back of the other so that her head dipped in deference. The woman nodded approvingly.

"It seems that ye have good manners to go along with that temper; however, it is I who should be showing respect toward ye, mistress."

Maura lowered herself, while Brina tried to keep her jaw from dropping open. The other women stopped what they were doing and turned to face her so that they might offer her the same courtesy.

"I am not yer mistress."

"Well, I heard the laird clear enough, and it is nae

in my nature to argue with what he set down as the way it will be. Only a wife might do that—in private, mind ye."

There was an unmistakable ring of authority in her voice, and it sent sadness through her because Maura sounded very much like Newlyn, her father's head of house. Brina was suddenly aware of how alone she was, and no amount of preparation through the years might have made the moment easier. Knowing something and feeling it were vastly different. Brina realized that her arms were wrapped around herself in an attempt to find solace, which was childish, and still she couldn't quite force her hands in front of her.

"A bath will make ye see things with a clear mind."

"A bath?" Brina heard her voice quiver with anticipation. She hadn't dared to long for a bath, for many a fortress did not consider bathing a necessity.

"Aye, we've a fine bathhouse here, and I find that there are fewer fleas when there is more bathing and washing."

Brina looked over to see that there were several tubs in the room, but they were all tipped up on their sides and facing the hearth so that the heat would dry them. Each was quite large and made of copper, which made sense because the metal was too soft for making weapons and therefore the least expensive of all metals.

"The air here is moist and filled with salt from the sea. We tip the tubs up to keep them from rusting."

A pair of the women pushed on the raised side of one tub, and it fell toward the floor. Brina expected a crash, but there only a dull thud because the stone floor was covered with wooden slats that absorbed much of the noise. Only half the floor was covered with wood, and as she looked closer, she could see that it was a sort of mat made from young tree limbs that had all been stripped smooth of their bark.

"A woman from the Prussias told the last laird about doing that to the floor, and I must say that it is a fine improvement."

"The Prussias?"

Maura nodded while she fitted one of her keys into a locked chest sitting on a table at the far side of the room. The lock clicked before it opened, and she lifted the lid to peer inside.

"Birch Stone gets a good many visitors because we're so far north that the ships coming around from the frozen waters up there stop here for provisions."

"I've never seen the ocean." The only ships she had ever seen outside a book were small boats made for traveling on the lakes.

"Ye'll see it clear enough on the morrow, and hear it too." Maura lifted several things from the chest and brought them over to a small stool that one of the other women brought toward the tub. She placed a chunk of soap on top of the stool along with a square of linen for washing.

It became clear to Brina that they were intent on treating her like their mistress. All five of them working to prepare her bath as though she deserved such service. She fingered the fabric of her underrobe, unsettled because she had never been waited upon. In fact, she had often assisted her sister and other female relatives at their baths because her future was to be one of service and devotion. She bathed last, after everyone else.

"I will haul water."

Maura shook her head. "There is no need of that."

"Yes, there is. I have never been waited upon. I do nae know what else to do except for my share of the work."

There were several looks shot between the maids, but a click from Maura's tongue sent their attention back to their tasks. "Aye, well, it will surely be a blessing to have a mistress who knows the duties of running a house from personal experience."

"But I will nae be running this house."

The head of house looked at her again, a deep frown marring her face. "I think we should nae be discussing what is a matter for the laird to decide, because he has said ye are the mistress, so ye shall be attended."

The woman was obviously slightly ill at ease with the fact that Brina had been promised to the church. Two of the other women looked nervous as well, but they all continued to prepare a bath for her without hesitation, because their laird had set her above them with his words.

Brina chewed on her lower lip, forcing herself to remain silent while she watched to see who might be receptive to helping her escape Birch Stone. She should have thought of it before fighting with Connor where all might see. The fox trapped its prey by creeping unseen through the dense portions of the thicket. If it ran through the open, it often ended up caught. She would be wise to recall what Bran had taught her and have patience until the time was right.

She was so deep in thought, a splash of water startled her.

The splashing sound continued, drawing a short gasp from her lips when she looked at the tub. One of the women had fit a trough against what looked to be the back wall of the tower. But there was a thick slab of wood that had been held in place by iron bars set into the stone. The trough fit beneath the iron on another curved piece that supported the trough. The wood was slid upward, and water was now flowing through the hole in the wall. The water traveled along the trough and into the tub, where it splashed down just like a river had been diverted.

Maura chuckled softly at the look of wonder on her face.

"Right clever, isn't it? And feel how warm it is."

Brina couldn't resist the invitation. She could feel every bit of grime clinging to her skin. She crossed the floor and trailed her fingers through the rising water inside the copper tub. Another little sound escaped her lips, only this was one of delight. The water wasn't hot, but it was not as frigid as the night would have made her expect it to be.

"How can this be?"

She looked toward the wall, impatient to understand how the water system worked. The answer was as clear as the heat hitting her cheeks from the huge hearth. The water must have been stored behind the wall.

"That is genius."

"And I'm pleased to see that ye have a quick mind." Maura pointed up. "With the roof being slanted, the men built a second wall alongside the outer one and left a space between them for the water to collect.

That hole there is near the bottom, and the weight of the water makes it simple to have it flow out. Even in the winter, the hearth melts the snow so that we have water every day."

Her skin began to itch. Chattan Castle had no such clever contrivance, but that had not stopped her from bathing often. Even when it meant that she needed to haul snow inside.

"It would have been a shame to cut all this fine hair."

Brina felt Maura behind her lifting her thick braid and working open the tie that held the ends tight.

"Ye'll make a bonny sight with it brushed out and shimmering on yer shoulders."

Would she?

Maura began to work the sections of her hair free from the plait that had kept it out of her way. It was true that if she had made it to the abbey, her hair would have been cut away at her nape by a pair of golden shears that would have been presented to her to kiss first. A custom designed to help a new nun banish all her vanities and embrace a future that did not include looking pretty or gaining attention.

But did that mean Connor might find her hair pleasing?

She frowned because she failed to understand why such a thought came so easily and quickly to her mind. She felt the loneliness wrapping around her again, worse now because it seemed that even her mind was not her own anymore. It wasn't that she longed for the life of a nun, but she was hungry to know she had a place, and Connor was a stranger. How did she place her trust in a man who had stolen her away from her own kin? The man was hunting for revenge, and it would be foolish of her to forget that fact. It was for certain that he was every inch a Highlander, and they were known for striking back at those they felt had wronged them.

She was but the tool for that vengeance.

There was a sputter as one of the women pulled a large kettle out of the hearth and water trickled from its spout. She grasped the handle with a handful of her skirt to protect her fingers and carried it to the tub. The wood was pushed down to stop the flow of water now, and the trough had been lifted away and set against the wall. It glistened in the candlelight that didn't quite illuminate all the shadows in the corners. It was amazing how the darkness changed the way a room felt. Brina tried to remind herself that the prickle of sensation moving over her skin was nothing but foolish imagination. She knew there were many who would argue with her about that, for even the church preached of sinister specters that inhabited the night.

Bran had taught her to ignore such prattle as mindless mutterings of soothsayers and storytellers who needed to entertain those who listened to them. That was not to say that Bran didn't believe in spirits; the old Highlander simply didn't fear the ghost that walked with the mists after the sunset, and he'd taught her simply to be willing to share the nighttime with restless souls.

"Let's get this robe off ye now."

Brina jerked back to the present, shamed by the fact that she kept allowing her mind to wander. The two

days without sleep were obviously taking more of a
toll on her than she thought.

"I'll manage myself, thank you…" She stumbled
over her last few words.

Maura clicked her tongue in reprimand, but Brina
stepped away from the hands that were intent on
helping her to remove her last garment.

"I cannae recall the last time anyone was near…
or in the room with me… when I was… bare…
completely." Brina turned so that she faced Maura. "I
thank ye, all the same."

The head of house nodded with understanding, but
she did not turn to leave the room either.

"If ye had made it to the abbey, ye'd have
discovered that there is no privacy for novices."

"Well… yes, I was told to expect such."

Maura smiled and reached out to grasp two handfuls
of the loose undergown. "So ye'll just be adjusting, the
same as ye would have if the laird had nae brought ye
to Birch Stone. There is no difference between this
bathhouse and the one at the abbey."

"There most certainly is a difference."

Maura chuckled beneath her breath and gave a tug
that was harder than Brina had expected from her
small frame. The woman didn't lack strength, and
the undergown was soon in her grasp completely,
leaving Brina in nothing except her bare skin. Her
newly brushed hair floated down onto her back in a
soft flutter.

"Now sit down and let us have those boots. They
need attention, else they will turn hard, which would
be a shame considering they look to be so well made."

Maura even pointed toward a short stool while two of the women came forward to begin untying her boots.

"Best to learn no' to be so modest. Ye have naught that any of us do nae have, and there will be no rumors about ye if there are a few of my trusted maids to testify that ye are sound and healthy beneath yer robes."

Brina felt her mouth go dry. Maura's words were softly spoken, like a mother did with her child, but there was no mistaking the hard truth in them. Gossip was a sin, but that didn't stop the church from listening to it when it came to women. She might find herself being questioned if rumors began to circulate that she hid her body. What one person labeled modest, another would call suspicious. Several of the Lindsey maids were sneaking peeks at her while they worked, looking for marks that might be considered unnatural. Even if Connor had declared that she was to be his bride, no one wanted bad luck around, and a woman with a witch mark might bring a failed harvest. Superstition held just as much authority as the church did sometimes.

"The boots are new; my father had them made for me before I left for the abbey."

"We'll get them cleaned up." Maura's tone was tempered with authority both from her position in the house and her years. Brina sat, and two of the maids immediately attended her.

They loosened her boots and removed them, then dropped them first into pails of water to help remove some of the mud caked onto them.

"Now into the tub with ye before ye catch a chill."

Brina sank into the water gratefully, her muscles enjoying the warm water. It was far hotter than she ever prepared for herself, because she was normally so tired that she simply wanted the task of cleaning herself finished. Two days on a horse had left her sore, and she arched her lower back with a soft groan.

"I suppose the laird was worried that yer clan would be close on yer heels if he lingered."

"Of course he was, for he took me from my father on the road."

There were a few stunned glances, but she didn't temper her words. The tale was no doubt being repeated by Connor's retainers in the hall where they broke bread.

"The early snow covered our tracks, though."

"Aye, the snow is unusually early this year." Maura spoke without thinking but frowned when she realized the wide eyes of several of her maids. The girls were clearly thinking that the snow was a sign from heaven, just as Brina had told Connor it was. The older woman shook her head and a thin finger at her staff.

"But no' so early that I cannae recall years in the past when such has happened before. It is no' unnatural," the head of house declared in a firm tone.

The women came forward and began bathing her, no longer worried that she had brought misfortune to Birch Stone. Connor's will was law here. She was his possession just as surely as if she were a fox he'd snared and put in a sack to bring home.

The women didn't miss any part of her, and Maura washed her hair personally. Warm water was brought to rinse her hair, and her skin tingled from the soap, but it was a pleasant feeling.

"Come on out with ye now and stop holding yer breath. I suppose it's to be appreciated that ye are so uncomfortable with being touched, for it proves that ye are nothing like yer sister."

"What do ye mean?"

Brina stood up and stepped over the edge of the copper tub. The wood was smooth beneath her bare feet, and she discovered that the space between the boards allowed for the water running down her legs not to puddle around her feet. It would surely make it less likely that she might slip on wet stone.

"I mean experienced." Maura spoke plainly and firmly, drawing the attention of her helpers. "Ye sat there biting on yer lip the entire time, mistress. The look in yer eyes is nae something that anyone can fake. Even the most jaded of women fail to mask their experience completely from other women. Ye'll understand better once ye share yer wedding bed with the laird. An experienced woman knows the look of another experienced woman." Maura cast a quick look toward the two youngest maids.

They nodded and muttered "aye" immediately, but Brina was too busy listening to the last part of Maura's statement echo inside her head.

Share a bed with Connor...

The idea was too large to break down into anything she might deal with. She suddenly felt every scrape and bruise on her body. The women tending to her were gentle, but it still felt as though they had burlap gloves covering their hands, for each touch brushed over someplace that the last two days had left painful marks on.

Brina lifted her arms to allow the women to slip a fresh gown over her head. She froze when it settled around her ankles, her eyes going to the soft color of it. In the meager light, it looked like some shade of green that was found only in spring. She fingered it and found it soft and clean feeling. One of the women knelt at her feet and offered her a pair of warm slippers to keep the winter chill from her toes. Two more of the women helped her ease a dressing robe over her shoulders. This garment was made of thick wool, and the inside was lined with fur. She had never worn such a thing, for it was a luxury even if she had brought home many a rabbit and then dried the pelt so that the fur might be used to line the dressing robes of her sisters. She had always made do with a wool cloak and arisaid. Her garments were always simple and undyed. She gently touched the blue fabric of the dressing gown.

"That color suits ye well."

Brina jerked her face up and discovered the head of house watching her. There was a twinkle in Maura's eyes. "Ye remind me of a child on Twelfth Night, yer face all glowing with wonder as ye look at yer gifts."

She had only ever received practical gifts during the winter holidays, because her father didn't want her to suffer when she was sent to the abbey and expected to give up all worldly possessions.

Brina looked down again to hide her thoughts, for she felt like every feeling she had was on display.

"Come this way, mistress, and we shall have you tucked beneath a thick comforter in no time at all."

Brina followed Maura toward the back of the bathhouse but turned when she heard the sound of flowing water. One of the women pulled on a rope that lifted the far end of the copper tub into the air. Another trough that was much wider sat beneath the tub, and as the foot of it was lifted, the water spilled over the edge, falling in a glittering wave toward the trough waiting below. There was enough of an angle to see the water rushing downhill toward another hole in the wall, and the sound of water splashing against the side of the tower told her how the water was being discarded.

So clever and it meant that she might bathe every day, not just on special occasions.

Brina froze, realizing that her hair was brushed out behind her and she was truly prepared to be presented as a bride. The only thing lacking was a priest to give the blessing, but many a couple sought the church's approval after they had consummated their union.

That would benefit Connor and the Lindseys in every way too. If she had no virtue, then wedding Connor would be in her best interest, for even the church would look scornfully upon a soiled nun. She would be required to do years of penance before being allowed to take vows. Among those who had no possessions, she would be the lowest of the humble.

That was assuming Connor would wed her after having her. Considering that the man had taken her in vengeance, there was no way to trust that he would in fact marry her once he had lain with her. It was entirely possible that shaming her was what he sought. It wouldn't be a unique form of revenge either.

Connor's promise rose up to needle her. He'd clearly declared that he wanted to wed her, so her thoughts were vindictive, considering that he'd spoken in front of his own retainers.

It seemed that the only thing she held control over was herself, and she decided that fearing the unknown sickened her. Raising her face, she looked at Maura but found that the head of house was already moving across the chamber toward one of the darkened corners.

"Where are ye taking me?"

Maura looked slightly guilty, as though she had been hoping to avoid telling Brina anything until she had arrived and it was too late to argue.

The head of house tilted her head to one side and huffed softly. "Well now, there are two sets of stairs that lead out of this chamber. The ones here that are tucked in the corner are private." Maura tossed her head toward the doors Connor had brought her through. "Behind those are the two men the laird left to make sure ye do nae do anything foolish, like try to leave the tower when there is snow flying."

Brina felt her pride rear its head in the face of knowing that there were guards set on her. Only the guilty needed watching. It chafed her to know that Connor considered her untrustworthy.

But you do plan to attempt escape...

Her inner thoughts needed to be smothered. It was her duty to attempt escape. If she failed to try, she would be shaming her father just as Deirdre had done because she failed to try and set herself back onto the correct path. Nothing good could come from wrongdoing.

"Ye look like ye haven't slept in days, mistress. I promise there is a warm bed above this floor."

"That sounds very pleasant indeed." And just the word "bed" made her notice how weary she was. Her bones actually ached with it, but her belly was tied into a knot so tight, it felt almost impossible to lift her foot and set it atop the first stone step. One of the women went ahead with a candle that flickered and cast shadows that danced between the stone walls of the passageway. It was narrow and clearly constructed for nothing except function. It was so small that no candles were left burning in it, because the holders would have scraped anyone using it.

She admitted that she doubted if she had any strength left to protest what might be awaiting her at the top of the stairs. In the narrow confines of the stairwell, each step echoed. Brina heard her own breath and was sure the others could hear her heart accelerating. They reached the second floor and turned to mount another section of stone steps.

Maura didn't stop climbing until they reached the fourth story of the tower. It grew colder as they went higher, and the wind whistled through the arrow slits that looked like crosses so that the archer might aim in all directions. The open slits were an eerie reminder that the fortress was built to repel attack.

It was also constructed to keep those inside secure.

Or imprisoned, in her case.

"This is a fine chamber." Maura held a slim door open so that it would not shut on her.

"A bunk in the kitchen would serve for as tired as I am."

"That would nae do for the future mistress of Birch Stone."

The chamber they entered was like something out of a little girl's dream. Brina discovered herself enchanted with it, because it was everything that she had been told to not expect from life. She admitted that being lectured so often had sometimes seen her thinking about just what luxuries were.

This chamber had them for certain. Only a few candles burned, but they were pure beeswax, for the sweet scent of honey floated through the air. She drew in a deep breath and smiled when the scent of lavender also teased her nose. The shutters were closed tight over the windows, and in spite of the wind whistling through the arrow slits, there was not a single rattle from any of the wooden shutters, telling her that someone had tended to them recently.

The furnishings were fit for the grandest noble, or at least they were the finest she had ever seen. Two large chairs sat near the fireplace with their backs carved with the crest of the Lindsey clan. They had plump cushions tied to their seats, and the fabric was rich in hues of green and blue.

"I'll leave ye to settle in, mistress. No one shall disturb ye, but the laird bid me warn ye that the night is frigid and ye should no' venture out. His retainers will nae allow ye to."

"Of course he did."

The head of house clicked her tongue in disapproval of her tone. "He's a good laird, who thinks of his clan before himself. Consider that before ye judge him too harshly."

Maura lowered herself before going back to the narrow door and slipping away down the stairs. Brina sighed and realized that she was at last alone. She glanced around the chamber, walking into the center of it and turning all the way around before blowing out another breath.

But her relief was not complete, because she looked at the outer chamber doors and frowned as Maura's words rose as clear as a bell in her thoughts.

She realized that she had not been thankful enough for her future as a nun, because it had afforded her much freedom and privacy that she only now noticed the blessing of.

A large bed was set off to the other end of the room. It was set with curtains that were drawn, except for one side where the thick bedding was drawn down. It beckoned to her, and she didn't bother to ignore the summons. She was too tired to do anything but pinch out the candles on her way toward the bed. Once dark, the chamber seemed stranger, but the bedding was thick and scented with lavender.

She slid between the sheets, muttering with delight as the comforter settled around her and began to warm her toes.

Sleep rose up to embrace her, but it was not a dark oblivion. Instead Connor's blue eyes were there, watching her with that piercing gaze she noticed so much. The man mesmerized her, and that was no mistake. She was drawn to him, feeling some need to look into his eyes while she ventured closer to him.

Deep in sleep, she recalled his kiss, her lips tingling with sensation that bled down her body, warming every inch of her just as his touch had done.

If that was wickedness, if longing for another kiss was the path to damnation, then she was surely wicked.

❧

Maura lowered herself but kept her chin level when Connor frowned at her.

"Ye're my laird and have my loyalty, but I'll say it plain that I've come to speak my mind to ye."

Maura was old enough to be his mother, and in many ways she had raised him. She'd done her best to fill the emptiness left when his mother died and his uncle took control of the Lindsey clan.

"Then tell me straight, Maura. Do ye disapprove of my bride?"

The older woman who had wiped the blood off his face after countless fights scoffed at him.

"If that were so, I would nae have taken her above stairs to await ye, but told ye to do yer own sinful deeds."

Connor hadn't anticipated how much he would enjoy hearing that Brina was ready for him. His cock twitched, surprising him, because just a few minutes past he had been certain fatigue was going to crush him beneath its weight.

"Then what is on yer mind?"

Maura clicked her tongue at his tone. Connor felt a twinge of guilt because she was the woman who had been there for him, and she rarely spoke her mind now that he was laird. He forced himself to bite back his next demanding question and wait for her to speak.

"Yer tone tells me that ye're eager for yer bride."

"That would be considered a blessing in most matches made for the sake of alliances."

"Aye, upon that point I agree." Maura stopped talking and pressed her lips together for a long moment while she eyed him. There was a wealth of knowledge in her stare, the sort a person only gained through experience.

"Ye have grown into a fine man, as large as yer father and maybe a wee bit more." She ran her gaze down his frame once more. "Which is why I feel I should say my piece to ye. That girl is nae petite, but she is still half yer size."

Connor felt his temper rise. "I will no' be rough with her."

Maura kept her tone even but firm. "That is no' what I am aiming to talk about, but rough to a man's thinking is different than it is to a woman's."

Connor felt his fatigue return, or maybe it was frustration. He shook his head. "What are ye getting at, Maura?"

"That girl was raised to serve the church."

Connor snorted with his displeasure. "I know that, but it was her or no alliance, which would leave us with the Douglas prowling our borders like hungry wolves."

"Ye are becoming cross for no good reason, Laird. I am nae here to debate whether or no' taking her was a good deed or a bad one."

Connor went to speak, but Maura held up her hand, and he snapped his jaw shut.

"I mean to tell ye what it means for a lass to be

raised in that fashion, for there is no reason that ye might think upon the matter if ye do nae have it brought to you by an experienced woman, and due to the circumstances, her mother is nae here either."

Connor felt his forehead crease. "Which leaves you, so go on with what ye have to say."

Maura grunted, obviously becoming cross with him. "Ye are twice her size, and while that is nae an uncommon thing in couples, that girl has nae been touched."

"I expect her to be a maiden, which was the entire point of taking her instead of her sister."

Maura shook her head and blew out a short breath that left no doubt that she was growing impatient with him. "Even a maiden is allowed more touching and flirting than a girl who has been promised to the church."

"Aye, I noticed that she's skittish already."

"Ye noticed, but did ye take any time to think upon the fact that a simple touch is alarming to her? Rush into consummating yer union, and ye might turn that girl fearful or, worse yet, resentful of intimacy for the rest of her days."

"Obviously ye didna see her in the courtyard when we rode in. Brina Chattan is no quivering lass."

Maura humphed at him. "I did see, and one has naught to do with the other, but I'm wasting my time if ye cannae hear what it is I am saying." She lowered herself but hesitated before turning to leave. "Mark my words, Laird; fail to seduce her like a lover, and ye will never have a contented wife. Ye will nae be the first to suffer a woman who feels shame every time she enjoys her husband. Yer aunt was that sort. That's the truth that ye do nae know, but I do. It ate away at her soul and turned her bitter because she never learned to trust your uncle after he stole her and forced her into his bed so that there might be no changing the fact that she was his. That's a man's thinking, but I'll tell ye a woman's." She lifted one finger up in warning. "Ye can steal a woman, but nae her affections. Her heart will be only hers, no matter what ye decide to do with her body."

His head of house left him alone with his thoughts, and Connor groaned. He turned his back on the doorway, trying to hide his unsettled emotions by facing the fireplace. There was nothing but a bed of coals blanketed in a thick layer of ash, giving heat but very little light. There wasn't any light in the room because he preferred it dark. He'd lived a large chunk of his life without candles, and it had made him strong. The dark was nothing to fear.

But allowing Brina to become anything like his aunt was…

He'd all but forgotten that his uncle had stolen her with her dowry from a ship bound for England. His aunt had been a Frenchwoman who was a cousin of the English king. Connor's uncle had claimed her and wed her, but the couple had never been content. He hadn't thought on it for years because there were many matches in Scotland that didn't begin on the most… legal of terms.

That memory filled his mouth with a bitter taste.

He lifted his forearm and looked at the scratches Brina had left on his skin. She might have been raised to serve the church, but there was a flame inside her that was neither humble nor meek.

It was that part that he was going to enjoy taming.

He took the stairs with silent feet and only slowed his pace enough so that the retainers he'd posted at the door of Brina's room might recognize him in the darkness. They jerked their heads about when they noticed motion in the stairwell, their hands moving out of instinct before their gazes settled on his face. They reached up and tugged on the corners of their bonnets before stepping aside so that he could open one side of the double doors.

The room was cloaked in darkness, but that didn't stop him from locating Brina in the bed. She hadn't closed the curtains, making it simple to spot her with the light from the fireplace coals.

He crossed to her, feeling the slightest quiver of anticipation move through his belly. The feeling startled him, but at the same time it pleased him greatly. He'd spent a great deal of time thinking of this moment, when he would see his bride sleeping in the bed he was proud to be able to provide for her. The sheets she slept on had never been used by another soul; neither had the bed. Everything in the chamber had been carefully selected for her arrival. The sight of her unbound hair shimmering against the plump, goose feather–filled pillow was the reward that he'd desired while planning the chamber.

He sat down on the side of the bed, careful not to jolt the mattress. Brina stirred, her breathing increasing for a mere moment before she turned her head and settled her cheek against the soft pillowcase. But her breathing never completely slowed back to the deep rhythm that it had been. He watched as she turned her head, almost as if she could sense his presence.

Part of him enjoyed that idea. It had taken him two solid years to reach an agreement with her father. The fact that those negotiations had resulted in Deirdre being named as his bride-to-be didn't stop him from feeling the glow of satisfaction spread through him now.

He was very pleased with the woman in front of him. More than pleased, for he felt drawn to her. The kiss he'd stolen from her burned a path through his mind, and even the fatigue of riding for so many days with little rest wasn't enough to make him eager to seek out his bed instead of sitting on the side of hers.

The delicate scent of her hair teased his nose. Connor reached down to touch the delicate strands, his fingertips gliding through them while a smile tugged his lips upward. Brina muttered and turned her face toward his hand. Her eyes remained closed, but she kicked at the bedding with soft motions that made slipping sounds against the sheets. His gaze was drawn to her lips. Even in the dark he could see the soft motions she made with them, almost as if she were dreaming of his kiss. He stretched his fingers out until he stroked the soft, tender skin. A delicate sound passed over those lips as she pressed the most innocent of kisses to his fingers.

Connor felt that kiss more intensely than any he had ever experienced. For the first time since he had heard of his parents' death, his heart felt warm. There was no logic to it, no way to truly grasp what he felt, only that it sat there burning slowly in his chest, melting ice that he hadn't really noticed. Brina was the source of the heat that warmed him. The idea of leaving tore at him because every fiber in his being dictated that he lie down beside her and bask in the glow.

But Maura's words rose up to needle him. Brina was an innocent. She lay so trusting in the bed he'd selected for her that he stood up before he lost the resolve to leave her. Many things were said about him, but he wasn't a rapist, and his head of house was correct about his bride. She wasn't ready to accept the passion between them. It was a complication he hadn't considered.

Connor made it across the floor and to the door before he snorted with his frustration. His men turned the moment he opened the door. Their expressions reflected their surprise to see him leaving, and he closed the door before he spoke.

"She's an obedient lass to her father, so expect her to try escaping. Mind yer hands with her, for she's shy of touches, but keep her within the inner walls and be sure that whoever takes the next watch knows that she's to be treated gently."

His men nodded their approval. Connor drew in a stiff breath and forced himself to move a few more steps away from the doors. Traditions kept Scotland from dissolving into a barbaric place where might made right. He could not think ill of her father for promising one of his daughters to the church. The church had its place and needed its share of devoted souls to keep it functioning.

Just as he had needed to claim his Chattan bride.

He walked up the stairs to the floor above where
Brina was sleeping. The chamber was not so lavishly
afforded, but it was clean and served his needs. Maura
had left a single candle burning on the long table
where he would lay his bonnet and kilt. He removed
the bonnet and grinned when he noticed that one
of the feathers was crushed from Brina's yanking it
off his head. With the door closed, he could chuckle
without worry that the sound would disturb anyone
or humiliate his newest guest.

His bride...

Connor enjoyed the sound of that word while he
dropped his kilt and shrugged out of his shirt. His
boots required that he sit down and unlace them, but
he enjoyed being free from his clothing. Getting fully
dressed after he bathed had been a chore he had nae
been in the mood to suffer. But the idea of seeing
Brina made him put every last article of clothing back
on. He doubted she was ready to receive her groom
in nothing save his skin.

Making her ready for that moment was something
that weighed on his mind. Deirdre would have arrived
ready to welcome him into her embrace. Connor
settled into his own bed and considered the fact that
Brina had been quite surprised to discover that a kiss
might be so enjoyable. He was sure that the priests
sleeping in his village church were going to be very
displeased to hear that he had taken Brina, but even
knowing that didn't banish the grin from his lips.

But the erection refusing to allow him to slip into
slumber did make him frown. His cock was rigid and
needy in spite of the chill of early winter. The snow

was going to be his best ally, for it would keep the Chattans from launching an attempt to retrieve Brina.

Well, at least the early snow would make it far more difficult for Robert Chattan to march his clan onto Lindsey land. He was still a Highlander, so that meant he wouldn't let a few feet of snow stop him if he was really intent on doing something to retaliate.

There would be nothing for the Chattans to claim back if Connor went back down to where Brina lay and deflowered her.

Connor frowned in the dark, not caring for that idea, but he couldn't deny that there were plenty of men who would do exactly that.

It was what would happen to his sister Vanora, the moment she was deemed old enough for marriage.

His thoughts were darker than the night, but they burned through any further hesitations he had concerning his marriage. Brina would be his bride, but he would not treat her unkindly. The early snow was a blessing that would give him time to court her gently.

But she would be his.

❧

Brina heard the church bell ringing and sat up.

It was barely dawn, or at least it seemed that way until she rubbed her eyes and realized that there were bed curtains drawn around the bed she lay in. The fabric was thick and kept the light dim where she had been sleeping.

Her mind was clouded with sleep, and she reached out to touch the curtains, unable to recall why she was sleeping in such a fine bed.

"Mistress?"

Brina froze, and her mind cleared instantly with that single word.

"Are ye ready to rise?"

It was Maura, and she tugged on the curtain, obviously having seen movement behind it. Once the fabric was drawn, Brina could see that it was in fact dawn. The church bell tolled again, stunning her with how simple it might be to end Connor's madness.

She slid out of bed and was frantically thinking of how to meet with the priest so that she might plead her case. Maura wasn't alone this morn but had two maids along to help dress Brina. They tugged her underrobe up and over her body before she realized their intention.

A startled gasp left her lips as she wrapped her arms around herself to cover her breasts and mons. The women cast quick, curious glances at one another.

"I told ye that the mistress is new to being served."

Both maids instantly lowered themselves and returned to the chore of dressing her. A fresh undergown was brought forward, but Brina did not extend her arms for it to be placed over her body. Instead she stared at the soft blue color of it.

"Blue will suit you well, mistress." Maura spoke quickly while the woman waiting with the gown offered it once again.

"I believe something plain will serve." Brina forced herself to say the words because she doubted that she would have the willpower to maintain her determination to return to the abbey if she allowed herself to wear pretty clothing. The bed would be hard enough to forget when she was once again sleeping on a narrow cot without any curtains to keep her nose from becoming cold. But Connor had burned her undyed gown, and only now did it cross her mind that she was left to wear only what he provided her.

"The laird didna have anything plain made. This gown is the simplest that was commissioned for his bride." Maura took the gown and gathered it up through the neckline so that she might easily drop it over Brina's head.

"I am sure that ye do nae wish to be late to Mass because ye were displeased with yer clothing."

"No, of course nae."

The blue undergown slid smoothly over her body in a single movement. Maura didn't give her any time to contemplate the overrobe that was brought forward. It was a darker blue, which meant it had cost even more, because more dye would have been needed to deepen the color. There was also trim sewn onto it, and once the hem was fluttering about her ankles, one of the women laced it closed up her front. Unlike her plain robe, this garment was tailored to her figure. With each eyelet, the robe closed over her hips and waist, until finally even the curves of her breasts were seen clearly. It was very fashionable; something that either of her sisters would have enjoyed full well.

She had never worn anything like it. Her breasts felt strangely sensitive with the fabric of both robes so close to them. She looked down to see the curves clearly displayed by the garment.

"'Tis chilly enough for an arisaid, but I think ye should wait to begin wearing the Lindsey colors until ye have wed."

One of the maids had already brought forward a length of Lindsey wool, but Maura sent her away with a flick of her fingers. She brought forth long lengths of ribbon that Brina looked at with confusion until she went behind her and began braiding her hair with the ribbons. She fashioned two braids instead of the single plain one that Brina was accustomed to.

"Yer boots need a fair bit of work to make them soft again."

A pair of leather shoes were set out for her, and stockings dangled from the hands of one maid while another fetched a stool for Brina to sit on. When she lowered herself onto it, the blue fabric became too beautiful to resist. She fingered it, tracing along the line of trim while noticing the tiny stitches that held it in place.

"Here we are, a veil for Mass, and forgive me, mistress, but we had best make haste or we'll be the last to arrive."

"Of course, ye are very correct."

The last piece of fabric was just a rectangle with the edges carefully rolled to keep it from unraveling. But it was a soft butternut color, and the weave so fine, if she held it over her eyes, she could still see through it. It didn't smell like wool either but slipped through her fingers as smoothly as water.

"It is silk."

Silk? Brina tripped over her own feet, drawing a frown from Maura.

"I'll have the cobbler see ye as soon as we finish breaking our fast to shorten those shoes."

The double doors were opened, and the sight of

Connor's retainers standing there distracted her from making any comment about wearing silk. Instead she felt her cheeks turn pink when they reached up and tugged on the corners of their knit bonnets. It wasn't the respectful gesture that sent heat into her face, but the way their gazes began to twinkle, just a bit in approval of her appearance.

She had never been pretty.

An ache tore at her as she passed the retainers and began hurrying down the stone steps. Pain rose up inside her from a thousand times that she had wished to receive the same compliments her sisters had.

A nun had to learn to live without such praise.

And so she had.

As they descended to the main floor, there were more sounds of footsteps, all of them hurrying toward the open doors of the tower. Outside, she could see the small church built inside the castle yard. Every fortress had one, for to forget to build a house of God inside your walls was like asking to be overrun by raiders intent on pillaging.

The gate that led to the outer yard was raised as well, and people were streaming in to the church from all directions. The bell was ringing faster and louder in warning that the Mass was beginning. Brina hesitated at the doorway, feeling like a child caught with fruit on her hands left there after stealing a tart from the kitchen between meals. Her clothing felt wicked and disrespectful to the father who had promised her to the church.

But Maura gave her a push that sent her stumbling over the threshold and into the sanctuary.

It would seem that she was attending Mass in blue today.

✑

Connor wasn't at Mass.

Brina was disgusted with herself for noticing, but at the same time her curiosity rose to a level that had her sneaking peeks behind her throughout the service to see if he joined the congregation late.

He never did.

The priest gave the final blessing, and she faced the aisle, intending to wait her turn to exit, only to discover that everyone was waiting for her to leave before they did. The entire congregation strained to gain sight of her, stretching their necks and angling their heads so that they might look through any possible hole in the crowd at her. Parents lifted their children up high so that the little ones might peer at her also.

Brina was sure that her cheeks were going to catch fire.

The moment she looked at them, they all began to offer her respect. The men reached for the corners of their caps, while the women nodded their heads, because there was no room for true courtesies in the tight confines of the church.

She took one step and then another one, stumbling her way toward the door as whispers began to rise behind her.

"Bonny thing…"

"Is nae wearing Lindsey colors…"

"She has blue eyes…"

"A bit thin…"

There was a sharp snap, and the voices died instantly. Maura offered her no repentance when Brina turned to see who had wielded such authority over the castle inhabitants.

"Everyone is pleased to have the laird's bride here."

"Everyone except my father."

Maura frowned, and her eyes even darkened. "I have faith that yer father and the laird will come to an agreement."

There were many nods from those around them, proving that everyone was listening. Brina felt as though there were a stone sitting on top of her chest, making her struggle for every breath she drew. But a quick flick from the head of house's hand and the congregation began to disperse, most of them going toward the open doors of the tower for a morning meal. Smoke was rising from the long buildings adjacent to the tower, telling her where the kitchens were. The scent of bread was already drifting on the morning breeze.

The priest caught her eyes, and she reached out to him. He took her hand and covered it with his opposite one.

"I will hear yer confession later today before ye come to take yer vows."

Brina was horrified, pulling her hand free. "But surely ye cannae be in agreement with me doing anything but fulfilling my father's promise that I become a bride of Christ?"

The priest tucked his hands into the wide sleeves of his robe. "The laird came to me early this morning, and I am well contented by his thoughts upon this very important matter. Yer father will send yer sister to the abbey. It is she who needs the stern hand of discipline to keep her from the path of damnation. I will marry ye."

Her throat felt as though it were shrinking. She heard Maura muttering something beneath her breath before the woman grasped her hand and began to lead her back toward the open doors of the tower. Snow clung to the roof ledges and sat in large clumps on the ground where it had not been trampled by those going to Mass. A light dusting of it continued to float down while they watched.

"A warm meal will make ye feel sturdy and strong, mistress."

Maura used the title, but Brina felt anything but in command of the woman. The head of house pulled her right up the steps and through the doorway of the tower, where the scent of warm food drew a growl from her belly. It was deep and long, betraying just how hungry she was.

But she froze in place at the entrance to the first floor of the tower where long trestle tables were hosting the inner castle's inhabitants for their first meal of the day. At the far end of the common room was a raised platform that played host to a long head table.

That was the high table, the laird's seat.

Connor sat there with several men who all wore two feathers upright on the sides of their bonnets. They stopped talking when she was sighted, and Connor looked up from a parchment he'd been reading along with Shawe.

She shivered as his gaze met hers. The reaction was instantaneous and beyond her ability to control. His gaze traveled along her revealed figure, and his lips twitched into a grin before he raised his attention back to her face. By that time she was nervously fingering the fabric of her gown as she tried to tell herself not to care about what his opinion was of her.

She shouldn't care a bit…

"Please join me, my lady."

He indicated the chair to his right, which was the only seat left vacant at the high table. The position proclaimed her as mistress of Birch Stone and his bride. The table was a formal one, set above the others to illustrate that those who ate there were considered of a higher station. Every man there had earned the right to sit beside their laird, and Connor had gained his seat by serving his clan. Even if she was bound to refuse him, she could not keep from admiring the dedication he had for his people.

She held the same respect for her father. At that moment she felt suspended between both men while they pulled her toward them, but in the doing of that, they threatened to rip her apart.

Brina shook her head. "I will be content at the lower tables, Laird Lindsey."

Connor frowned, as did several of his captains.

"Yer place is here, Brina, beside me."

He was using her Christian name deliberately. Only her father and siblings used her first name in public. Connor was making it clear that he felt he had the right to call her by such an intimate name, even in public.

Such was the right of a husband.

She shook her head to dispel the idea. "I disagree, Laird Lindsey."

The hall quieted.

"Are ye saying that ye still refuse to wed me, Brina?"

He was irritated and possibly worse, for his face was flushed slightly and his eyes narrowed.

"I cannae do less than honor my father's word."

She could feel the weight of the stares of his captains and the women who served the hall. There was a loud scraping sound as he pushed his chair back, made more noticeable by the lack of other noise in the hall now that everyone was standing still, waiting to hear what would happen.

He moved down the steps that kept the high table elevated, but even when his feet were on even standing with her, she still had to raise her chin to maintain eye contact with him. For the moment he was every inch the Highlander laird. There was no hint of leniency in his expression, and he hooked his fingers around the wide leather belt that held his kilt in place while he braced his feet shoulder width apart.

"Yer father is nae here; I am." His voice held a challenge now, one her pride eagerly rose to, because her honor was not something she would allow others to discard so simply.

"I should imagine that every father wearing yer colors would expect his grown daughter to heed his word, even when she is away from his sight." Her voice was firm and even because she realized that she did not fear him. She should have, for the man was large and his arms cut with muscles that spoke clearly of his greater strength, but there was no fear that he would strike her for daring to voice her opinion. There was a ripple of whispers among those eating.

His eyes filled with his temper. "Then we have a battle between us, lady, and it is one I intend to claim victory from."

Five

A RIPPLE OF CONVERSATION WENT THROUGH THOSE watching, but Connor reached out and captured her hand before she had the chance to answer him.

"Begin the meal without us."

Connor tossed his words over his shoulder while he pulled her along with him. He took her down a hallway and into another room, where there were no curious eyes upon them. He released her hand when she tugged on it, and stood with his hands braced on his hips while he watched her from beneath hooded eyes.

"What do ye gain by refusing to kneel for the church's blessing, Brina?"

His words were softly spoken, but when she looked at his face, she discovered that he was anything but calm. In his eyes, she could see his temper smoldering.

"I gain the knowledge that I am nae a disobedient daughter. Isna that what all children are expected to be? Do ye somehow think that women do no' have honor?"

He snorted at her and began slowly to follow her

across the room. "Sometimes adjustments must be made. Yer sister made it necessary for me to change my plans, but I see no reason why you and I cannae have an agreeable relationship. Yer father will adjust his thinking."

Heat flickered in his eyes and drew another gasp from her lips. His gaze made her overly conscious of the way the blue gown molded to her figure. It was designed to make her pretty, but that was a woman's word. To a man, she was attractive, and Connor's expression left no doubt in her mind that he was being drawn to her.

Brina heard him growling softly with his frustration. The sound drew a short laugh from her.

"Are ye frustrated, then, sir? Good, for that is something that ye have ensured that I have a bellyful of."

He considered her with something glittering in his eyes that looked like a promise. "I believe that is the first compliment ye have offered me, lass."

"What are ye talking about?" She scoffed. "I insulted ye."

"Aye, refusing to sit beside me was insulting, lass."

He chuckled, the sound low and deep. Brina discovered herself fascinated by his change in mood. She had never pleased a man either.

"Now, admitting that I frustrate ye, that is praise, for it confirms that ye are drawn to me."

"I said nothing of the sort, and furthermore, it is clear that we cannae even converse clearly, so ye should leave."

Her face heated up, and she turned away from him without thinking about what she was doing. Brina stared at the stone wall for a moment before she recalled exactly what had happened the last time she presented Connor with her back.

The man didn't deviate from his previous actions either.

She turned around, but much too late to avoid being pinned against the wall by his larger body. Yet he didn't touch her but flattened one hand against the stone surface behind her, right next to her shoulder so that his outstretched arm caged her.

"Oh, but I disagree with ye again, for I believe we are doing a fine job of conversing."

She leaned back away from him because it was becoming harder to focus on the point she wanted to make.

"You enjoying quarreling, Laird Lindsey? Is that what ye are telling me?"

His lips were set into a grin again. "Do ye nae recall my name, Brina?" He drew his words out in a lazy manner that teased her.

"Formality would be best between us." She drew in a deep breath. "And distance."

"Why does it matter where I stand?"

Brina blinked, trying to restore her clear thinking. "Because my thoughts become muddled when ye are so near." She was talking without thinking again, and she pressed one hand on top of her lips to still her words when she witnessed how much her confession pleased him. His blue eyes sparkled with it.

His lips twitched up farther, and she discovered her attention focusing on his mouth. A tingle of memory traveled across her lips, awakening a yearning to feel his kiss against them once again. He reached out and gently pulled her hand away from her lips.

"I confess that ye have the same effect on me, lass."

His voice was low and deep, coating her senses like honey.

"There… ye see? A fine reason for ye to stop coming so close to me. Neither of us can reason properly." She went to move away from him through the one side that was not blocked by his arm, but he moved his right hand and cupped the side of her face, bringing her to a halt while she felt her heart begin to accelerate.

"Or it is a good reason for us to marry, so that we might enjoy what happens when we are close to one another and need do naught save follow our impulses."

He didn't allow her the opportunity to reply but tilted his head so that their lips might fit together. The kiss was tender. So soft and slow that she quivered. She felt his breath against her lips before the first connection of his flesh against hers. Her heart thumped beneath her breast with a rhythm that was far faster than it should have been while she was standing still.

That action sent blood rushing through her veins and past her ears, so that she heard little else. But her mind was focused on the warm touch of his lips on top of her own, and she shivered with delight as he pressed his mouth against hers. The hand cradling her cheek turned her gently, and their mouths fit together more completely. His thumb pulled her chin down, opening her mouth. The tip of his tongue swept along her lower lip before it began to tease her own. Just the tiniest flickering touches, but they sent sensation roaring through her like floodwaters. She was grateful for the support of the wall behind her when the quivering in her limbs threatened to rob her of the ability to stand. Temptation called to her, dangling a promise of more delight if she would simply surrender and return the kiss.

"Ye see, lass? We have passion between us, and that is a rare thing. One that should nae be discarded so simply," he whispered against her ear before placing a soft kiss against the skin of her neck. It was the simplest of kisses, one she might have bestowed upon a child, but there was nothing innocent about it. Heat flowed down her body from it, and she heard her own tiny moan of rapture.

It was that sound that broke through her muddled thoughts. She felt as though she were in a stupor, intoxicated beyond the ability to think clearly.

"But that is exactly why I must tell ye no." She lifted eyelids that felt heavy, and stared into his piercing blue eyes. "My sister followed passion, and it brought ruin."

"Bugger me." He cursed bluntly.

Brina felt her eyes widen before she laughed.

Connor looked at her as though she had gone mad, but she covered her mouth with one hand and tried to smother the giggles that rose from her chest. Connor snorted, his fingers curling against the stone wall he leaned against.

"I would have expected ye to become offended, no' bloody entertained by my profanity."

He was distracted, and she slipped past him in that moment, dancing nimbly across the chamber while he turned and crossed his arms over his chest.

"Well, it is just that it is the first time I've ever heard anyone use profanity. Besides, what ye said is quite impossible." Her cheeks heated as she considered exactly what he had said. "Well, I mean to say that it would be impossible for me… to perform such an act upon you, because…"

He lifted one eyebrow. "Because ye do nae have a cock?"

She felt her eyes narrow because he was teasing her once more, and part of her didn't care for the fact that he thought her so naive. "Ye are trying to shock me by saying that so plainly."

He shrugged. "Since ye seem so determined to return to the life of a nun, should nae I speak honestly to ye?"

"There is a difference between honest and crude."

"Ah…" He held up one finger, and his lips rose into a grin that was quite attractive on him. "But since ye were amused by the fact that I said… bugger me."

"Ye do nae need to repeat it. I heard ye clearly the first time."

His grin became a full smile that flashed his teeth at her. "Now, Brina, if ye are going laugh at the fact that I said… bugger me… why can I nae discuss the reason why it amuses ye?"

"I do nae want to discuss it."

"Only laugh because ye do nae have a cock and could nae bugger me so I should choose better words to describe my frustration with ye?" His eyes flashed with hard intent. "But the truth is that when I kiss ye, you forget that ye have an objection to being buggered?"

She had to clear her throat before any words would pass through. "That is the most audacious thing anyone has ever said to me. Of course I have an objection to ye buggering me... Ohh... never mind that." She let out an exasperated sound that gained her a chuckle from Connor. His face was flushing dark red as he laughed at her stumbling over the words that he'd ground out so easily.

She slapped the top of her skirts. "Oh, have done with ye. Connor Lindsey, ye gain too much enjoyment at my expense."

He sobered, but there was still merriment sparkling in his eyes. "That's a solid truth; one I'm looking forward to increasing tenfold."

Tension began to wind its way through her once more, and she watched as he noticed. Brina forced her gaze to remain on his face, in spite of the fact that she was tempted to turn her back on him.

Such was a coward's way of making everything his fault. Part of her very much wanted to be touched again and swept toward that place where she didn't have to think but only feel.

Connor must have read the desire off her face, for he suddenly drew in a stiff breath. He took one step toward her but stopped and considered her from behind a pensive expression.

"Come here, lass. Come to me this time. I can see in yer eyes that ye want to."

Brina fingered the fabric of her gown, torn so badly between what she knew she should do and what she wanted that her eyes burned with unshed tears.

"That would make me no better than my sister

Deirdre." He frowned, but she held up a hand to quiet him. "My father was most clear with all three of us as to what he expected. If I fail to honor his word, how could ye ever accept any promise I made to you?"

There was the soft compression of his leather boots against the stone floor while he closed the distance between them. He loomed over her again, but she didn't fear the man, only her own lack of discipline.

"I would accept yer word, Brina, because I am the one who prevented ye from honoring yer father."

"That does nae absolve me of my duty." But it did send a tiny feeling of achievement through her, because he was not a man who trusted lightly. "And… well… I simply…"

He placed one fingertip against her lips to still them. His eyes flashed with a warning that sent a shiver down her spine, for it was the same look he'd had in his eyes when he had stolen her away from her father's retainers. This was the Highlander in him, not the man who had just been teasing her so playfully.

"Ye honored yer father by riding out of his gates as he directed ye, lass. That is yer past, and I am yer future, even if it isna what was planned. Ye are here. Now kiss me, Brina, for I can see in yer eyes that ye long to."

His hand slid around her face to cup her nape in a gentle hold that was still very solid. This time his kiss was harder, pressing her mouth until she allowed him to tease her tongue with his own. It was a bold invasion; one that shocked her but also sent sensation shooting through her body. Her nipples began to tingle and contract into hard points that pressed against her clothing. Connor closed the distance between them, his other arm wrapping around her body to bind her against him. She shuddered as her curves pressed against his hard form. There were too many points of contact to think about; instead she was overwhelmed by the sheer intensity of how good it felt to be held.

She wanted to be closer, her hands settling on his chest and smoothing up to rest on the tops of his wide shoulders. His tongue thrust deep into her mouth, and she stroked it with her own. She wanted to kiss him back and tried to mimic his actions, moving her lips in unison with his.

"Ye see, lass? We'll wed and soon, for I swear that I will nae stay away from ye for much longer."

The hand that had cradled her nape moved, sliding down her chest and right over the soft mound of her breast while his gaze held her captive. He didn't stop until he was cupping her entire breast in his grip, the hard point of her nipple unmistakable behind the soft fabric of her robes.

"And ye will welcome me, Brina Chattan, make no mistake about that, for I swear that I plan to seduce ye. Ye can wed me a maiden or after I charm my way into yer bed; I do nae care which way."

His tone was too smug. She snarled softly at the arrogance displayed on his face, and shoved him away from her with both hands planted firmly on top of his chest.

"Ye are a barbarian."

He grinned but backed away from her. "I'm a Highlander, lass."

"Well, so am I. That means I am no' without self-discipline when it comes to my…"

"Yer passions?" he offered with another smug smirk.

She growled at him, slightly surprised to hear such a sound come from her own lips while someone else was there to witness it.

Connor laughed, but the tone was not kind. It was deep and packed with the promise of his doing exactly as he'd sworn to do.

Seduce her…

"Ye are a Highland lass, and that is exactly why I have no doubt that behind the wall of duty that yer father made ye build with yer honor is a lass who will kiss me back. As ye just did."

Her hand rose without thought to cover her lips, but it wouldn't be so simple to conceal the fact that he was speaking the truth. The sting of that knowledge burned its way through her mind. Her belly suddenly rumbled again, drawing a frown from Connor.

"Ye may eat at my side, or we'll retire now and share a more personal meal, as a new couple would be expected to do."

There was no hint of relenting in his tone. It was the laird talking now, his expression telling her how he had managed to command one of the largest clans in the Highlands. It was in the solid confidence he displayed and the fact that she didn't doubt he meant every word completely.

"The table, or I'll likely be hung at dusk for smashing yer skull in with a stone when I can no longer endure yer lurid suggestions."

He laughed at her, and even his eyes sparkled with merriment. "Spoken like the hellcat I labeled ye."

She snarled at him but ducked beneath his arm,

because she was starving and it was an excuse to have others around them. But the man's amusement echoed in the hallway, tempting her to turn around and take issues with him again.

Fine, let him call her a hellcat, for it was better than being so easy to bend.

⁂

Connor left with his captains the moment she finished eating. Her pride was bruised by the demonstration of his power over her. She bristled beneath the glances that moved over her the entire meal, tasting little of the fare placed in front of her.

"Come along, mistress. We've plenty to keep every set of hands full."

Maura seemed intent on keeping her close, but when Brina turned to look in the opposite direction of the head of house, she was met with the diligent stares of the retainers Connor had set to watch her. They nodded at her respectfully but never looked away.

"Something to do would be appreciated."

"That we have in abundance, thanks to this early snow."

Maura led her to the kitchens, and they were in an uproar. Women worked at every available space. The hooks used to hang pots over the fire were all spouting more than one pot. More kettles with long legs were set in the coals themselves, and the reason was clear.

All around, there were piles of late-harvest fruits and vegetables. Squashes and pumpkins filled the hallways, while younger boys brought sacks full of apples and other late-autumn fruits that they also had nowhere to put except in the hallways. The cook looked overwhelmed by the amount of food waiting to be processed before it rotted. An early snow could very easily translate into empty storerooms before spring arrived with a new crop.

The cook used a rag to wipe sweat off her brow while she looked at Brina to see if the laird's bride could offer any wisdom that might help.

Well, she knew how to work, and that was for certain.

Brina looked at the lads who were about to dump their apples into a corner that was already full.

"Not there. There must be chambers in this castle that can be used for some of this until we have a chance to preserve it. Store them in the hall, away from the hearths."

Many of the women nodded, while the cook offered her a pleased look. Brina hung the delicate silk veil on a peg and took up a plain linen square of fabric that she tucked about her head before joining the frantic effort to stew and process all the food. Hours flew by, and before she realized it, the sun was setting and the church bell had begun to ring again. She had never sat down to eat a midday meal but had snacked on the smaller choppings that were on the table. No one else had left the kitchens either, but they did now, gratefully tugging off their soiled aprons and heading toward the doorways, eager to have something else to do.

There was suddenly quiet when there had been none the entire day long. Brina simply closed her eyes and drew a deep sigh, but Connor's face appeared in the space that having everyone leave opened up in her mind. She'd avoided thinking of the man for hours, but now every sensation he'd unleashed on her that morning returned to stoke the fire that had burned so uncontrollably inside her beneath his touch.

Oh… bugger it all!

❦

Robert Chattan, laird of the clan Chattan, was closer to a true rage than he could ever recall. In his entire life, he had never been so angry.

Cory stood firmly in place, facing his laird after delivering the news that more snow was falling.

The bells on his outer walls began to ring, drawing another curse from his lips.

"What arrives now to vex me?"

One of the men closer to the door looked out and came across the floor at a run to answer his laird.

"Looks to be Laird Cameron. The snow must have caught the man on the road."

"The snow seems to have caught us all with our arses hanging out in the breeze."

He turned around and caught his remaining daughters in his sights. They sat near the large hearth that warmed the great hall, both of them looking bored nearly to death, but that did not gain either of them any mercy from him. They'd sit there until their feet fell off from lack of use if it meant he might be sure what they were about.

"Well, this is a right cheerful gathering."

Quinton Cameron was a dark Highlander. The man drew his blood from the Saxon more than the Norman, for his hair was black and thick, and he even kept a beard, one that he did not allow to grow long. But his eyes were blue, hinting at his Celtic blood.

"Cameron, my friend, ye are welcome. Even if my home is nae so cheerful a place at the moment, it is better than the snow."

"It was nae the snow that drove me in, my friend."

Robert found himself chuckling in spite of his dark mood. "I'd be disappointed to hear it was so. According to the gossips, ye are on yer way to becoming a legend with all the things ye mange to get involved with. It would spoil my image of ye to hear ye run inside because of a bit of snow."

"Well, I am nae sure I am no' happy to be warm, man." Quinton Cameron took the mug of ale that Deirdre offered him, giving her a wink, which she frowned at. He watched her return to her seat near her sister and the older women presiding over them both.

"I see it's true, then." Quinton Cameron spoke plainly, without any pity for his host's pride.

Robert sank back against the chair, feeling older than his years. "Aye, and worse, for now I've lost me youngest to Lindsey. The man took her right out of me own hands and swears he'll have her to wife now that Deirdre is no longer pure."

Quinton stopped with his mug only halfway to his lips. "Connor Lindsey took a girl promised to the church?"

"Aye, and the shame of it is, I am to blame, for I failed him by no' being able to control my eldest daughter."

Quinton watched Deirdre for a long moment while he drew a long sip from the mug she'd given him before turning her back on him. "I disagree, Robert.

Melor is every inch a Douglas. The man knows how to deceive well and good. Ye should nae blame yer daughter for it."

"I suppose I'll take yer word on Melor Douglas since ye spend more time at court than I do, but ye are nae a father, and I'll tell ye straight that I expect better from my children. Ye will too someday when ye're finished watching the shadows at court and take yerself a wife who keeps yer home warm enough to make ye enjoy being there with her."

Quinton Cameron shrugged. "The king needs his loyal lairds near him these days."

There was dark meaning in his words that Robert didn't bother to comment on. The court was a place of intrigue and danger that he had no liking for. Give him a battle, where he might look his enemy in the eye, instead of a place where a man shook yer hand but dumped poison in yer drink that same day.

"I wish the king were more than a lad, for he could solve this issue between me and Lindsey without the bloodshed that I see as my only recourse."

Quinton frowned. "Ye do nae mean to march on Lindsey? Ye did promise him one of yer daughters."

Robert glared at Quinton. "I'm an old man, Cameron, and when ye get to my age, ye begin to have more of a care for just how the Lord is going to receive ye when ye arrive. I promised Brina to the church."

"But ye promised Connor Lindsey an alliance through marriage to one of yer daughters, and I'll tell ye straight that I call the man friend. He passed up others in favor of his agreement with ye."

Robert wasn't intimidated. Many men would be, for the Camerons were a fierce lot. It was wise not to anger them if you could avoid it.

"That does nae make it right to steal my Brina. She's a good lass, the only one who has given me the proper respect due her sire, and I'd be a poor father to sit here drinking me ale while she's imprisoned. Even if Lindsey did ask for her, I told him no, and I have to keep my word."

"Ye told him no?"

Robert Chattan nodded. "Aye, I did, because I told ye, Quinton Cameron, I'm too old to be offending the Lord by sending him a daughter who will nae serve his church honestly. Lindsey wanted me to exchange the pair of them and send Deirdre on to the abbey because he would no' suffer the doubt that she would nae be true to him."

"That's a reasonable solution, man." Quinton lowered his voice so that his words remained between them. "One that will keep blood from flowing. Scotland needs her clans no' bickering between each other, or we'll find England invading us while we're busy trying to kill one another."

"Ye think I should send Deirdre to the church, then?"

Quinton took another long look at Deirdre Chattan. He was no stranger to women who had charms, and there was no mistaking that Deirdre knew how to use her body and enjoyed it. As far as he was concerned, that was not necessarily a shame, even if the church preached against it, but one woman couldn't be allowed to start fighting between the Chattan and Lindsey.

"I say send her dowry to the church, and if she

wishes to take her position there, let her worry about gaining forgiveness."

"And if she will nae go?"

Cameron frowned. "She'll remain here, maybe wed a man who will have her with no dowry."

"That would only satisfy the church if Deirdre came with the dowry that was promised to Lindsey. Brina is my third daughter and comes with less. That means Lindsey would have to agree to having what comes with her and no' what we agreed upon. The man is already angry. I believe hearing that will turn him toward being enraged."

Quinton Cameron leaned forward. "That's an interesting point, but I believe Connor would have to accept yer terms, since he stole Brina. I believe I'll ask him for ye."

Robert Chattan frowned and shook his head. "I didna say those were me terms, and now my middle daughter claims she has a true calling. This house has gone mad."

"Young Kaie wishes to be a nun rather than wed Roan?"

"Aye," Robert growled. "Yet another problem to face, for the McLeod will likely no' take it any better than the Lindsey did that the daughter they have been promised is discontented with her lot. If I send Kaie to the church, I doubt Roan McLeod will be pleased to have Deirdre."

Quinton stroked the side of his beard while he considered the situation. "Roan will nae be pleased, and that's a fact."

Robert snorted, but Quinton held up a hand. "What of Erlina?"

Robert Chattan's face turned red. "Her hellion of a mother has taken her off to Monroe land and will nae even pen a single sentence to me. That is no answer."

"Having another daughter would be a very fine solution to this quarrel."

Robert Chattan sat forward and slapped the tabletop. "Erlina is my bastard."

"So wed her mother and offer her to Roan."

"I'd have to have her taken into church bound and gagged, for the woman swears she'll never marry." Robert shook his head. "And the Monroe give her shelter, so enough said on that matter. Kaie will wed Roan McLeod, and I will march on Lindsey land just as soon as the weather clears enough."

Quinton held up a hand. "I'll ride up there first and see if peace might be restored."

"I did nae give the man permission to wed me daughter; the only way peace can be made is if he returns Brina the way he took her. If ye want to tell him that, ye may."

Quinton Cameron stood up.

"If it keeps the pair of ye from drawing steel on one another, it's worth the ride through the snow. I told ye I call the man friend, so it would be better if I rode to his gate instead of ye."

Robert was silent a long moment. "Yer point about the English is well made. I'll listen to ye, even if part of me wants to march up there and have it out with Lindsey for no' respecting my decision on the matter of which one of me daughters he might have to wife."

Quinton hid his true emotions behind a practiced facade; he was experienced in the art of maintaining an expression no one might see past. That was how a man stayed among the living at court. He forced himself to remain in place while he itched to ride out to Lindsey land immediately, but arriving dead tired would not be in his best interest. He wanted to keep both the Chattan and Lindsey laird for friends, and he wasn't jesting about needing the Highlanders to remain at peace or risk invasion from England.

The English had a young king who was now of age to rule, and he favored peace with France. That would free up the English armies to invade Scotland, since James II was only a boy. The Highlands needed to remain united, or there would be no Scotland left. There was also Roan McLeod to consider too, for the man would not be happy to discover a woman in his bed who longed for the life of a nun. That was the sort of thing that a good friend passed along before the wedding sheets were pulled back and a man discovered himself wed to a woman who would always shun him.

So he'd ride to Lindsey land and make sure there was no blood spilled, or he'd take Brina Chattan away from Connor himself, and he'd make sure news of young Kaie's true calling made its way to Roan.

※

Brina paused at the doorway to the tower. From her vantage point, she could see that everyone was already inside the church; even the two retainers set to watch her stood in the doorway with their attention on the service inside. Something drew her attention from behind the tower, and she couldn't quite decide what it was.

A sound that was being carried over the curtain wall on the evening wind. The sky was crimson as the sun set, and the wind blew bitterly cold. She pulled a cloak off a peg near the doorway and gathered the thick fabric around her. The garment was too long and obviously made for men who had to venture up onto the walls at night to keep watch.

She held the fabric up in front of her and began climbing the steep steps cut into the wall that faced the high ground behind the tower. As she climbed, she realized that these walls were but protection for the cannons that were set into bunkers every ten feet along the back of the fortress. It was no longer a curtain wall meant to keep invaders from scaling it, because the land dropped away here and no army might attack from this direction. That wasn't to say that the walls were not thick and built with keeping the castle secured in mind; it was just that they cut away at sharp angles so that the cannon might be aimed in a full half circle out and over the edge of the cliff.

What the cannons faced stole her breath. Bathed in the ruby light of sunset was the ocean. Dark green water was riddled with white foamy caps. The sun was a brilliant half-sphere of golden light that stretched out its beams over the surface of the sea. There was the sound of water crashing down somewhere she could not see from her position on top of the wall, but she smiled and smelled the salt in the air while she drank in the wonder of the ocean, a sight that no drawing on paper might ever have prepared her for.

It was far more majestic than she had ever thought possible; the sound that had drawn her up onto the

wall was those white-capped waves breaking down on
the shoreline she could not see. She strained to catch
even a glimpse of it, because who knew if she would
ever have the chance again.

"Are ye truly trying to escape this direction?"

Brina jumped, a squeal crossing her lips as she
turned to discover Connor lunging toward her with
his hand outstretched. She recoiled from the fury
etched into his expression.

But that was a grave mistake, for she was too close
to the steeply slanted edge of the cannon bunkers.
Ice clung to it, and her shoes slipped right out from
beneath her when her weight landed on her feet.

"Connor—"

She reached for him even as she realized that it was
too late for rescue. She felt herself sliding down the icy
side of the stone surface, the angle of the wall her only
salvation, because it kept her from dropping straight
toward the ground, where her bones would surely be
snapped under her own weight.

Connor lunged toward her, his body surging across
the distance between them. His hand captured her
wrist, but she was already too far down for him to stop
her. He came over the edge of the wall, his cursing
filling her ear.

Every second suddenly took forever to pass. She
felt each beat of her heart and waited in between
them, with enough time to wonder if the last one was
the moment when her life ended. She felt her gowns
rising up and her bare skin burning as she twisted and
turned in an attempt to stop her descent.

But most of all, she felt Connor pulling her against

his body and rolling her on top of him to shield her from the scraping ice that tore at the tender skin of her thighs. His sword made a horrible grinding noise against the stone wall, but it was comforting because it meant that the thick leather scabbard was taking the sharp bite of the icy stone surface instead of their flesh.

The ground that seemed to be taking so long to reach suddenly stopped their fall with a bone-jarring impact. Brina found her cry smothered in a spray of powdered snow that flew up all around them, clogging her nose and eyes as it flew into the air. Every joint erupted with pain while her body bounced and rolled with Connor holding her tightly.

She gasped and sputtered as she tried to draw breath through the ice that plugged her nose and mouth. A hard hand scraped it aside in one motion, allowing her to draw a deep breath. Connor only allowed her one before he was yanking her away from the edge of the cliff they had landed on.

"Holy Christ, woman! Ye're lucky ye aren't dead."

Connor was furious, but Brina was still staring at the ledge she had almost rolled over. Beyond it was a fall that would no doubt have killed her, but the waves she had longed to see crashing onto the shore were in sight. She stared at the raw power of the water as it rose up, up, and then curled back down toward the earth to strike it with a roar as if it were being taunted in its attempt to fly.

"What's wrong with ye, woman? How could ye think to escape in such a foolish manner?"

Connor pulled her to her feet, pressing her back

against the base of the fortress wall and depriving her of seeing the shore any longer.

"Ye're the one who startled me, yelling at me like a lunatic."

His hand was curled into her cloak, holding on to her, while his face looked as though his temper were hot enough to melt the knee-deep snow they stood in.

"Ye were standing on the edge of the wall, woman."

"Well, I wanted to see the shoreline... I've never seen the ocean before."

He looked at her with surprise on his face, words failing him for a long moment. "Ye weren't trying to escape?" He sounded incredulous at the very idea, and her temper rose up in defense.

"I do nae lie, Connor Lindsey, and that has been a frustrating thing, because I'd have escaped ye already if I could."

She kicked at the snow, because her legs were beginning to hurt, but one of her shoes was missing, and her toes ached when they collided with the snow that was now hard instead of powdery.

"Besides, I didna think tumbling down the surface of the wall was a way out of your castle, but I never had to think of way to escape from a castle until now... because I've never been a prisoner before..." She looked around, suddenly realizing they were standing outside the fortress, and in spite of scrapes and bruises, she was very much alive.

"Except that now the fact is proven to ye."

"That does nae convict me of attempting it. Ye startled me. If ye had nae yelled at me, I would nae have jumped away from ye." She reached out and slapped at the hand holding her.

He snarled something before bending his knees and lifting her up onto his shoulder once again. It was an intolerable position, and she kicked as she growled at him.

He didn't smack her bottom this time. Instead he clamped a solid arm across her thighs and began carrying her around the point of the fortress wall. As soon as they left the point behind, the curtain wall rose straight up once again.

"I swear to Christ, woman, ye're blessed by every angel there is, for I had that wall slanted for those cannons just this last spring. Before that, it was a straight drop down like the rest of the curtain wall surrounding Birch Stone."

He set her on her feet and glared at her. Brina narrowed her eyes and propped her hands onto her hips.

"Ye do a lot of swearing at the Savior."

He rolled his eyes at her. "I thought this morning ye found my profanity amusing."

"'Bugger ye' is entertaining."

"No unless ye are planning on doing it, since I've gone to so much trouble to bring ye to my bed."

He was in a temper, and she suddenly understood why. The cliff face rose up, cold and unscalable. It was just like another curtain wall, impenetrable from their position at its base.

"Are we locked out of yer own castle?"

He blew out a snort and glared at her. In the fading light, she recognized the scowl on his face and couldn't stop herself from laughing. "It seems I am nae near yer bed after all."

"Ye're daft, woman. It's freezing out here, and in the dark no one will know we are down here."

Brina couldn't help but continue laughing. "I've no' ever heard of a laird being tumbled down the side of his own fortification."

"Well, I've got beardless lads who know enough no' to go up onto the forward battlements when there's ice on the stones."

Brina turned away from him to hide the hurt that slashed through her. It had been foolish to go up onto the wall when it was icy. She faced a solid cliff that the curtain wall was built up against. There was no way around it, and with dusk almost completely fallen, she forgot about her quarrel with Connor, because their situation was grave indeed. With both of them missing, she doubted the men set to guarding her would raise any alarm, assuming, of course, that she was with their laird.

The snow had not melted, and she looked at it now with mounting dread, for it heralded a night ahead with freezing temperatures that could very likely kill them both.

She heard him sigh, and a warm hand clasped her shoulder to turn her back around.

"I didna think that ye had never seen the ocean, but I should have, for yer father's hold is inland."

It was a fragile attempt at an apology, one that struck her as tender, and she suddenly realized that she was lonely for such attention. Maybe she had been intended for the church, but she had still had friends at Chattan Castle. At Birch Stone, she had only guards who watched her with suspicious eyes and women who served her while trying to decide if she would ever have any power in the clan and worried about what she thought of them.

"I heard the waves and didna know what the sound was."

He nodded. "At least ye were wise enough to take that cloak with ye. That will be our salvation in another hour."

He turned around and faced the cliff face. He began to pull on bushes and other plants that were covered with snow at the base of the cliff. He threw what he grabbed aside and continued to yank more out of the earth.

"I swear that I never thought to be using these cells myself."

"Cells?"

Connor turned to look back at her. "Aye, no' all the lairds of this castle have been merciful ones."

He knocked a tree branch aside to reveal a large iron ring that looked as though it was set into the cliff side. Connor kicked at the ground, moving more rocks and plants until the path was clear for him to open the door.

"I'm only grateful that I didna have the door removed. I thought about it and decided it wasna wise to destroy something that might someday have a use. Even if I hoped never to condemn any soul to imprisonment here."

"Who would put anyone in a cell on a cliff side?"

Connor struggled with the door, until at last it opened with a grinding sound. She looked up, hopeful that one of the Lindsey retainers might hear the sound up on the walls.

"With the wind blowing the sound of the surf over the walls, no one will hear us until morning when it reverses, lass. The cell was built by my uncle because he intended to keep the lairdship by any means."

"Why did he even inherit it, when ye were alive?"

Connor offered her a hard look. "Because my parents didna wed until after my birth, and he used that fact to question my legitimacy. He took control of the Lindsey while the matter was sitting before the nobles, something he helped to ensure by making sure those powerful men knew he was nae interested in them attending to the matter quickly. That would give him time to see if fate would snuff out my life before I became a man capable of pressing the issue."

She gasped. "Yer uncle was dishonest..."

Connor turned to look toward the cell. "Still, sleeping in the stable was warmer than this promises to be."

Stable...

Brina covered her mouth with her hand because the hard muscles along his back suddenly impacted her as something beyond the fact that he was a Highlander. His body was hard because his life had been horribly difficult. Being labeled a bastard was a harsh thing, and it would have set him apart from others just as clearly as her undyed robe had.

"At least we shall have shelter in here."

The last of the light washed into the cell, showing a dismal place that must have been a horrible fate for anyone condemned to it. There was a stone bed made from flat rocks piled carefully against each other, and the remains of a pallet lay curled and rotted on top of it.

"We're in luck, it seems." Connor stepped inside and picked up a wooden chair roughly made of large sections of wood. A center cut of a tree had been hollowed out to leave a short back on it. He swung it against the wall, and it shattered into sections. The large section of wood would burn for hours.

The ceiling of the cell wasn't high enough for Connor to stand up straight. He arranged the broken chair pieces against the wall and reached for the rotted remains of the pallet to use as tinder.

"At least it's small enough in here that the fire should keep us from freezing." He opened the pouch hanging from his belt and pulled a tiny flint stone from it.

"I'll strike the flint. Ye need to pull the door shut to keep the wind from blowing the flames out." Brina spoke up and gained a grin from him.

"Aye, and a few of those tree limbs for green wood are better than nothing on a night such as this one promises to be."

The wind was whipping into the cell, making it bitterly cold. Connor handed her the stone, but she had to step up onto the stone bed to allow him enough space to get back to the door. The cell was no more than four feet across and six feet deep. Brina shivered as she considered anyone who might have been locked inside it. She knelt next to the pile of wood and fabric to strike the flint against another stone she picked up from the floor. Sparks flew out, blinding bright. She hit the stone again and several more times while she heard Connor pulling a large limb inside before the door ground closed. Once the wind was blocked, the sparks caught on the dry pallet remains, yellow flames eagerly licking over the wood. Connor left the door open a few inches to allow the smoke to escape.

"At least it is dry in here." She tried to hand back the flint, but Connor grasped her hand in his larger one.

"I'm more grateful for the fact that I went searching for ye, lass. Ye would nae have known this cell was here."

There was too much concern in his voice for her to bear. It made it too difficult to think of him as someone she must leave. With the cell door closed, it was so tempting to huddle close to him and share the warmth of life, because the cell was a blunt reminder of just how easily the world around them might snuff out that flame.

She didn't want to live in cold, unnoticed servitude...

"Come here, lass..."

His voice had dropped to a deep timbre that beckoned to her. He was suddenly the only spark of light in a dark wasteland. She couldn't suffer the cold any longer, not now that she knew what his embrace felt like, and the darkness seemed to offer her a place to indulge her needs, because she couldn't see anyone watching her.

His arms wrapped around her, but this time they didn't bind her to him. Brina reached for his shoulders, sliding her hands over his chest until she could wrap her fingers gently around his neck beneath the collar of his doublet where it was open. She quivered as her hand met his warm skin, and she heard him draw in a stiff breath because her fingers were chilled.

"I'm sorry..."

"Do nae be." He pressed her upper body forward to trap her arms in place when she began to withdraw her hands.

"It seems I have waited forever for ye to touch me."

The skin of his neck was warm and soon chased the last of the chill from her fingers. She trembled because the touch felt more intimate than any she had shared with him.

"We have nae known one another very long, Connor," she whispered, because the cell was so tiny that it made every sound louder and more noticeable. She heard his breath and could feel his heart beating beneath her forearms where they lay against his chest.

"And yet I discover that it seems like it has been a year since the last time I tasted yer kiss."

Just the word "kiss" made her long for another one. Her heart accelerated with anticipation, while her body seemed no longer to feel the cold. The reason was Connor; he was warm and his embrace sheltering. The hand on her back gently smoothed from the center of her shoulder blades to her waist. Tiny ripples of delight spread out from the motion, and she shivered, her eyes closing so that she might become immersed in the sensations moving across her skin.

She felt his breath against her lips before he kissed her. A soft warning that sent a bolt of awareness through the delicate skin. The moment between when she felt that brush of warm air and the first touch of his mouth on hers felt like an hour. She quivered and stretched up onto her toes to gain what she desired.

The contact made her knees weak, but she forced them to support her, refusing to relinquish the kiss to her inability to endure the flood of delight flowing through her body.

And it was her kiss. Connor didn't take command of it, only tilted his head so she could press her lips fully against his. She gripped his neck tighter so that she might deepen the kiss, allowing her lips to part and the tip of her tongue to tease his lower lip.

He shuddered and his chest rumbled with a low growl. He took command of the kiss, his mouth moving across hers in a steady motion that drew a small hum of enjoyment from her lips. That sensation flowed down her body, and she felt her nipples contracting behind the pair of gowns that she wore. She didn't seem to be close enough to him, her body yearning to be pressed even tighter against him. The sturdy wool of his doublet frustrated her, and she pulled her hands down until she could unfasten the first button. It gave with a soft popping sound.

She pulled her head back and listened to the sound of her breathing. It was agitated, and her lips were wet from his kiss. She expected Connor to follow her, and his hand clasped her nape, but his fingers merely massaged the tense muscles. It was such a gentle motion but made it impossible to think. She didn't want to anyway. She wanted to allow the delight to continue flowing and discover how much more intense it became. Her fingers could feel his warm skin hidden behind the doublet and shirt that he wore. She pushed them inside the opening, sighing when she was rewarded with a soft sound from his lips.

It was stunning how empowering that sound was. Deep inside her, a sense of confidence rose up she had never anticipated having or enjoying so much. She smoothed her hands up to his neck again, sliding her fingers along his skin and smiling when she felt him tip his head down so that she might reach all the way to where his hair began and even up into the silky strands.

"I enjoy yer hands on me, Brina."

The tone of his voice left no doubt that he did. She shivered as she contemplated how to touch him. The desire to please him was growing strong, and along with it came a yearning to be stroked in return. Her nipples ached. They were hard points, but not because of the temperature. Both soft globes clamored for attention from his hands, and she found herself pressing up against him in an effort to gain that contact.

"But I confess that I want to return the favor and put mine on ye."

She shivered in response to his words, her feet refusing to remain on her toes. She sank down, her hands gliding down across the wide planes of his chest.

"Tell me to touch ye, Brina. Tell me that ye crave it and that it is nae something forced upon ye."

Her breath caught in her throat, betraying how much she enjoyed his request. He plucked one of her hands off his chest and turned it over so that the delicate skin of her inner wrist was facing up. He leaned down and pressed a kiss against it that unleashed such a wave of need, it made her gasp.

"Ye are nae forcing me…"

"Ah… but that isna telling me to touch ye, sweet lass." He lifted his head, and the firelight bathed his features in scarlet and orange, making him look as barbaric as the stories of wintertime liked to paint ancient warriors.

She found him fascinating...

"I... do nae know what words to use..."

He drew in a stiff breath.

"So... ye tell me... Connor..." Her words were bold, but she felt desperate to continue.

"I enjoy the sound of my name on yer lips." The husky tone of his voice made her shiver, but it also sent her lips curving with satisfaction.

"I want to cup yer breasts in my hands and glide my thumbs over those hard nipples that ye pressed against me. Tell me ye desire that."

"Ye could feel my nipples?"

The last word came across her lips as a mere whisper, but he chuckled as he heard it.

"I can see them too, and the sight pleases me, Brina. I'll no' lie about that. I want to touch them and show ye how much ye'll enjoy having my hands on ye."

"But why have me tell ye to do it?"

He chuckled again and kissed her wrist once more. But then he opened his mouth and grazed her skin with his teeth, bestowing a gentle bite that made her jump.

"Maybe I've decided to listen to ye command me for a change."

He reached out and captured her, though, picking her up and placing her where he had stood, which was farthest from the fire. Her skirts swirled around her ankles along with the fabric of the cloak, and she felt her eyes widen as she realized how close she had been standing to the flames.

"So ye want me to command ye, but only so far as it pleases ye to have me tell ye what I wish."

He shrugged. "There are some things about me that ye shall just have to accept as my nature, lass. I'll always look after yer well-being, but it's harsh of ye to think unkindly of me for that."

"I do nae think unkindly of ye." The words were spoken before she thought about them. "That is no' to say that I am complacent with this plan of yers."

There was a soft chuckle from him that sounded very much like a promise.

"By complacent, do ye mean to tell me that ye are nae ready to submit yet, Brina? Be careful, lass. I do enjoy a challenge from time to time."

One of the smaller pieces of wood broke and fell. Connor turned to make sure that it did not roll away from the corner where he'd built the fire. He reached out and began snapping the branch into pieces. Brina stared at the demonstration of strength in his hands.

And yet he'd been so tender when touching her…

"We need to conserve our body heat."

He turned back to face her.

"Of course, that would be wise."

His gaze studied her for a long moment, his expression giving her no hint as to what he was thinking about. Disappointment was lashing at her for starting a conversation that had interrupted their kissing.

The word "interrupted" sent heat into her cheeks, because thinking about it in those terms meant that they would be resuming their kissing at some point.

Her nipples tingled in response to that idea.

"There is really only one way to pass the night ahead, since there is snow falling."

He reached up and untied the lace that held the pommel of his sword at his left shoulder. Once it was free, he unlatched his wide belt so that he could set the sword aside. He placed it against the ledge where the pallet had been. His plaid was loose now, but Brina ordered herself not to blush, because his shirt was long enough to cover him down to his thighs, and it was only logical that he would use the length of wool to wrap around himself.

But even with the fire, the night promised to be too cold for their location. Wind whipped in through the space that the door was open, and it ruffled her hems, making her shiver when it touched her ankles. There was a reason that raiding was a springtime event, and that was due to the deadly reality of being out in such weather.

"We'll have to share our body heat if we plan to survive."

Her eyes widened even as her mind confirmed that he spoke the truth. Bran had told her such once on an afternoon that seemed so very long ago. Families often huddled together in the winter for the same reason.

"Yes, I've heard that said."

"Good." He reached forward and unlatched the cloak where it was closed around her neck. The leather closure opened easily, and he lifted the cloak off her back. She felt it become loose instantly, her arms going around herself to keep as much heat as possible.

"It will be easier if I wear this and wrap it around you."

His voice was low, but there was no mistaking the

satisfaction in it. Connor had raised his plaid up to
cover his head, and now the deep hood of the cloak
rested on top of the Lindsey colors. He shook the
heavy wool out before lying down on the hard stone
bed the cell afforded them. The scarlet light from the
fire bathed him, sending her heart beating at a near-
frantic rate when he lifted his arms and the wool in
invitation toward hers.

"Come here, Brina, and I'll keep ye warm."

❧

Chattan Castle

"Ye frown too much for such a sweet-looking lass."

Deirdre turned around and scowled when she
discovered just how close she was to Quinton
Cameron. The man was huge, and still she'd practically walked right into his chest where he was lurking
in the shadows.

"That's on account of the fact that I am nae sweet
nor a lass any longer."

The man emerged from the shadows concealing
him, and a tingle went down her back. That little
sensation annoyed her completely, for it was exactly
the sort of thing that she loathed about her body now.

Her flesh had a weakness toward men that would be
her downfall if she failed to quell it. The fact that she
was more of a woman made her notice that he wasn't
looking at her with the sort of innocent knowledge he
would have sent toward her sister Kaie. No, the man
was interested in taking her back into the darkness for
something that lasses had no knowledge of. Quinton

Cameron was a fine example of what she liked, his body large and hard, but that was exactly the sort of trap that nature enjoyed seeing women fall into, a trap she would not fall prey to again.

"So go on with ye. I have nothing kind to say to ye."

He chuckled at her insulting words.

"I agree. Ye are nae sweet, but that does no' stop me from wondering if yer lips taste like honey. I'm no' a lad interested in playing the games of youth."

"Ye'll never know—"

He sealed out the rest of her response with a kiss that was as hard as he was. His hands bound her against him, while her body twisted and strained to escape. She dug her fingernails into his shoulders but only gained a snort from him, which died when he renewed his assault on her mouth.

His kiss was hard but not brutal. Deirdre discovered that she knew the difference, thanks to Melor, and that renewed her determination to escape from Quinton's embrace. She raised her knee, but this man was prepared for her attack. He turned her away from him so that her knee only struck air, and she was forced to stumble to regain her balance.

"Yer lips are sweet, but ye're a hellion, and no mistake about it."

Deirdre tossed her head to swing her hair behind her shoulders. "One with naught to offer ye, thanks to yer words to me father."

Quinton's eyebrow rose. "Oh, ye have something to offer me, lass."

"No, I do nae, nor will I ever, for there is one

blessing to no' having a dowry, and that will ensure that I will nae have to suffer a man trying his hand at mastering me."

Those words were torn from her soul, and she spit them out like the foulest of curses.

His eyes narrowed. "Be very careful, lass, for I am a man who does nae pass up a good challenge. Toss one at me, and ye might just discover how wrong ye can be proven."

Deirdre hissed at him and propped her hands on her hips in defiance. Arrogance was rising off him so strongly, she was practically nauseated by it.

"I shall never lie with a man again. Ye are all the same with yer possessive nature toward women. I'll go to the abbey in my sister's place and right happily. I shall be glad to go where I will never have to tolerate a man's touch again."

She flounced down the passageway, never looking back at the man who watched her. Quinton Cameron didn't sleep alone unless he wanted to or he was too busy to charm what he wanted from the lass of his choice. There were two maids in the kitchen who were sending him hopeful glances every time he entered the hall, which proved that he wouldn't have to suffer a swollen cock tonight either.

But he was uninterested in anyone but the woman who had just cursed him and every other man. He chuckled because he'd insulted her as well, but he wasn't too sure that Deirdre Chattan wouldn't come to enjoy being known as a hellion, for she was no lass, but a woman who had grown past the need to have the world agree with her.

Quinton chuckled again because that was something they had in common. He might just tell her too, for the entertainment of watching what she made of it.

Aye, maybe he would.

⤜⤛

Brina trembled.

She felt the vibration moving down her limbs, where her knees felt unsteady. Her mouth went dry, but her feet began moving before her muddled mind made any sense of the situation.

Of course there was nothing to do but go to Connor and allow him to wrap his body around hers.

Her belly twisted with anticipation, but something else made her blood move faster, and she realized that it was excitement.

It took her only another step to reach the ledge. She turned her back on him and sat down. She could feel the heat from his body before she was completely lying alongside him. He wrapped his arms around her, easing her back until she felt him touching her from her toes to her head, the heavy wool of the cloak closing around her to seal the heat from his body next to her own. She could feel the steady rise and fall of his breathing, so similar to her own, except that hers was more agitated.

"So at last ye come to my embrace."

Six

"STOP MAKING FUN OF ME."

Brina tried to shove her elbow back toward him but his arms tightened around her, confining her arms so that she couldn't put any true strength into the motion.

"Why is it that men are expected to be experienced while a woman who is finds herself called horrible names? I know that is the way of the world, but the least ye might do is no' tease me for being innocent."

He blew out a soft sound near her ear. "Now why would ye deprive me of the enjoyment I gain from teasing ye, lass? This night promises to offer few other entertainments. But I was nae teasing ye because ye are innocent; that is a mark of honor for ye."

"Ye mean it is what makes me valuable to ye."

"Maybe, but ye should be a wee bit kinder toward the fact that I'm driven to taking a wife who has no rumors clinging to her skirts, because I want there to be no further question as to who is the rightful heir to the Lindsey clan."

"I never said I had no compassion for yer plight. It is a just cause." Her voice was low, and his hands smoothed along her arm, unleashing sensation that was enjoyable.

"I've seen bad times on Lindsey land, Brina. I'll keep that from happening again if I can."

His body curled around hers, and she decided that it was too hard to think about their conversation. Her heart hadn't slowed down, and sleep was only a distant idea that wasn't even interesting to her. She caught his hand and slid her fingers along his. He was warm, and his skin slightly rougher than her own, but that only struck her as right.

Maybe this would just be the best solution...

No one would believe that she was still pure now that she had passed so much time at Birch Stone. No matter what happened, no one would consider her innocent, even if she had a midwife swear to it. The world was run by men, and they would assume that Connor had claimed what he wanted from her.

So why not taste what she would be accused of having sampled?

"Thank ye for keeping yer promise."

He nuzzled at her neck, a soft kiss making her lift her chin so that he had more of her skin to tease with his lips.

"Which promise, lass?"

"No' to rape me."

He was a good man, who had treated her better than she might have expected, when considering the circumstances.

He moved slowly, his hands rubbing gently along her body. He used the slowest of motions, but her head lifted sharply because she suddenly realized that she was exactly where he wanted her.

"Ye're attempting to gentle me," she said.

He made a soft sound of male amusement near her ear before one of his hands glided over the top of her hip. "Aye..." His hand continued onward, petting the length of her thigh before stopping at the limit of his reach. He then began to retrace the same path. Her body quivered with mounting excitement, every inch of flesh that he'd touched eager for a second stroke from his hand.

"I'm set on demonstrating just how much ye have to gain by yielding yer trust to me."

His words were a dark whisper that shimmered like a loch on a hot summer afternoon with the promise of pleasing her body.

"Most men do nae care how a woman yields to them, only that she surrenders."

"I care." There was a hint of smug pride in his tone.

"I know," she muttered softly. It was the thing about him that she liked too much.

He drew his hand up and over the curve of her hip, sending little ripples of enjoyment down her leg and across her midsection. His fingers soon smoothed over the tight muscles of her belly while she felt a soft kiss press against her cheek.

"Come closer, Brina."

His hand opened, his fingers stretching out to cover her belly, and he moved up behind her so that her bottom was pressed firmly against his cock. The soft fabric of her gowns and his shirt didn't prevent her from feeling the rigid outline.

He cupped her face, turning it toward his own. "I regret no' a single thing, Brina, for the fates brought ye to me, and I am pleased by what fate has decided."

His hand glided up her body before stopping to cup one of her breasts. She suddenly longed to be rid of her clothing, for it prevented her from feeling his skin against her own. A need to experience that contact began to pound through her.

"Ye are my bride."

"But—"

He smothered her protest with his lips, rising up to lean over her so that he might kiss her and press her down onto her back. His hand remained on the side of her face to keep her where he wished, but the truth was, she wasn't interested in moving away from his kiss.

Maybe it was the danger of freezing lurking just a few feet beyond the shelter of his embrace, or the knowledge that her bed at the abbey would have been cold and hard, she wasn't sure which, only that his kiss was full of life, and she wanted to be close to it.

One of his legs curled over one of her thighs, and his knee separated her legs. She had never been so conscious of her sex before. Suddenly the folds were a place that begged for a stroke from his fingers, even if she had always been forbidden to consider such a thing.

For the moment, nothing was beyond her reach. Connor was hard and warm, and she lifted her hands to investigate every ridge of muscle she had viewed on his chest. He trailed his fingers down the side of her face and along the slim column of her neck until he reached the top of the lace that held her overgown closed. The lack of light didn't seem to keep him from being able to loosen the lace and pull it free from the eyelets.

"I wanted to welcome ye to Birch Stone in that fine bed I had built for ye, but I will nae reject the gift of this night."

"Tumbling down the side of yer castle is a gift?"

He hovered over her, his breath teasing her lips, which were still wet from his kiss.

"It sent ye into my embrace of yer own free will, and that is a gift, one I plan to enjoy full well."

Her underrobe only had a single button at the neckline. He pushed it through its loop and parted the edges of her last garment with his fingertips. Her breath caught, and she watched his gaze return to hers. The fire bathed them both in crimson light that didn't mask the hunger in his eyes. His hand slipped completely beneath her robes to lie against her skin while she quivered.

"Being able to touch ye is a gift, Brina."

"I enjoy it too…" She spoke without thinking, her back refusing to remain still, because she wanted to feel his hand on more than just one spot. Her nipples felt harder than she could ever recall them being, while the soft globes of her breasts yearned for a stroke of his fingers.

But that wasn't all she wanted. Her body was filled with too many longings for her to understand all at the same time. Connor didn't suffer from that same lack of comprehension though. He slid his hand down her chest until he cupped her breast with a knowledgeable hand.

She arched beneath him, her back lifting so that her breast was pressed against his palm.

"I can see that you do, lass."

Her eyes closed because there was so much sensation flowing from that touch that she couldn't continue to try and process what her eyes saw as well. There were too many signals rushing through her body and into her mind.

She had never imagined that a man's touch could feel so good.

He brushed her gown aside, baring her breast to the night air, but his hand kept it warm. And then she felt his breath against her puckered nipple. The cloak was still over his shoulders, so when he bent his head down and closed his lips about the puckered tip of her breast, the heavy fabric kept her from feeling the icy breath of the night air.

That allowed her to experience nothing but the heat. It flashed out to cover every inch of her body from the point where his mouth drew on her nipple.

"Connor, you shouldn't..."

He lifted his mouth away, and she cringed with disappointment, her body jerking with lament as her flesh demanded that she silence every protest.

"And why no', lass? Ye liked it."

He wasn't asking her; he was stating a fact. One that was as solid as his body.

But she didn't want to move him.

"Shall I taste its twin?"

His tone was liquid sin, she was sure of it, and still she couldn't resist its allure. Lifting one hand, she grasped the edges of her gowns and pulled them aside so that her opposite breast was bared.

She heard him draw a short breath and felt a rise of confidence inside herself. There was a sense of power that grew from knowing that she could affect him just as much as he did her.

Connor didn't hesitate very long. He bent down over her offered breast, his breath warming the skin a moment before she felt his lips graze the hard tip. He didn't suck it inside his lips immediately this time but toyed with the sensitive peak, the tip of his tongue flicking over it before he sucked it.

She cried out, a soft sound that was a combination of delight and need. She bent one of her knees, because her sex felt too compressed, as though the folds were swollen and the small bead that was covered by them too sensitive to remain between closed thighs. She reached for her partner, her hands threading through his hair as she arched, and her breast rose up in complete surrender to his lips.

Connor lifted his head away, and she heard her own cry fill the tiny cell, a flicker of promise in his eyes. She felt his hands moving down her length until he grasped her skirts and tugged them up. He only pulled the front of her gowns up, leaving her lying on the back.

Her eyes widened as she felt his arm brushing her knees and then her thighs. Deep inside her belly, excitement was raging like a fire that had too much tinder. She needed to think before she lost the ability to reason when he touched her again.

But Connor didn't give her the opportunity. He leaned down and pressed a hard kiss against her mouth. There was nothing soft about it, his lips commanding hers to open while she felt her gowns slither up to bare her mons. She gasped, and he took advantage of her open mouth, his tongue thrusting inside to tease hers with a bold penetration that drew a soft moan from her.

The sound was born from need. Her passage felt too empty, when she had never noticed it wanting to be filled before. She wanted to be touched, and her body wasn't interested in waiting either. She moved beneath him, reaching up to hold his shoulders close to her while she mimicked his kiss, moving her lips in unison with his.

His chest rumbled with another sound that told her he enjoyed the contact between them as much as she did. That was her undoing, for it sent her hands into his hair again, almost frantically this time because she wanted to pull him into the storm assaulting her. She wanted to feel him against her, harder and closer, because she could not bear to be alone.

"Easy, lass…"

His words were a mere whisper and drew an irritated sound from her. She didn't want to slow down, but the first touch of his hand on her inner thigh drew a harsh gasp from her. Connor didn't retreat in response to the sound, his hand remaining firm on the sensitive skin, soothing her with a gentle motion that filled her with delight. It felt so perfect, as though she had been blind and suddenly could see. Her skin was made to feel pleasure from the touch of a hand.

He pressed her thigh aside and rolled over her in the same moment. She lifted her eyelids, startled by the motion, but his hands framed her face, brushing the small bits of hair that had worked loose from the fabric wrapped around her head.

His breath was warm against her lips again, and she could feel his heart beating quickly against her chest. The cloak settled over them, and his weight pressed down on top of her, feeding the yearning that had made her clutch at him. It was satisfying in some deep way that she didn't understand but could feel swirling through her like intoxication from too much whisky.

His larger frame spread her thighs wide, and she felt the brush of his cock against her folds. It was strange how she understood exactly what it was that glided through the folds protecting the opening to her body. It was instinct along with the half-heard whispers that rose up from her memory. Things she had overheard and ordered herself to ignore but had never truly forgotten. The reason was simple; deep inside, she hungered to know another's touch. That need had always been burning inside her, never truly snuffed out by the duty she knew was hers.

But she wanted to know what it felt like to have him inside her...

Right, wrong, or possibly wicked—none of it mattered.

"I meant to seduce ye gently, in a soft bed... with fine things about ye..."

His voice had turned husky, with strain edging it. His fingers trembled against her face as though he was struggling to maintain control.

"I don't want soft." Not a single bit of it. She craved hardness, and the head of his cock made her passage ache. It was a deep feeling of need and hunger that assaulted her without mercy. She twisted in its grip, her hips rising up to seek out what she craved.

Connor growled, his body pressing down on top of hers more. "I swear that ye leave me helpless at times, lass, with the way that ye speak so plainly. I pray ye never change."

He thrust forward, and his length began to penetrate her. The folds of her sex were slick and wet in welcome, allowing his member to burrow inside her. But her sheath wasn't wide enough, the walls of her passage refusing to stretch around his girth. Pain burned white-hot along her insides, and she felt tears stinging her eyes because it was so intense.

Connor muttered something next to her ear that she failed to understand as the torment ripped at her. He moved, withdrawing from her and leaving only a burning sensation to mark where he had penetrated her. Brina drew in a deep breath, feeling it cleanse some of the hurt away, but Connor wasn't finished. He thrust smoothly back into her, gaining more ground this time, and she felt her body tearing in order to accommodate his hard flesh.

She cried out, unable to contain the agony eating at her. His cock felt too large, but it was firmly lodged inside her passage. Her thighs clasped his hips, a reflex against his gaining any more depth, but she could feel that he had penetrated her completely.

Tears escaped from her eyes, but he caught them with his fingers, smoothing them away while he offered her words of praise that her brain didn't really grasp.

Brina opened her eyes. Her brain finally made sense of what he was saying. His words were soft endearments, muttered softly against her hair. Such tender words surprised her because she would have expected him to be crowing with his victory.

Instead he praised her spirit.

"Easy, lass, ye're a Highlander just as surely as I am. It's in yer blood, Brina. That is why ye crave me as much as I do ye."

He pulled free, and she drew in a deep breath that flew out of her lungs in the next instant as he moved back into her.

But the pain was missing this time. Her sheath took his member without the blinding hurt, only a dull ache remained.

"I promise ye, Brina, it will nae hurt like that again. Now there is the pleasure that I can show ye."

His hips began working, driving between her spread thighs. For the first few thrusts, she could only remain still, part of her dreading that he hadn't spoken truthfully.

Yet he had. Each stroke began to rekindle the need that had burned so brightly inside her.

"Lift yer hips for me, and it will be even better…"

His voice was like a spell, leading her off into the darkness for something that was forbidden but worth the possibility of being caught.

Her body responded before she thought any further on it, her hips lifting to take his next thrust. She gasped as his penis slid along the small bead hidden at the top of her sex. Pleasure shot up into her belly from the contact, awakening an enjoyment of being stretched by his hard flesh.

"That's the way, lass."

It certainly was. Pleasure filled her with each thrust that she lifted to take, his cock sliding deeper into her, and his body pressing against that little bead. Enjoyment surged through her, swirling and increasing. Her belly began to tighten, and she reached for her lover, pulling his shoulders close while she arched to receive every plunge of his body into hers. Reasons and thoughts fell away while pleasure and the need to gain more of it filled her fuller and fuller until they burst in an explosion that drew every muscle tight. Her body strained toward Connor, her fingernails biting into his skin while rapture burned a path through her. Brina heard her cry echoing inside the tiny stone cell, but she was powerless to prevent herself from muttering several more times while the sensations whipped through her.

Connor growled, and the sound made her eyelids lift. It was a savage sound that pleased her, for it was edged with satisfaction that no words might ever convey. He drove his member deep and fast, his flesh feeling harder with every downward plunge, and then suddenly his face drew taut, and she felt his seed burst against the mouth of her womb. He shuddered, pleasure crossing his features in a savage display that she stared at because of its raw beauty. It wasn't the sort of handsomeness that sonnets spoke of, but something far more primitive that pleased her in more ways than any words ever had.

Connor caught his weight on his elbows, just shy of crushing her beneath his greater size. Their breathing filled the cell, with only the wind to mix with it.

He pressed a soft kiss against her lips and then a row of them across her cheek before he withdrew from her body and rolled her onto her side once again. Satisfaction bathed her in a warm glow that his embrace complemented perfectly. Her strength failed her, but she didn't lament it, because Connor wrapped her in his arms, and that was everything she needed.

Her eyelids closed with her lover still gently lowering her skirts to cover her legs. Nothing mattered except the rapture still glowing inside her and the secure embrace keeping her in that moment of pure bliss.

Nothing.

❧

The door scraped open, the sound shattering her sleep. Brina tried to sit up but had to battle against the cloak that was tucked around her body. The sturdy wool pinned her arms against her chest, while the ends were tucked beneath her, which made her fight against her own body weight.

Connor's sword was missing, and she heard his feet snapping the hard layer that had frozen on the top of the snow during the night. She finally succeeded in gaining her freedom from the cloak as he released an owl's cry that was shrill and loud. Pushing the fabric aside, she stood up and shivered in the frigid air. The fire had long since died, even the coals losing their heat against the winter chill.

Yet she hadn't felt it, not even awakened once during the night. She blushed, her cheeks heating scarlet when she took a step and felt her passage ache. It was a deep, dull hurt, but there was no ignoring it.

Another owl's cry drifted down from atop the curtain wall. Connor answered it as she neared the open door. In the morning dawn, he looked completely confident in his surroundings. His kilt was belted back in place about his narrow waist, but he had some of it resting over his shoulder. She might have expected that to be raised over his head, but it wasn't. Now that he'd risen from his bed, the man was ready to face the day completely. He had his head tilted back so that he might look up the walls now that the wind wasn't whipping around them, Brina could hear men running along the top of the wall. Connor let out another shriek.

A moment later a rope ladder was tossed down. It thumped and skidded against the stone surface of the wall, the sounds loud in the dawn quiet. She must have moved, because Connor suddenly jerked his head toward her. For the briefest of moments, his expression was hard and unyielding, but he grinned when recognition registered in his eyes.

"Morning, lass. It seems that daylight has brought us the rescue that darkness denied us."

"Ye could have cried out last night."

His expression remained guarded. "With the wind, I doubt that anyone would have heard me."

"Yet ye didna try…" She should have thought on it last night.

He reached out and gave the ladder a sharp tug. It didn't move, and he nodded with approval before turning to close the distance between them.

"It matters no'; it's the truth that I am well pleased with how the night passed." His hand came out to stroke the red stain resting on her cheeks, and for a moment she was taken back to the time that they had clung to one another. The touch of his fingers against her face brought it back instantly, and a ripple of awareness went down her body. His blue eyes watched hers, and her eyelashes fluttered because it felt like the man could see directly into her thoughts.

She heard him grunt, a small, extremely male sound, and his fingers lifted away.

"What does matter is that we have discovered that we are well suited to each other."

There was the solid ring of authority in his voice, and when she looked back at his face, she discovered herself facing Laird Lindsey. A creak on the ladder told her why. Shawe jumped to the ground, his boots crunching on the snow.

"Sweet Christ, Laird, we didna think the pair of ye were down here when ye failed to attend supper."

Brina felt her cheeks heat, because it was obvious what the Lindsey retainers had thought she and Connor were doing.

They had been correct.

"Aye, yer mistress slid down the face of the cannon bunkers. Have the lads tie up a sturdy chair so that we can hoist her up."

"I can climb well enough." And she didn't care if it was considered unfeminine. The men turned to face her with suspicion on their faces. Brina stared back with firm conviction in her stance. Connor looked down her length.

"Ye'll have to raise yer skirts."

"I know that."

His head tilted, and his eyes narrowed. "Is that a fact? How do ye know so much about climbing?"

Brina began answering before she thought. "I've climbed a fair number of trees because that is the best position from which to hunt rabbit with a bow."

Connor frowned. "Yer father had ye trained to use a bow?"

"Aye."

She said it with pride and heard Shawe whisper a soft word in Gaelic, but Connor's expression turned hard.

"What's the harm in knowing how to catch a rabbit?"

The men who had followed Shawe down the ladder looked toward Connor instead of answering her. Brina propped her hands onto her hips and felt her pride rearing its head once more.

"Oh… as if I care what ye think of it. My father warned ye that I was nae raised up to consider the egos of men. He had me taught how to see to my own needs."

She grabbed up a portion of her skirts and tucked them right into the bottom of the opening in the front of her overrobe. It wasn't easy, but she pushed a measure of the cloth through the space beneath the last set of eyelets. It raised the front hems enough for her to see her toes. Lifting one foot, she set it firmly on the bottom of the ladder and grasped the sides to begin climbing. Once she left the ground, the ladder began to sway from side to side like a pendulum as she made her way up the wall. When she looked up, the top of the wall suddenly seemed much farther than it had from the ground.

She heard a short grunt that she knew without a doubt belonged to Connor, and then the ladder remained straight.

"I can manage just fine on my own," she said.

"So I see."

There was an edge of frustration in his voice that

she didn't want to linger long enough to consider. Brina returned her attention to climbing and made it up to the top of the curtain wall, where several Lindsey retainers reached over and pulled her the last few feet.

Connor was a mere moment behind her, except that he wasn't hauled over the edge of the wall but jumped those last few feet to land solidly beside her.

"What else did yer father have ye trained in?"

Brina felt her lips rise into a small smile. It was definitely smug, but she discovered that she enjoyed knowing that he was unsure of her for once.

"Practical things, Laird Lindsey. My father made sure that I was ready to assume my place at the abbey as a productive member of the convent." She tossed her head. "After all, my life was never supposed to include the luxury of depending on a man for anything. My father made sure that I was ready to greet that future."

He wasn't pleased with her tone, but he did smile at her words. His lips rose into an expression that spoke clearly of his satisfaction.

"We'll have to discuss yer skills later, to determine which ones will be useful in yer future here at Birch Stone for I find that I like knowing ye are nae helpless."

Connor didn't give her any time to deny his words. He looked past her, and she recognized the retainers who had dogged her footsteps the day before.

"I hope ye listened well and are ready to do a better job of looking after my bride today." He turned back to look at her with a glare that was edged in suspicion. "She is more capable than she appears, do nae allow her sweet face to beguile ye."

"That is nae a sin." Her tone was less than respectful and far from meek. There was a challenge in it that she would have done well to temper, but she failed to. Connor stepped up to her without hesitation.

"No, it isna, but leaving ye to dupe my men would be, lass, for I will nae have ye running because of some sense of misplaced shame. Last night will no be a sin once we kneel in front of the priest."

She gasped because every man heard his words. She could feel the weight of their stares on her and witnessed a few grins appearing in response.

Connor's gaze moved to the stain darkening her cheeks. There was a calculating look in his eyes that spoke of why he held the respect of the Lindsey clan.

The reason was that he was no fool, and he was, without a doubt, every inch a Highlander. A man who took what he wanted and held it, even against the odds.

"It was nae necessary to say that in front of all."

He reached out and stroked her face, the touch delicate and soft. A hint of tenderness flickered in his blue eyes that struck a soft spot deep inside her heart. She looked away because it was unnerving the way that he could so easily take her back to their moments of intimacy with only a look. She heard him blow out a stiff breath.

"I believe that it was, Brina. For I intend to see ye later this day in the church sanctuary. It is best that ye understand that every soul wearing me colors knows ye should seek the church's blessing beside me."

It was a solid promise that annoyed her because of how much pleasure it gave her. Surrender shouldn't be so simple, and yet she discovered that she was more frustrated by the fact that she was duty-bound to resent enjoying his embrace last night.

Life was not fair, and for the moment she wanted to rail against it.

❧

"Not a soul thought that ye would have managed to get yerself into such peril, mistress."

Once again, Maura was speaking in a tone that held a great deal of authority.

"It is by far a great blessing that the laird thought to be so close behind ye."

"I would nae have slipped if he hadna startled me."

There was silence in the bathing chamber as all three of the maids who the head of house had insisted attend Brina's bath stopped what they were doing to stare at her. The moment became uncomfortable because Brina could feel the disapproval being aimed toward her.

That only doubled her discomfort, making it feel like shame, because Connor had earned respect from his clan, and that was something that could not be ordered or taken. If the women in the room had no true devotion toward their laird, they would find some task to take them away from attending to her. The only reason that they remained when there was so little to do was that they sought to please Connor by making sure of his wish that she be treated as the mistress of Birch Stone.

"I mean no disrespect toward yer laird. I was fortunate to have his assistance last night."

Maura nodded approvingly. "I imagine so; it was bitterly cold last evening. Anything left in the fields is lost for sure now."

"We'll have to pray for an early thaw." The women nodded in agreement as they set about filling a tub for her bath. The sound of running water was still slightly amazing, in spite of the fact that Maura had told her there would be water even with snow outside the castle walls.

Brina was grateful for it today. She longed for a bath and suddenly understood why some religious orders shunned washing as a luxury. Just looking at the clear water in the tub felt good; having it glide along her skin was going to be decadent.

One of the women pulled the blue overgown from her, and there was a soft sound of surprise from the woman standing behind her. Brina turned to see what had startled her, only to hear another gasp from the woman in front of her. She turned back around but found both women looking at the back of her underrobe.

"Well, it's good to know that ye have settled matters between the laird and yerself."

Maura reached out and plucked the back of her gown up between her fingers. Brina turned to see that the light blue fabric was stained dark brown for a good foot. The head of house flicked her fingers at the woman in front of Brina, and the gown was whisked up and over her head in a moment. The head of house handed the garment over to another maid before she reached forward and boldly wiped the top of Brina's thigh with the linen cloth that was waiting to dry her after her bath.

Brina jumped, but Maura held up the fabric, making sure that the light streaming in through the open windows illuminated it. She gave a satisfied grunt before turning it to show each woman in the room.

There were suddenly smiles around the room, and the women hurried to make sure that the waiting bath was perfect. They dipped their fingers into the water to check the temperature and moved the drying rack closer toward the hearth to ensure that the underrobe she would wear after bathing was cozy.

"Karen, send down to the cook and tell her to make supper special."

"That is nae necessary."

Brina might as well have saved her breath, for Karen lowered herself and was out of the door before she finished protesting. The maid's steps echoed down the hallway with a pace that spoke of the woman's excitement. It wouldn't take long for her to spread the word throughout Birch Stone that the laird had consummated his union.

"Let's get ye bathed, mistress, for I'm sure ye'll want to be getting on to church before the day grows much older."

It could be that simple.

Brina tumbled that idea over and over inside her mind while she was bathed from her head to her toes. She was too preoccupied by her thoughts to protest.

Oh aye, simple, because she had only to turn her back on her duty to her father. The problem was, she was beginning to see staying at Birch Stone as an option.

❧

Father Luke-Paul was waiting for him. Connor saw the man standing in the arched doorway of the church. The priest had his hands tucked into the wide sleeves of his robe while he stood as still as one of the carved statues that adorned the inner sanctuary.

Connor lowered himself to one knee at the threshold but didn't linger there. He pushed back up to his full height while Luke-Paul surveyed him.

"I made it plain that I plan to wed the lass from the moment I took her."

The priest's eyes narrowed slightly, showing that he didn't care for the arrogance in Connor's tone. Connor didn't lower his head. He wasn't sure that he could feign any sort of remorse for the fact that he'd had Brina before they took the blessing of the church, for he wasn't sorry.

Not one bit.

But he was thankful.

Luke-Paul frowned. "That is a truth. I will have to compose a lecture for yer bride on the merits of nae arguing against God's will."

"I did steal her, Father."

There was a faint flicker of amusement in the priest's eyes that didn't change his expression. "Ye are both Scottish, and that is a common enough practice. I will hear yer confession."

He turned and led the way into the sanctuary, saving Connor from upsetting the man further with the grin that split his lips. It was cocky, to be sure, and no doubt Luke-Paul would have felt the need to compose a lecture for him on the ideals of virtue if he had seen it.

Connor didn't care. He'd sit through any sermon the man deemed necessary, for he did not regret claiming Brina.

Her cries of delight still echoed inside his head, and they stirred a need to curse the sun for not making its way across the sky faster. He was as impatient as a newly tried lad to get back beneath her skirts, his cock stirring beneath his kilt to throb with need.

It was more than lust. He felt that truth even as he knelt in submission to the church and began his confession. His words were disjointed because his mind was not on the matter of his soul and its position in the afterlife. Instead he was focused on the bride he wanted to learn more about.

But for a man of the church, Father Luke-Paul held more knowledge than any celibate should. The priest drew out the confession and announced a penance that was going to take a fair amount of time to complete. Connor ground his teeth but nodded.

Bugger it.

∞

Connor was on his knees when Brina entered the church doorway.

The sight stunned her, and she stood in place, her eyes adjusting to the dim interior of the sanctuary.

He was not a man who knelt easily…

She couldn't stop the rise of her own pride in response. Oh, it was surely pride, because what else could she call the enjoyment she gained from knowing that such a powerful man was attempting to satisfy the church so that he might wed her?

He might have doubled his offering to the priest or promised to build something for the church with the labor owed to him by his clan members. Such was the normal practice for lairds who stole brides. A bartering of material things before the church gave its blessing in spite of any obstacles that might have impeded the union.

Instead Connor Lindsey, laird of some of the fiercest Highlanders in Scotland, was on his knees while a priest watched from an alcove.

It brought tears to her eyes because it was more sincere than any words he might have uttered could ever have been. A man might say many things when he was intent on seduction, but how he conducted himself after he had won the victory he sought spoke much about his true nature.

Connor Lindsey was truly a man of honor. That was such a rare thing. Many men claimed it, fought over it, but in truth they only maintained their noble facade when there was someone about to offer them attention for it. Here in the dimly lit pews, there was only a priest who would keep his silence in accordance with his vows on just how the laird gained his absolution.

Connor was doing his penance, just as any man beneath his authority would have instead of using his position to force the priest to marry them.

Aye, he had honor, and it made her proud to know that he considered her worthy of being his bride.

From behind her, a bell began to ring, and very quickly after that a second and third joined in. Connor jerked, jumping to his feet and turning in a swirl of

Lindsey plaid. He froze when his gaze settled on her, surprise taking command of his features for a brief moment before more bells joined the ringing. He covered the distance between them with long strides.

"Go into the tower, lass, until I discover who is at my gate."

Fear tore through her, the distaste in his voice shattering her fascination with discovering him in the church.

She reached out, clutching at his forearm. Her action surprised him, bringing him to a standstill when she was sure that nothing else might have distracted him from his duty to protect his clan against whoever was riding toward Birch Stone.

Horror threatened to choke her while images of her father and other members of her clan lying bloodied in the snow rose up to torment her. Being inside Birch Stone would give the Lindsey an advantage that would see many of her kin dead if not all of them, if it was her father approaching.

"My father is a good man." She forced the words past lips that threatened to tremble and reduce her to a weeping weakling at his feet.

More than one stolen bride had discovered that the only way to keep her kin from being cut down when they came to protest her abduction was to wed her captor, looking willing and contented in spite of the circumstances.

"I refused to return home without ye, Brina, because I want an alliance with the Chattan. It isna a feud that I'm looking to begin."

He covered her hand with his larger one, offering

her a firm squeeze before he lifted her fingers off his arm and looked past her toward his men.

"Take her into the tower and keep her there, lads."

❧

Brina realized she had never truly known fear.

Not a single time in her entire life. Every minute felt as long as an hour. Connor's men took her to the tower, but she refused to go any farther than the doors. The retainers looked at her and then at one another, but the older one shrugged and leaned up against the wall, content to allow her to remain where she was because it would satisfy what their laird had ordered them to do.

"Mistress? Come into the hall. Better not to dwell on matters that men must tend to."

Maura's voice held a measure of kindness that didn't soothe her. Brina walked across the width of the tower, then stopped at one of the windows that had its wooden shutters open to allow fresh air inside. She wasn't high enough to see out of the inner castle, but she could see that the gate was lowered to seal off the inner yard. Voices came from the hall behind her, telling her that most of the inhabitants had crossed through that gate to take shelter in the tower farthest from the approaching riders when the bells had rung. She could hear children and women behind her, and in spite of the fact that they were keeping their voices low, the number of them made the hall quite noisy.

She turned and walked across the length of the tower until she could see out a window on the opposite side. Now she had a view of the church. The large double doors that had always been open were now shut, and every window was covered with thick wooden shutters.

"We've no way of knowing who is coming up the hill, mistress. Save yer worry for a time when there is clear trouble."

Maura stepped in front of her, refusing to allow her to pace back to the other window, but Brina was not in the mood to be bent beneath the woman's greater experience.

"For all that yer laird has his honorable reasons for taking me, my father is equally bound by his integrity to object. Why am I the only one who can see this has the making of a feud that will only take lives that would be better used to make the future good for everyone. I cannae take my own happiness in such a manner."

Maura lifted a hand to cover her lips, while her eyes filled with worry. She drew in a deep breath.

"Well then, I suppose 'tis a good thing that ye and the laird settled matters between ye last evening."

"Settled?"

The head of house drew herself up and propped her hands onto her hips.

"I saw yer gown myself, and I'll swear to the fact that ye are nae suffering yer courses. Ye were pure when ye went to his bed."

Maura raised her voice, making sure that the men behind her heard every syllable. Brina's face heated up as they nodded with approval.

"There will be an alliance, and if it is yer father out there, the laird will deal with him. I have faith in that. It's in yer favor that ye think of others before yerself, but ye do nae know our laird very well yet. He will bring to us what he has promised. A bright future with an agreement with yer clan that will ensure peace."

An alliance. Of course. That was her purpose. Brina turned and entered the great hall. She hesitated at the door as so many heads turned to her. Younger children peeked between the shoulders of the adults, while conversation died away. She forced herself forward, and a few of the older men reached up to tug on the corners of their bonnets, but they were few. Most of the Lindsey clan simply regarded her as a recent acquisition, one who would bring them what they wanted. Maura might call her "mistress," but she was nothing of the sort.

She preferred it that way…

The image of Connor kneeling in the sanctuary surfaced in her mind, lending her the strength to make it to the end of the hall with a level chin. She would earn respect from the Lindseys or live without it. She heard Connor's retainers following her, their boot heels making soft tapping sounds on the stone floor. Even when they masked their steps, she could see on the faces of those in front of her that they were trailing her.

Connor didn't trust her, and yet the man had boldly demanded her trust last night. Frustration rose up, and it mixed with the fear still brewing inside her.

But what bothered her the most was the fact that she was growing very trusting of her captor. She might refuse to admit it to anyone else, but that did not change what she knew to be true.

A grinding sound began to echo through the hall,

stopping Brina in her tracks. A hush settled over the inhabitants, which allowed them to hear the sound more clearly, and then laughter erupted all around her.

The inner gate was being raised, and relief washed over everyone except for Brina. She turned to watch those who had crowded onto the benches all heading out of the tower now that the threat had passed.

"Ye see there, mistress?" Maura smiled and she nodded. "All is well, and I'm right pleased to tell ye that the laird takes no chances on the well-being of his clan. He has that gate secured every time riders are sighted, just to make certain of that fact."

"The raising of that gate does nae mean that my father is nae outside the walls."

But it did mean that Connor wasn't going to order his archers to let loose their arrows.

Once more the man was true to his word. Brina turned around and walked past the retainers set to guarding her.

Oh yes, Connor Lindsey did keep his word in so many ways. She was likely to go insane before the week's end from the man's persistent nature.

Or wed him…

"Mistress, ye're to remain in the tower."

The older of the men reached out and neatly hooked her forearm when she went to follow the other women out into the yard. His touch startled her, but more so because she had been so deep within her thoughts that she hadn't taken notice of where she was going.

"Do nae call me mistress when I am no such thing here."

She stepped to the side of the doorway, and

the man folded his arms in front of his chest while frowning at her.

"Ye're to marry our laird; that makes ye the mistress."

Brina scoffed at his logic. "Just because a man is a Scot does nae make him a Highlander, or do ye consider those who live in the Lowlands Highlanders?"

"No one does, and that's a fact sure enough…"

The man snapped his lips together when he realized that he'd agreed with her logic. He lifted one hand.

"But that is nae to say…"

"Do nae concern yerself with my feelings. I prefer honesty, and it is clear enough that yer clan does nae consider me their mistress but are only calling me such to please yer laird. I have no' kept the books or seen to the stores so that all will be fed throughout the winter. That is what makes a mistress of a castle, nae simply… well…"

She slapped her hands down on top of her skirts again and fixed him with a hard look. "It is a fact that I have nae acted as mistress of this castle, and I cannae accept being called by a title that should be earned."

"That is something that will change when we wed, Brina."

Connor stood in the doorway, his voice deep and hard with authority. He aimed a stare at her that was unwavering with his intent. "And if ye want to argue about what ye are here, Brina, I am the one ye should be talking to."

She raised her chin in the face of his disgruntled tone. "Then dismiss yer men, for I am no' accustomed to ignoring those around me as if I am better than they."

Connor's eyes flashed. "I agree that ye are nae

accustomed to many things, but I believe ye are doing a fine job of learning new ways." His eyes narrowed slightly. "I've taken notice of just how well ye are adjusting. Last night ye did very well."

Her jaw dropped open, but she snapped it shut as her temper blazed.

Connor stepped inside. "Quinton, allow me to introduce Brina Chattan to ye."

He turned to look at another man, who was stepping through the double-wide doorway. He looked like Connor's opposite. They were both huge, but where Connor was light haired, Quinton had hair the darkest shade of black. Most men had brown hair, but this one was a true black, and he even kept a beard that was cut short.

"This is Quinton Cameron, Laird Cameron, and he's kindly agreed to witness our vows."

There was too much arrogance in Connor's voice, and she glared at him in defiance. Laird Cameron watched her with an expression that told her he expected her to yield as well, and her self-discipline failed in the face of their presumptuous attitudes.

"Except that I have promised ye that I will nae wed ye."

Laird Cameron actually grinned, but Connor wasn't amused by her words. She watched his eyes grow dark with frustration.

"Excuse me, Cameron. I need to have a word with my bride-to-be."

"Aye, I can see that well enough."

The Cameron laird offered her an amused grin before he walked past her, his retainers trailing him.

"Yer *mistress* does nae need ye for the moment." Connor drew out the title before walking toward her and grasping her wrist with his hand to turn her about to face one of the narrow passageways leading away from the tower. He kept her in front of him, turning two corners before guiding her though a doorway that led to a small workroom. She didn't get the chance to investigate what was in the room, because he propelled her into it and followed her with a frown that made her back away until she felt the stone wall against her shoulders.

He pressed her up against the wall, his expression as solid as the stone behind her. She heard him draw in a stiff breath and hold it, as though he was fighting for patience.

"We settled this matter last night, Brina."

His voice was unyielding, but she refused to buckle.

"The only matter that was made plain was the fact that I am as weak as my sister when it comes to the passions of the flesh. A fact ye should consider before continuing with this notion of wedding me."

He ground his teeth to smother some word.

"It means that ye are my wife, and I find myself very content with that. Why must ye continue to argue against it?"

Brina shot a hard glare straight back at him. "Because my word isna worth anything if I dishonor my father when I give it to ye. I cannae believe that ye would accept my vows knowing that I swore to do my father's will when I left my home. I cannae keep one promise and no' another. That isna how honor works, Connor Lindsey."

She heard his teeth grinding again, but he pressed his lips together instead of speaking whatever sprang to his mind.

"I respect ye for yer diligence, Brina, but there is naught else ye can do in this situation. My actions have made it impossible for ye to follow the path yer father set for ye. I promise that I will tell yer father that ye held true to yer word."

She lifted her chin. "And I am just to be content with ye shouldering the burden?"

"Aye. I am yer husband."

"No, ye are nae." She shook her head. "Ye are my lover because I was too weak to resist yer touch, but I will nae wed ye without my father's blessing."

He snorted, his temper glittering in his eyes. "Ye will wed me, Brina, and that is the end of it. Yer father will be brought to agreement on the matter, which is exactly why Cameron is here. To help me do the business that needs doing between men."

She opened her lips to argue, but he pressed a fingertip on top of them to seal them shut. She could see that his mood was turning dark, maybe even dangerous, but she still refused to lower her eyes, because he would consider that submission. The man she had witnessed kneeling in the church was not one who would have a woman too lacking in courage to look him in the eye. Maybe she could not wed him, but that did not mean that she couldn't be worthy of him.

He growled at her.

"I have a guest that I must see to, but be very sure that I will nae change my position on this matter. Ye can decide how our lives will be. If it must be by force, I will set my men to guarding ye until ye have done with this foolishness."

He pushed away from her, and took several long strides across the chamber floor before turning to look at her once more.

"Ye belong to me, Brina, and I will nae give ye up, no' even for the king if he were to ask."

"I am nae your chattel." She hesitated for a moment. "At least no' until my father gives me his blessing to wed ye."

He laughed, but it wasn't a pleasant sound. Instead it sent a shiver down her back as he closed the distance between them and framed her face with his hands. His touch undermined her efforts to refuse him, her body quivering in weakness once more. It was a tender hold, and that sent emotions through her that she was not able to push aside. He might break her so easily, but he didn't, and that touched her heart.

"Ye are mine, sweet lass, because ye clasped me between yer thighs and rode with me toward a climax that sent ye crying out with the pure rapture of it. Do ye think that ye shall be content to live without me? I swear I would haunt yer dreams if ye were to attempt it."

He pressed a hard kiss against her mouth. One that challenged her will just as much as she tried to refuse his.

"So spit all ye like during the bright light of day, hellcat, because once the moon rises, I will stroke ye until ye purr for me."

"I am no' a hellcat."

He chuckled and backed away from her, his lips set into a grin that infuriated her with how smug it was.

"Ye are indeed a hellcat, but one that I look forward to taming this moonrise."

Taming?

"Ohhh… go on with ye! There is naught that ye have to say that I care to listen to! Take yer bragging to yer men. Women have no taste for such boasting."

He laughed at her, his amusement echoing down the corridors while her temper strained against her common sense.

She wanted to attack the man. Run after him and strike at his body until he surrendered to her.

Brina felt her cheeks turn scarlet, for the truth was clearly etched into her mind. He'd turn and face her. All her temper would transform into passion, and nothing she had ever promised her father would matter once Connor kissed her.

She'd kiss him back too…

It was shameful, but too exciting to ignore.

❦

"Now, Connor, my friend, I have to admit that I'm surprised to see ye stealing a girl promised to the church. That is going to cause a stir for certain."

Connor shot his unexpected guest a hard look. "The church can make do with her sister since Melor Douglas has shown his true colors and refused to wed the lass."

Quinton narrowed his eyes. "Ye sound almost sorry for her."

"And why no'?" Connor sat down next to his fellow laird. "I never wished her any ill fate. She'd be here if she hadna made the choice to take a lover in spite of our contract."

"Ye're no virgin yerself, Connor."

"And ye are playing both sides of the coin, Quinton Cameron."

Quinton shrugged and sat back in his chair. "I do nae consider virginity so great a thing that a lass should be thought soiled because she had a single affair. Deirdre Chattan has passion in her. The right man could keep her attention."

Connor pointed toward himself. "I cannae be that man."

"Ye mean that ye choose no' to be."

Connor flattened his hand on the tabletop. "Ye are forgetting my sister in yer reasoning, Cameron, and that is something that I find distinctly unfriendly. My bride must be pure to protect my position and make it harder for the Douglas to keep Vanora. I need my alliance with the Chattan secure so that I can challenge the lieutenant general for my sister. The man is a Douglas; he's likely to want to side with his clan over me if I do nae show up in a position that will worry him enough to consider my case."

"Well… ye have a fine point there, but the lieutenant general is no' likely to restore yer sister to you. The man has all the power of a king, since he's got the young lad under his control."

"Which is exactly why I stole Brina. I need the Chattans standing behind me and the Camerons when I ask for Vanora to be returned or disinherited."

Quinton snorted. "The disinherited part will get the lieutenant general's attention for sure."

Connor frowned. "I hate having to say such a thing, but the Douglas will no' want her if there is nothing coming with her, and she's twelve now, so my time is running out."

"Aye," Quinton agreed. "They'll have her married in another year and bedded by the time she's fourteen. Those greedy bastards do nae care very much if the lass is too young for childbearing.

"So ye'll stand behind me?"

Quinton chuckled. "I've already given my word on that, Connor, and I do nae need ye questioning it."

"I'm asking about ye witnessing my vows with Brina."

His guest became silent, and Connor felt his temper begin to rise. "Then explain why ye are here, Quinton, if it is no' to lend yer name to my union with the Chattans."

Quinton drew in a deep breath. "Ye're right to be suspicious, even if I have no liking for it."

Connor snorted, but his friend held up a hand to keep him quiet.

"Robert Chattan was set to march on ye, but I told him I'd come in his place, because the Highlanders need to remain united, or we'll see our country being invaded by the bloody English for sure with a lad on the throne."

"Well, that's a solid truth."

Quinton nodded. "Aye, so I came up here to listen to yer reasons for stealing the man's daughter, because I call both of ye my friends."

"And?" Connor didn't care for the way Quinton

was hiding behind an expression Connor knew concealed what his friend was truly thinking.

"And I think ye made the best choice, considering the circumstances. I'll witness yer vows…" His face split with a smirk. "Providing ye can get a lass who was raised to serve the church to the altar. Personally I'm thinking that ye would have had an easier road with Deirdre."

"I know the way to convincing Brina."

Quinton Cameron laughed, his voice low and full of amusement taken at Connor's expense.

"I heard that well enough, my friend, but I still say ye're likely to get little sleep tonight while ye attempt to bring that lass to heel."

Connor suddenly grinned back at the man trying to tease him.

"But that's the part that I'm looking forward to, Quinton, and I do nae care if ye take offense, because she's worth it, believe me."

His friend leaned back in his chair. "In that case, my friend, ye'd better hope I can smooth things over with her father so that ye can gain his blessing, for that lass wants it, and I believe that she will nae be content until she has it."

"Aye… but as I said, Quinton, she's worth every bit of frustration she puts me through, and demanding her father's blessing on our match is yet another reason why I will nae relinquish her to any man. Brina belongs to me."

❧

Quinton Cameron sat drinking alone. His fellow laird

had left him at the high table, and he couldn't truly take offense, because he agreed with Connor.

Brina Chattan was a prize worth seeking out.

He drew a sip of ale off the mug a maid set before him. The lass lingered over the chore, offering him a long peek down the front of her robe. Her breasts were plump, and her nipples large, but his cock wasn't interested.

There were matters on his mind that required his full attention, even if the sun was setting and the gates closed until dawn. Keeping the Highlanders united was a goal that sank into his thoughts and didn't allow for anything else.

Except for a brief recollection of Deirdre Chattan.

His cock did stir, and it drew a frown from him. He didn't have time to become enamored of any woman in particular. If he were wise, he'd find a way to get the Douglas to return Vanora to him and lock her in his own fortress until she was old enough to wed. Connor wasn't the only Highlander laird who understood the need for an alliance with his neighbors.

But Deirdre's face refused to be banished, even when he lifted his mug again and drained it. Vanora Lindsey was merely an idea, but the taste of Deirdre's kiss clung to his lips along with the way she had struggled against him. She was a woman who knew the power of her own spirit, one who might be broken but would be so much more of a prize to the man who managed to win her.

Part of him was very interested in being that man.

Seven

MAURA WAS QUIET AS SHE DIRECTED HER STAFF toward helping Brina disrobe. Brina could sense the woman's displeasure with her, but there was nothing to say, for it seemed that they were destined to be on opposite sides of the issue of the staff calling her mistress.

She had that in common with many a stolen bride; that was for sure.

"I had a tray fetched up from the kitchen since ye didn't join the laird for supper."

"He had a guest and didna need a woman sitting by his side."

The truth was she had been sickened by the sight of the retainers set to guarding her. Brina looked around the chamber, recognizing that she had chosen to imprison herself instead of being watched.

She wasn't sure which she detested more.

"Thank you for the tray, Maura. It was kind of ye to consider me."

"Ye're the mistress…"

The head of house's words trailed off when Brina

simply ignored her. It was by far one of the most impolite things she had ever done, but she couldn't seem to stop herself from walking toward the windows that were closed shut for the night. Her hair fluttered behind her, released from the plait that had held the strands throughout the day, and the veil that had covered her head to provide warmth and modesty was now neatly draped over a clothes rack.

"Well, I'll bid ye good night, mistress."

Brina smiled for a brief moment because Maura was a stubborn woman. Maybe even as hardheaded as she was being. The doors to the chamber closed, leaving her alone for the first time that day. She sighed and turned around to look at the chamber with all its lavishness. Candles were lit and casting their yellow light over the long table and twin chairs. The bed curtains were drawn closed on three sides, making the turned-down comforter and sheeting look inviting.

But she discovered that she longed for the cold cell at the base of the cliff, with Connor there to wrap his warmth around her...

She snorted and turned back toward the shutters. Reaching up, she loosened the bar that held them in place against the wind and weather. The moment she did, the sound of the ocean rushed in on a cold draft of night air that sent a shiver down her back.

Brina laughed and pulled both sides of the shutters wide open so that the sound of the surf filled the chamber. Her nose turned cold instantly, but she was too enchanted by the sight of the ocean to worry about it. Moonlight cast the rippling waves in silver as far as she could see, while the moon itself was only a crescent on the horizon.

"Ye're mesmerizing, Brina Chattan."

She turned around and felt her thin underrobe flaring up to expose her ankles and calves, because the light fabric wasn't held down by a thicker outerrobe. Her hair flowed around her as well, and Connor's gaze was on it. His lips thinned, but in a sensual manner that captivated her.

He liked what he saw, and it made her feel pretty.

Connor stood near the door, his sword in one hand instead of tied to his broad back. He held one side of the doors open, and two maids carried in trays that they set on the long table. They began to set out the items they had carried, their attention purposely directed to the surface of the long table.

"We do nae require service."

Both of them raised their attention to her, the younger maid failing to maintain her stiff composure. Her lips twitched up into a knowing smile that was accompanied by a twinkle in her eyes. Brina blushed, but this time the heat surfaced in her face because she knew full well what it was like to have Connor next to her.

Inside her...

Connor cleared his throat. Brina looked at him because the sound was so delicate. She realized that was for her benefit, a gallant gesture she would not have thought he had in him.

Except that he had always tried to be gentle with her...

The maids lowered themselves before hurrying out the door. Connor closed it with a single motion of one arm. Brina stared at him and the amount of strength that he had in his body. Truly she shouldn't be surprised to discover him using such a soft sound to get the maids to leave, because the man had always controlled himself with her.

Of course, that knowledge only drove home just how helpless she truly was against his greater strength and position. He was more than just a Highlander; he was a laird and a powerful one too. His friend Quinton Cameron was equally dangerous, and together, they might swear that she had taken marriage vows, and there would be few who would be interested in challenging them.

"Now do nae look at me like that, Brina. Ye have little to be so unhappy about."

"I never said I was unhappy."

He walked across the floor and placed his sword next to the bed.

"Ye only fight with me over a matter that should bring ye peace. Would ye rather that I keep ye here and deny ye the respectable position as my wife? Ye wouldna be the first daughter who suffered that fate because of the shame her family brought to another."

His words were harsh enough to make her wince. But what stunned her into silence was just how truthful they were. Much of Scotland's history was written in vengeance. There would be many who considered Connor justified in taking her.

Brina frowned when she looked at the sword a second time, and it gained her a grunt from Connor.

"That's correct, lass. I'm sharing that bed with ye."

There was a hard edge to his voice, an exasperated tone that drew her attention to him.

She also noticed that he was without his doublet. Only the undyed fabric of his shirt covered his skin. Beneath her thin robe, her skin began to warm and awaken with hundreds of places that recalled how much she enjoyed his touch. The long, gliding strokes of his hands along her limbs before he had begun to touch her in more sensitive places.

"I simply cannae wed ye without my father's blessing. It is a matter of honor, Connor, no' my wishes."

One of his eyebrows rose. "Is that so, Brina?" He reached down and pulled on the end of his belt until the twin steel tongues that held it closed popped free of their leather holes.

"Does that mean that ye will lie with me tonight, willingly? Maybe even be eager for my touch?"

She scoffed at him. "Ye do nae need to tease me, Connor Lindsey. Ye know full well that ye didna need to rape me last night."

His loosened belt allowed the neatly folded fabric of his kilt to sag. He caught it before it slithered down his legs to puddle on the floor. With a practiced hand, he looped it all over his forearm and turned to deposit it on a side table she realized had been left bare just for his plaid.

"It is a very fond memory for me, Brina, one that I hope will nae be alone in my mind. So is the fact that ye told me that ye do nae lie, and I see it is so."

She was frustrated but satisfied in the same moment. The satisfaction grew because she enjoyed being praised for being truthful. Actually she simply enjoyed earning Connor's respect, and there was no way to hide from that fact.

His shirt hung down to his mid-thigh, but her imagination was quick to remind her what lay behind that single layer of simple fabric. He surprised her by sitting down.

"Come and help me remove my boots, lass."

So that he could take her to his bed…

She couldn't help but think about it. Excitement was beginning to pulse through her, running along with her blood to every corner of her body. Connor watched her with an expression that was more playful than she could recall having seen on his face before.

"Didna ye train to be of service, lass?"

She propped her hands on her hips with frustration. "Ye know very well that the kind of service ye are asking for is nae the sort that I was training to do beneath my father's roof."

Brina suddenly stopped speaking as she noticed just where Connor's attention was centered. He was staring at her breasts and the very noticeable mounds they made with her hands on her hips. The thin fabric displayed the puckered peaks of her nipples, even hinting at the darker skin because the fabric was so delicate a weave.

He smirked at her, and she turned around but gasped when her memory offered up just what he'd do when presented with her back.

Connor laughed and reached down to unlace one boot. His amusement echoed off the wall behind her as he pulled the boot off. The fact that he did it so confidently and with such ease spoke of a man who hadn't been raised with service being lavished upon him.

"I admit that I was looking forward to having ye tending to me, but if ye are too timid to do so, I'll see to the matter myself."

"I am nae timid."

His eyebrow rose once again, and he extended his foot with the lace hanging free from the antler-horn buttons.

"Then prove it. If I wanted to hear someone tell me tales that have fact mixed with fiction, I'd have remained below."

He was daring her. The challenge was as plain as the sound of the surf coming from behind her. She knew it and yet couldn't seem to smother the impulse to go to him. The desire to prove that she was not intimidated by him was too powerful to resist, and she leaned over to grasp his boot before thinking any further about it.

The front of her undergown gaped wide open, and Connor looked right down her body while she slid the boot off his foot. But she held it up and lifted her chin in spite of the smirk that decorated his features.

"Ye have hard nipples. Is that from the chill or the memory of how ye enjoyed having my lips sucking on them last night?"

"The chill," she snapped back at him. His lips didn't turn down into a frown but rose higher so that his smirk became a wide smile that flashed his teeth at her.

"Well now, if that's the case, you should be in bed where I may warm ye, Brina."

He didn't give her time to consider her answer.

Connor left the stool behind in a flash of motion and swept her off her feet in the next instant. He cradled her against his chest, sending a jolt of enjoyment through her at the demonstration of his greater strength. She failed to understand it but couldn't deny that his greater size and power impressed a part of her mind that she had suspected might issue opinions.

"I had this bed made for ye, Brina."

He angled her beneath the thick rod that held the curtain and laid her on the creamy sheet. The bedding was fresh, and the scent of salt came through the open window. But her senses were also drawing in the musky hint of his skin, and she recalled it vividly from last night when he had been deep inside her and it had felt as if there was nothing between them except pleasure.

"Everything in it, I selected myself."

"Ye're a good man." She meant it too and felt regret ripple through her for the facts that kept her from doing exactly what he wanted.

"No, I am simply a man who has known what it is like to sleep in the stable on a bench that was not big enough for a child, much less a man."

He looked at the canopy above their heads and reached out to pat one of the corner posts that held that fabric above their heads.

"But ye understand that as well, dinna ye, Brina?" His gaze returned to hers, and his blue eyes were piercing. "Fate has an interesting sense of humor to pair us together when we had each accepted to make do with much less."

His words were hypnotic, drawing her deeper into

his eyes while her body hummed with anticipation. She didn't want to fight with him, but that didn't mean she was feeling submissive either. Fire was licking its way across her skin, chasing the chill away while the scent of his skin teased her with how near he was.

It wasn't close enough.

"Let's no' talk. We can never agree when we talk." Her voice was steady and strong, each bold word increasing her confidence. "Touch me, Connor, before I think of the reasons why I should refuse ye."

There was a flash of agreement in his eyes that she only saw for a moment before he angled his head so that he could press a kiss against her mouth. It wasn't a soft kiss, but one that was full of passion and need. Her body didn't heat up gradually this time. The memory of last night swept her into a vortex of hunger that became acute almost instantly.

She reached for his shirt, pushing it upward even as she kissed him back. He pulled his lips away from hers so that she could lift the shirt over his head and pull it down the length of his arms.

"I insist on returning the favor, Brina."

He slid one arm beneath her waist and lifted her up and onto her knees. The position allowed him to tug her underrobe up, baring her legs and then her body before he removed it completely. Her hair fluttered down to lay against her back and part of her front. Her skin was alive with heightened sensation, making her extremely aware of the delicate fibers settling against her form.

"Ye're beautiful, Brina, and I admit that I enjoy the fact that I know I'm the first man to tell ye that."

Her arms had risen up to cover her breasts. Excitement was still flickering in her belly, making it impossible to become fearful, but she was a bit apprehensive. He reached out and plucked her hand away from where it hid one of her breasts from his view. Connor pulled it gently toward him, turning it up so that he might lean down and kiss the delicate skin of her inner wrist. Pleasure rippled up her arm and into her chest.

"And ye humble me with yer genuine responses." He lifted his head, his eyes full of male enjoyment that she might have mistaken for smugness if there were others about to hear him.

But inside the drawn curtains, with only one side still open to catch the last of the heat from the fire, there was no one to impress with his words.

Except her.

Her cheeks filled with heat, and he chuckled before leaning over to kiss the scarlet blush.

"Ah... the most perfect compliment that I might ever receive from ye, Brina."

He pressed a row of kisses along her face until he claimed her lips once more with a kiss that was full of rising passion. His hands pulled her to him, and she gasped as their bare skin met, the amount of sensation threatening to drown her.

It was a fate that she went to willingly. Her hands threaded through his hair, while her mouth followed his lead, kissing him with the hunger that seemed to sprout up from the seeds left from last night.

His hands traveled down from her nape, where he'd held her in place for his kiss. Now he slid his hands over her shoulders and down to cup both her breasts while he pressed her back into the bedding once again.

She sighed with delight, the feeling of his hands cupping her soft breasts a hundred times more enjoyable than the memory of it. She arched up, offering her nipples to his mouth, and Connor did not disappoint her. He captured one puckered point, sucking it between his lips and drawing a moan from her. The contact was hot but intensely pleasurable too.

Connor didn't linger very long but continued to press kisses along her belly, going lower and lower, until her eyes opened wide when she realized that he was hovering over her mons.

"What are ye doing?" Her voice was husky and unrecognizable, but the chuckle that answered her was one she recalled from the darkest hours of last night when Connor had been her lover, and she his consort.

"Did ye think that we had explored all the delights lovers might know last night, Brina? I assure ye, we did nae, but I plan to."

He pressed one of her thighs up and out so that her sex was spread. She felt the folds that protected the tiny bead that had given her such enjoyment last night open and allow it to be brushed by the night air.

She shivered, the sensation almost too intense to endure.

"Connor, ye cannae."

He pushed her other thigh aside and settled on his elbows between her knees. "Oh, sweet Brina, I assure ye that I can and will."

His fingers glided along her inner thighs, sending torrents of delight through her. The walls of her passage felt empty and needy, while the folds of her sex begged for a stroke from his fingertips.

Connor didn't disappoint her. His hands grazed over the top of her sex, the softest of contacts at first, but she arched and heard her own voice echoing off the chamber wall.

The next touch was firmer, his fingers slipping between the folds of her slit until one fingertip glided over the small center of her pleasure.

"Here's the spot I was seeking."

He drew a lazy circle over it, and she shuddered because it truly was the center of her pleasure. Need and hunger became roaring demands from her body as he toyed with the little bead. Her hips arched to press it more firmly against his touch, but he moved his fingers to pull her folds completely away from her bead.

"Connor…"

Brina had no idea if she was protesting his actions or praising them. She felt caught in the whirling center of the storm, suspended between pleasure and where hunger became pain.

"I'm going to taste ye, lass."

His voice was a low growl that sent a shaft of excitement through her. It was so intense that the first touch of his lips against her center nearly sent her into the pulsing rapture that had claimed her last night.

But not quite.

She was still quivering, her hands curling into talons among the bedding beneath her when Connor pressed a kiss against her open sex. She cried out and didn't care who heard her. The sensation was so intense, it made her heart beat at a frantic pace as she felt the flicker of his tongue over her center. His hands kept her in place because she had no control over her body. She twisted and arched in response to the flicking tongue. The pleasure drew her muscles taut, so tight, it felt as if they might snap as he continued to feast on her. The need to have him fill her passage became so strong, she snarled with it.

Connor lifted his head and looked up her body. He teased her with a single finger now that did nothing to relieve the pressure pulsing in her belly.

"Connor... I need more."

Her teeth were bared as need reduced her to serving the needs of her flesh.

His eyes flashed something at her that set her temper to boiling.

"And I need yer oath that ye will wed me."

He pressed harder on her center, driving her hunger to a pitch that almost frightened her with how badly she wanted release. His eyes were hard and unyielding as he tormented her flesh, keeping her twisting beneath his touch but taking her no further while his demand hung over her.

"Damn ye to hellfire, Connor Lindsey!"

She snarled at him, more furious than she had ever been. Frustration tore through her like a storm, and she curled her hands into fists with her rage.

"You want trust but torment me in order to get it!" She felt her fist connect with his shoulder, and satisfaction rose with the pain that traveled along her arm. It broke through the spell binding her to his touch.

"It is unfair!"

She sent her fist toward his jaw, rising up off the bed to do battle with him, but he raised one hand and captured her blow, his fingers closing around her hand with enough force to keep it prisoner. The hunger he'd stoked to such a burning intensity inside her was cruelly twisting and clawing at her insides. It was impossible to remain still, and she kicked and struggled against him and the bed while wrestling with the desire to simply give him what he demanded so that he would satisfy the raging storm of hunger trapped inside her.

"I hate the position ye have put me in."

But he faced her with an expression that was firm and unyielding in its determination.

"You should nae be able to use my body against me. What is an oath worth when it is sworn under such conditions? Is that what ye truly want from me? I believed ye to have more integrity than this form of torture."

In an abrupt change, her mood became one of lament. The fight drained out of her, leaving her moaning with the need that still nipped at her body. It was an agony, one that made her shiver and pull her arm back so that she could hug herself for the small amount of comfort it might provide. The yearning was more than physical, it was deeper, in that place that craved the intimacy they had shared last night.

"Ye have that right to be angry with me, Brina. Even if I do nae care for how it makes me feel to admit it, ye are correct, I want an oath from ye that ye truly mean."

He rolled over and settled against the bed with the

plump pillows at his back. She still wanted him too much, her body quivering in response to the sight of his erect member. Her passage wanted it inside her, and even her temper didn't have the power to wipe that aside. But he snarled something in Gaelic that kept her still and waiting to see what he had to say.

"Being a laird comes with as many responsibilities as being born the daughter of a laird does."

His quiet tone drew her attention, cutting through her emotions with how honest he sounded. They were suddenly not so very different from one another, and that made it impossible for her to maintain her fury. Instead she felt a kinship with him that struck her as tender. She felt it in her heart, and there was no denying it. Somehow the idea that he was willing to explain his reasons to her lifted her out of the role of captive and set her on equal standing with him. It was a small offering of respect that she realized she needed more desperately than anything else.

"I can agree with ye on that, Connor."

He nodded, a gleam of approval appearing in his eyes.

"Marrying for a strong alliance is my duty, Brina, and before ye say anything about yer sister, I'll tell ye a fact that ye do no' know. Ye know I have a sister that the Douglas stole away after killing my Uncle and Aunt. Vanora is twelve now and the Douglas have a firm plan to wed her soon and attempt to take Lindsey land through her dowry. They've no care for the fact that she is too young to be bedded."

"Sweet Mary…"

Connor shook his head. "There is naught holy

about it, Brina. It is a greedy attempt to extend their borders. I negotiated with yer father because I need to have the Chattans standing firmly beside me when I demand my sister be returned or disinherited."

"Disinherited?" Such was worse than being sent to the church, for even a holy order wouldn't have a girl who came with nothing.

"It's the only thing I can think of that will force them to relinquish her instead of wedding her too young, without a care for the fact that she might well die in childbirth without needing to."

"That's horrible."

He pressed his lips into a hard line, making no further attempt to defend his actions. Brina could suddenly hear the wind again and the ocean. But what she yearned to feel was the warm skin of the man lying so close and yet so far away from her. The world was too cold a place, and taking solace in his embrace was very appealing. She suddenly felt like she was squandering the opportunity to be cherished when there was no promise of having another offer extended to her. They had the night, and who knew what morning would bring.

"Ye're correct that I should nae be using my greater knowledge of bed sport against you, but it is the truth that I have no taste for bending ye to my will. Ye are an honest lass, one I admire for the spirit that refuses to allow ye to yield to something ye consider in conflict with yer duty. I can understand that, lass, for my life has its burdens too, but ye're here now, and life as my wife does nae displease ye as it would a lass truly devoted to the church."

He lifted his hand and offered it to her with the palm facing upward.

"So perhaps I'll try asking ye to wed me because it would bring me joy, and I promise ye that I will secure yer father's blessing, but that will take time."

Her breath caught in her throat, and her hand was in his before she thought about it. Every bit of conscious thought evaporated, leaving behind only the need to be near him, the distance between them too harsh to endure now that she felt like they were kindred spirits.

He wrapped her in a solid and secure embrace that was a haven from the ugly matters surrounding their lives. Brina lifted her face, seeking his kiss, and Connor didn't disappoint her. His mouth took command of hers, pressing her to open her jaw and allow his tongue to thrust boldly inside. She quivered against him, her body eager for the hard thrust of his flesh against hers.

He didn't roll over her though. Instead his hands cupped her hips and lifted her up and onto his lap. Her own weight spread her thighs around his hips, opening her sex so that the hard length of his member lay against her slit. She gasped and pulled away from his kiss, only to discover him grinning at her. From her position, she sat above him, his head even with her breasts, his blue eyes filled with appreciation of the view.

"What are ye doing, Connor?"

"Taking the opportunity to have ye ride me."

Her pleasure center throbbed, and her passage renewed its demand that she feel him stretching her once again. But the image that his words painted in her mind sent a surge of wicked anticipation through her.

"Aye, ye are thinking of it, aren't ye, lass?"

He lifted her high enough so that his cock sprang up beneath her. The head of it settled against the opening to her passage, and Connor slowly allowed more of her weight to lower. Brina realized that she could control her own descent with her thighs, and she braced her hands on his shoulders as he guided her down onto his length. Her passage ached only a fraction of the amount that it had the night before, and there was never any true pain. Instead she moaned as his hard flesh filled her, satisfying the need that felt as though it were intent on driving her insane.

"That's the way, lass. Ride me, take what it is ye desire."

There was a hard edge to his tone, a challenge she was eager to rise to. She watched his eyes flash with hunger, and she lifted herself off him, only to feel his hands push her back down.

Pleasure spiked through her, sending her back up the moment she felt him completely lodge inside her. Beneath her hands, she felt his chest vibrate with a chuckle that was dark with passion. Her breasts bounced with her motions, and his gaze shifted to them, his lips thinning while he watched them. His hands tightened on her hips, urging her faster, and she did not resist. All the need that had twisted so tightly inside her demanded that she rise and fall with a growing wildness. She craved the burst of rapture that had satisfied her so completely last night, and she could feel it brightening in the distance, twinkling and beckoning to her.

Pleasure surged through her a moment later, tearing aside every thought or idea as it ripped through her belly. Connor surged up, rolling her over and onto her back in the middle of the bed. The ropes creaked beneath the mattress as he thrust hard and quick into her spread body. Brina was lost in a storm of delight that wrung her like a piece of cloth, the hard, pounding thrusts of her lover only drawing out the pleasure.

He suddenly groaned and thrust deep inside her. She felt the spurt of his seed, hot and thick against the mouth of her womb. Her eyes flew open, and she discovered Connor's blue ones watching her while her passage tightened around his member, intent on milking every last drop of his offering. Another burst of pleasure went through her. This time it was deeper and duller, but when it finally released her, satisfaction glowed warmly through her body. There wasn't a single place left untouched by the rapture, and when Connor closed his body around hers, his arms binding her against him so that she heard his heart beating with the same accelerated pace as her own, she allowed herself to slip away into slumber, because the moment truly was perfect.

❧

Connor didn't sleep as quickly. He nuzzled against the head of his partner, inhaling the sweet scent of her hair. It spread around her like a cloud, and he gathered it up, laying it over her shoulder so that it would not become tangled. He wasn't cold, but he pulled the covers over her and listened to the sounds of the surf coming through the open window. It was a sound that he'd listened to in the stable, and it stirred up the memory of the goals that he had once used to keep himself alive.

For the moment, one of them was sitting firmly in his grasp. Brina would wed him, and Robert Chattan would stand beside him against the Douglas. He should have been focused on the alliance, but instead he was more interested in the way Brina felt against him.

She wasn't the first woman he'd lain with, but she was the only one who interested him enough that he was happy to lie there and listen to the sound of her breathing. He was more content than he could ever recall being, a sense of happiness settling over him as the candles began to burn low. He never rose to extinguish them but closed his eyes and drifted off into slumber along with Brina.

❧

The window shutters were still open, and Brina could see the faint glow of dawn illuminating them when she lifted her eyelids. Maybe it was the fact that they had retired so early last night or the sheer abundance of emotions that had coursed through her, but she was wide awake now at the very first hint of day. Her mind was fully alert, beginning to tumble the things that she wanted to do, and she felt eager to begin, too much so to remain in bed.

"Where are ye going so early, Brina?"

Connor's voice was slurred as he turned to eye her with sleep still clouding his vision.

"I never went to confession yesterday."

He groaned. "Aye, I suppose we should get to that." His lips rose into a lazy smile that was not repentant but satisfied instead.

She pressed a hand flat in the center of his bare chest. "You went yesterday."

The bed shifted as he moved, all signs of sleep vanishing from his expression. What remained was something very serious, and it touched her heart.

"I want to wed ye, Brina, no' simply have the world be told that ye are my wife. So I will join ye so that we may be truthful."

"With your friend Quinton Cameron here to lend his name to it, there would nae be many who would question whether we truly took vows or no'."

In spite of the fact that she'd thought it, hearing it aloud made her shiver. It would be so simple to bend her.

A warm hand smoothed over her shoulder, taking the chill away. She looked into his eyes to find them full of determination but lacking the glare of superiority that would have seen him treating her as his chattel. That was the honor that she had witnessed in him yesterday, that facet of his personality that made it impossible for her to resist him.

"Honor is nae something that I talk about but fail to hold myself to."

"I've noticed that."

She angled her head down and pressed a soft kiss against his hand.

"I'm going to confession now." She slid out from beneath the covers, shivering in the early-morning air. There was no sound from behind her, and that drew her attention back toward the bed. Connor still lay there, the bedding slid down to his waist to expose his bare chest.

The room suddenly filled with the sound of his amusement. "Careful, lass, yer expression is nae one of repentance, but of contemplation of more sinning." He grasped the edge of the coverlet aside, exposing his member and the fact that it was thick and hard.

"Come back here."

"But…"

Her voice was husky already, her body favoring his invitation over the penance that would be waiting for her once she reached the church.

"Come back to this bed and leave yer confessing until ye have a nice long tale of sin to entertain the priest with."

"Connor Lindsey! That is unchristian of you to say."

He grinned, patting the surface of the bed. "It is the truth, one ye can see plainly, for I notice that yer gaze keeps traveling to my cock. What's more in line with the teaching of the church than speaking only what is truth?"

"It's wicked."

His hand clasped his erection, and her mouth went dry. She had already turned to face him, and her nipples drew into tighter points that had nothing to do with the morning chill.

"It is honest." His hand worked up and down his length, drawing her a single step closer to him. "Come here, Brina. Lie with me instead of doing what ye have been told ye should. Do what ye want to instead of what everyone around ye tells ye to. For this moment, no one else matters but the pair of us. Let us enjoy that, for the day will arrive soon enough with its demands. Come here and tell me what ye would have of me."

His words were empowering. She felt free for the first time in her life, her shoulders lacking the weight of responsibility. There was nothing but the man in front of her and her desire to share the hour of predawn with him. Later the sun would rise, and along with it, the struggle to survive and maintain balance between their clans and the church would return.

But for that moment, she walked back to him, her bare feet making soft sounds against the floor before she climbed back up into the bed. His body was warm and welcoming, the thick coverlet falling back over her as he slid his arms around her and locked her into an embrace that shut everything out except for the pleasure that their bodies produced when they touched.

Nothing else mattered.

❧

Connor began snoring.

Brina raised her head, her own mind muddled by sleep, which made it hard to decide what the soft sound was. She looked at her partner and heard the soft sound once again.

Her lover slept deeply, and she realized that he was finally at peace with having stolen her. For all his confidence, he had not cared for the way that he had brought her to his home.

He hadn't told her that, not with words, but she felt it in the way his body was so relaxed with dawn brightening the room. Highlanders rarely slept past first light, but she could hear him snoring as she slid from the bed once more. With a careful hand, she closed the bed curtains.

Brina shrugged into her underrobe and overrobe. She brushed out her hair and quickly braided it, listening for Maura as she hurried through dressing. Putting her boots on felt as though it took forever, and the light seemed to grow brighter every second. She left the shutters open because closing them would no doubt make enough noise to disturb Connor.

There was a bubble of happiness sitting inside her chest. It made her giddy in a fashion she had never felt before. Making sure that her lover might sleep seemed to matter a great deal, and she smiled as she slipped out of the chamber and pressed the door shut with only a tiny sound.

Maura was halfway up the stairs, with her maids in tow.

"Mistress?"

"I'm off to confession."

Maura frowned, looking behind her. "Ye need yer escort, mistress."

Brina nodded and watched the head of house's eyebrows raise.

"Tell them that I've gone to church, for I expect a stiff penance for missing yesterday, and I want to begin straightaway so that I can take my vows once the laird is ready."

Maura smiled, the first genuine one that Brina had seen on her face.

"Well then, I'll no' stand here yapping with ye, mistress. Go on and settle yer accounts with the priest."

Brina passed her and the maids, her pace quick and
fueled by her excitement.

She was going to wed Connor Lindsey, and that
was the truth. Fate had spoken, and she was no more
fit to serve the church as a bride of Christ than Deirdre
was. So she would take the happiness that had begun
to flow through her and be grateful for it.

Life was too uncertain to argue with.

～✦～

The priest did indeed set her to a stiff penance. Brina
finally stood up and felt her knees protest how long
she had been on them. But her feet transmitted just
how cold the stone floor still was because she was
without shoes or even stockings.

The priest had taken her boots to teach her the
value of humility. That wasn't so uncommon for a
bride. There were still many men who insisted that
their future wives wed them in their underrobes to
show the proper amount of respect for the fact that
the husband owned everything, right down to the
clothing she wore.

Being forced to be barefoot wasn't teaching her
anything but a resentment of the men who thought
women were chattel.

When she turned around and discovered the priest
watching her, Brina bit her lip to maintain her composure. She lowered herself before walking toward one
of the back entrances to the church, where the silver
bowls and chalices were stored. She had chores to
do now that her prayers were concluded. Every soul
owed the church hours of labor. That was how the

great cathedrals and abbeys were raised and decorated with such fine carvings and statues.

She picked up a cloth and began to rub it over a silver plate that was dull from use. It was still very early, but there were other silver dishes waiting on the table for others who came to confess their passion to the clergy. Her fingers were stiff from being in one position too long as well, but the polishing soon warmed them up. There was no comfort for her feet except to rub them against one another and twist them up into her skirts.

Beyond the open doorway, she heard the outer gates rising and the faint stirrings of more of the castle's inhabitants. There were steps in the sanctuary, telling her that she was no longer alone in her quest to gain the church's approval so that she might get on with the rest of the day. She looked down at the plate, rubbing harder at a persistent dark smudge.

A pain shot through her skull that was so blinding, she never realized that it was going to rob her of her consciousness. Her mind simply went black, every thought ceasing along with it.

She sank down into an oblivion that was suffocating, and the only thing she managed to think was that maybe she was dead.

❧

"Ye hit her too hard."

"As if ye have any more practice in the striking of women that ye can lecture me on the manner in which it should be done."

There was a hard grunt from one of the Cameron

retainers before he conceded the point. He allowed Brina to lie against him, her body limp, but he listened to her breathing to make certain that she was in fact senseless and not just trying to dupe them. Her breathing remained even and slow, and he nodded once again.

"Let's finish this bit of business. I've no desire to be caught doing this deed."

"On that we agree." The other retainer draped a long cloak over her shoulders. The garment was made for a full-size man, and it covered the lass completely, even hiding the hem of her robes.

That was exactly what they were aiming to do—disguise the lass and smuggle her out of the castle. It was a brazen plan, but since she had risen so early, it was actually achievable.

He raised the hood and pulled down a length of leather that had been sewn to the front of the fabric to tie about the neck clasp. The lace was a hasty addition that would keep the hood from falling down to reveal the fact that they were stealing the Chattan lass.

Quinton Cameron was waiting when his men brought his prize out of the back of the church. The last hour had seemed almost endless while he had waited for the gates to rise. There was still no sign of Connor, and for that he was both grateful and resentful.

He didn't care for the plan that he was enacting, but he couldn't think of another way to achieve true peace among the Highland clans.

That idea was his driving force.

One of his men had Brina riding behind him, and his other men made sure that the cloak was hanging down to cover every bit of her.

"Let's be on our way, lads."

Quinton looked toward the gate and the Lindsey men guarding it. They checked both incoming and outgoing parties. Connor was a wise man who didn't take any chances with the security of his castle.

Quinton felt his men close around him as they approached the gate, but he pulled up on the reins to face the retainers without any hesitation.

"Morning, lads, I'm sorry to be quitting this fine place."

His men began to file through the gate, none of them stopping, but they kept their pace slow.

"Yer laird knows a thing or two about welcoming a guest. We'll be back soon, with a bit of luck."

The retainers grinned, enjoying hearing that their laird had impressed another.

"Having the Camerons here is a good thing."

The retainers guarding the gate suddenly looked past Quinton toward the horse that was burdened with two riders. One was slumped against the man sitting tall in the front, but there was no saddle on the animal so that they might both fit. Instead the horse behind them carried the second saddle.

"What goes wrong with that man?" The Lindsey retainer stepped back, a hint of concern appearing on his face. Even in winter, the plague was still something that no wise man took any chances with.

"Just a little too much Lindsey hospitality."

The Lindsey retainer stepped up again, but the frown remained on his face.

"That's a slip of a lad."

Quinton laughed. "Aye, beardless too, which

explains why a bit of ale put the lad down. He's my brother's boy and a wee bit too tender still, but he's family, and someone has to show him the way of being a man." Quinton caught the retainer's eye and offered him a shrug. "That's no' something a lad needs his sire about to witness."

The Lindsey retainer grinned and nodded. "Well, best of luck with the boy."

"Well, it will be the lad who needs luck, for I've no time to be nursing him."

Quinton Cameron lifted one hand, and there was a surge of leather and horses through the open gate. He joined their ranks while the Lindsey retainers watched them ride forth into the rising sun. The landscape was covered in snow, which no doubt accounted for the speed that the Cameron retainers set. They pushed their horses and lowered their heads so that they might cover more ground even more quickly.

The Lindseys who had been waiting to cross into the castle or out of it stepped back into the road now that the mounted men were gone. Carts rolled past as the trading of goods began just as it did every day except the Sabbath.

◈

Connor listened to the priest, but he was more interested in seeing Brina. There was no sight of her, but his gaze fell on her boots sitting near the base of the front pew. He didn't care for knowing that she was barefoot with snow on the ground, but he also couldn't help but be pleased that she was doing her penance without running to him to beg for leniency.

There was more than one laird who had to suffer a brat for a wife when his contracted bride arrived full of vanity and the idea that her comfort was owed to her simply because of who her parents were. The sort who would cry for pudding when there was barely enough bread during the last weeks of winter.

Brina was nothing like that. Even if her stubbornness had nearly driven him insane, he could still admire it. He made his way from the sanctuary, forcing himself to allow her to finish what she had set out to do.

The stamp of horses' hooves against the wooden bridge that led out of Birch Stone drew his attention. He climbed the steps in front of the tower to look through the inner gate toward the outer one. A flurry of Cameron plaid was streaming out of the castle, the horses moving fast.

Connor frowned. Apparently he would not have his friend there to witness his wedding after all. It was disappointing, but he refused to allow it to distract from the overall joy filling him. Brina Chattan was going to be his wife before the sun set.

That was what mattered.

❧

"Give her to me."

Quinton took up Brina's limp body, frowning at the way she still slept. He peered at her face, but her color was good. Birch Stone was well in the distance, and he kept his ear turned toward it in case Connor had discovered his loss.

It was a loss to be sure. If his friend didn't come quickly, he just might have to keep the prize himself.

"We do nae sleep tonight, lads."

His stallion danced on nervous steps beneath him, adjusting to the second rider. Quinton closed his arms around her as he urged his mount forward. His men didn't question his order but followed him instantly. Every man among them understood that the Lindseys would not take kindly to their actions.

Well, his friend would have to come to terms with it. Quinton still called Connor a friend, even if the man was likely to curse his name to hell and back. Scotland was in a precarious position with James II being so young. The lieutenant general was a Douglas, who every man knew wanted the crown and not just the power.

But more importantly than that, Connor Lindsey was too hopeful by far to think that the Douglas would give up Vanora when he cemented his alliance through marriage. Quinton didn't have that same sense of certainty. But he spent more time at court and understood the evil that inhabited men such as the lieutenant general.

It would take more than a wedding in the Highlands to force the Douglas to relinquish the only sibling of the laird of the Lindseys. It would take a dangerous gamble that he doubted Connor would be willing to make with the woman it was clear he was falling in love with.

So Quinton would do it for him. Quinton refused to think about the possibility that Connor might never forgive him. True friendship went further than worrying about whether the man you called friend was going to be pleased to hear what you had to say. Connor wouldn't like him, but Quinton knew without a doubt that his plan was the only hope of maintaining peace in his county.

So he would carry through with it.

❦

Connor suddenly frowned and stood up. His captains instantly stopped talking, in spite of the fact that the meeting happened every day before supper and was vital to the continued defense of Birch Stone. They turned their heads to see what their laird was staring at.

Connor watched the two men he'd set to guarding Brina enter the hall. It was late in the afternoon, and there was still no sight of his bride.

"Where is yer mistress?"

Both men frowned, but Connor didn't wait to hear their reply. He strode down the aisle, closing the distance quickly.

"Still in the church, Laird."

"The entire day long?" Connor felt suspicion prickle along his nerves. "What is that priest doing with her? Her sins are surely no' the worst he's ever heard."

There were a few chuckles in response to that.

Connor turned his stare back to his men, and the amusement behind him died. "Ye saw her there?" Even if he was suspicious, he couldn't challenge the church without good cause, at least not more than he'd already done by stealing one of their intended daughters. He was on precarious footing and knew that unsetting the balance was not the wisest thing he might do.

That was the only reason he had suffered the entire day without seeing Brina. Even if he disagreed with her penance, he would need a good case to challenge the priest, or risk beginning a rebellion among his own kin. There were many who believed his position was a half step below the church, not above it. That knowledge had made it possible to understand why Brina had resisted him so steadfastly.

"We did not see her leave, and our relief stands steady at the doorway to accompany her when she does finish her penance. Her shoes are still in the sanctuary, Laird."

That drew nods from many listening, but it didn't cut through the unease twisting his insides.

"Enough of this. Brina has nae fallen so far from the path as to spend the entire day atoning for it. Becoming my bride is nae a sin." Connor headed toward the back of the tower. Shawe caught up with him before he made it to the doorway.

"Are ye sure ye want to risk the wrath of the church, Laird? She's bound to be finished soon, and ruffling the feathers of the priests might belittle everything she's accomplished today."

Connor cursed. "I already ruffled those feathers when I stole her, man. If a full day is nae enough for them, they can extract their vengeance on me. I'll nae allow this to continue."

But his men were standing at the doors to the church, their attention on the inside of the sanctuary, though they shifted every now and again to watch the yard around them as well. There was nothing about their diligence that he might find fault with, but the feeling of unease in his gut persisted.

"Maybe she's changed her mind about wedding ye." Shawe spoke low to keep his words between them.

Connor debated his friend's words, because it was a possibility. The night before replayed across his mind. His temper rose as he considered that Brina might renounce him once she was forced to face a priest who would no doubt remind her of her father's vow and the fact that refusing to serve the church would forever stain her soul.

The church was just as greedy as the Douglas when it came to keeping what they believed belonged to them. Those shoes sitting by the front pew might have meant something very different than what he'd believed that morning.

"She will wed me," Connor insisted. "And if she's for some reason changed her mind, the woman can simply readjust her thinking again or at least give me the opportunity to make an argument in my own favor."

Shawe chuckled, but Connor wasn't feeling so lighthearted. The church was quiet now, shadows beginning to darken the corners. Connor strode down the aisle, stopping when he stood beside the pair of boots that still sat where they had been that morning when he arrived. They hadn't moved, and his suspicions grew. He caught a slight movement in the passageway that led away from the sanctuary. One of the priests stood there, clearly shocked to see him.

"I expected ye earlier and with yer intended bride to take yer vows." The priest leveled a disapproving look toward him.

"My bride was never seen leaving this church."
Connor pointed to the boots. "And her shoes are
still here."

The priest looked shocked, as though he had failed
to see them. Shawe stiffened beside him, drawing in
a harsh breath, while the priest looked between the
footwear and Connor's dark expression.

"I have nae seen yer bride since she gave me her
confession this morning."

"Search the church, and I mean every last inch of
it, including the confessionals."

The priest made to protest, but Connor's men
didn't wait for the man to form his stunned thoughts
into words. They fanned out, opening every door
and curtain, until the entire church had been searched
from the loft where the bell ringer slept to the privy.

Connor stood with his hands clenched into fists.
The bite of betrayal rode him hard, growing with every
moment that he waited for Brina to be found. When
his men all stood in front of him, waiting on his next
action, there was nothing to hold back his temper.

"Ready the horses, Shawe. We are riding after them."

"After who, Laird?"

Connor turned to shoot a dark look toward Shawe.
"Quinton Cameron, that is who. Brina would never
have made it past the gate without his help."

But what Connor wanted to know was if had she
left or had she been taken. He needed to think that
she had been taken, even if doing so would pit him
against a man who might be the worst enemy he could
make. There would be plenty of men who would tell
him a woman wasn't worth that. There would be even

more who would counsel him to tolerance because of the blood that would most certainly flow from a feud between the Cameron and the Lindsey.

Connor struggled to rein in his temper, but it eluded his grasp. Instead all he could think of was the look on Brina's face when she had told him that she would wed him.

Call him a fool, but he was going after Brina, and he would kill whoever stood between them. For the first time in his life, he understood how men might be driven to illogical extremes for the love of a woman.

He would have her back or die in the attempt.

Eight

HER HEAD FELT AS THOUGH IT WERE GOING TO SPLIT like a ripe pumpkin. Brina kept her breaths slow and tiny because even the sound sent pain through her skull. As she hesitated in opening her eyes, other points of discomfort made themselves known. Her feet were still bare and her toes almost frozen. But not quite, because she was aware of the excruciating burning coming from each of them. Brina lifted her eyelids and closed them when a bolt of white-hot pain went through her head once more.

"I wondered when ye'd join us."

Brina stiffened and felt the body she was lying against help her sit up. She was being bounced up and down and realized that she was on the back of a horse.

She opened her eyes and forced them to remain so in spite of the pain. Her vision was blurry at first, her mind unable to make sense of what she saw. She rubbed her eyes, gasping at the shooting pains that renewed their assault on her. Dragging in a deep breath, she stared at the rope tied around her wrists.

"I'm glad to see ye regaining yer wits. My horse is getting tired of carrying us both."

She turned to stare at Quinton Cameron as she felt the man pull up on the reins of his stallion. It was a huge horse, and the ground looked very far below her dangling feet.

"What are ye doing?"

Her voice was shrill, but alarm was racing through her as she looked around and didn't see a single Lindsey plaid. Darkness had fallen and she couldn't recall anything of the day, beyond the finishing of her prayers.

"What have ye done, Laird Cameron?"

A horse came up beside them, and he lifted her up and deposited her on it. Brina found herself reaching for the reins and throwing her leg over the back of the animal so that she wouldn't slide over it completely and end up beneath the hooves of both beasts.

"I've stolen ye."

"What?"

She shrieked, horror sending her voice up a few octaves. Several of his men growled at her, shooting her warning looks she refused to buckle under.

"Keep yer mouth shut, or I'll tie it shut, Brina Chattan. I've no time for a hysterical woman." He grabbed the reins of her horse and looped them over the back of his saddle so that she had no way to control the animal.

"Ye're going to the palace with me because Connor is too trusting in honor keeping yer father from starting a feud."

Quinton turned his back on her, obviously finished

with explaining his actions to her. His men were
riding hard, their horses close together as they cut
through the darkness. She lay over the neck of the
horse she rode, her hands grasping the bridle where it
was secured around the animal's head, because it was
the only place that she might gain a good grip. She was
suddenly thankful to Bran and her father for promising
her to the church and making it possible for her to
learn how to ride astride.

The speed Quinton kept them at made it impossible to do anything but cling to the horse. Her fingers
ached and became icy cold because she didn't have any
leather gauntlets such as the Highlanders riding with
Quinton did. She looked at them with resentment
filling her, but that did nothing to cut the chill of the
winter night.

What weighed on her mind the most was that every
pounding hoof took her farther away from the man
she had thought to wed. Fate was truly cruel, for it had
allowed her to taste true happiness only to swipe it from
her grasp while she was still looking at it in wonder.

She was left with nothing but pain slashing across
her heart, which sent tears into her eyes, the wind
whipping the droplets along her cheeks.

Sometime near the darkest part of the night,
Quinton lifted his hand, and the horses stopped. Their
breathing filled the air while he listened to the darkness and pointed toward the sound of running water.
His men guided their horses in that direction, but the
animals went without much urging, eager for a drink.

His men slid off their horses, and the animals waded
into the water while they drank. Brina felt someone

reach up and lift her off her horse and deposit her on her feet. The sharp rock covering the ground dug into her bare skin while her knees wobbled.

"See to yer needs and do nae make me chase ye."

Quinton Cameron spoke quietly, his words similar to Connor's when he had first stolen her, and yet there were vast differences between the two men. She suspected that she hated this man, something she had never done before.

"Go on, unless ye want to see what is beneath me kilt."

Beyond him, Brina noticed that several of his men were not waiting for her to make it behind the rocks before they relieved themselves. She snorted at his vulgarity but left the area because wetting herself would only make her more miserable.

Quinton didn't give her long to tend to her comfort, appearing just moments after her robe had fluttered down.

"What were ye doing without shoes beyond the door of yer bedchamber?"

Brina growled when a rock jabbed into her unprotected arch.

"What are ye doing stealing me away from a man who welcomed ye as a friend?"

Quinton frowned at her, and she heard the way he snorted at her tone and the fact that she had answered his question with one of her own.

"If ye do nae care for my words, leave me here."

He crossed his arms over his chest, looking like a looming demon in the darkness. One that had decided to toy with his prey before he pounced on it.

"Do ye fancy being eaten by wolves, then, lass? If I left ye here, Connor would certainly nae call me friend ever again."

"And do ye truly believe that he'll do so now that ye've stolen me?"

She watched the man's lips rise into a grin. "Are ye saying that he has a reason to come after ye, lass?"

He reached out, and she saw the flash of his dirk in the meager starlight. She lunged away from him, but not before she heard him cutting a piece of her overrobe from the hem.

"Ye're insane." And she was talking too much, allowing her unsettled mind to share things with him that she would be better off keeping to herself. She watched him in the darkness, but he seemed content with his trophy and put the dirk back into the top of his boot.

"No, lass, what I am is a man who will nae see the Highlanders fighting among themselves for any reason. If that means I must steal ye away from a man who welcomed me into his home, I'll do it."

"That much is proven."

"Aye, it is."

The hard certainty of his dedication to his course sent another wave of despair through her. The chill in the air only added to it. Brina forced her chin to remain level, because it was so tempting to allow the moment to drag her down into hopelessness.

She refused, clinging to the memory of how little time had truly passed since she had felt Connor's arms about her. She would have more faith in him, in the feelings that were swirling around inside her for him. Call her insane, she did not care, because love was lodged solidly inside her heart for the man who she had been willing to wed in spite of her life's expected path.

She prayed that she got the chance to tell him so.

❧

Connor looked at the ground, holding his hand up to stop his men. Something had caught his eye, and he turned his horse about to investigate what it was. Dawn was beginning to turn the horizon pink, which provided enough light for him to make out the scrap of wool fluttering from where it was pinned to the trunk of a tree. The dirk holding it there was marked with the crest of the Cameron clan.

"Does the bastard want ye to know where he's heading?" Shawe asked.

Connor reached out and pulled the dirk free. He stared at the weapon, trying to force himself to think beyond the rage that had been controlling him so far.

"I think so, but I dinna ken just why."

Or how Quinton might think that they could be anything except enemies now. Still, the dirk was something, a message from the man he'd called friend for so long. It cast a new light on the situation, clouding his thinking with confusion.

"We'll discover the answer at Holyrood."

But there was something else brewing. Connor looked toward Shawe.

"I've something else for ye to do, Shawe."

His man looked curious, a few of his more experienced retainers leaning in to catch the conversation.

"Take some lads and ride off to Robert Chattan.
Tell the man that he needs ride for Holyrood."

Shawe nodded and pointed at the men he wanted
guarding his back.

Connor turned his horse toward the road once
more. He tucked the dirk into his doublet and allowed
the stallion its freedom. The animal wasn't interested
in standing still. It surged forward, intent on keeping
warm by maintaining a brisk pace. His men flowed
around him, their expressions grim and determined.

Whatever Quinton wanted, Connor was going to
make sure the man learned that he had a few demands
of his own.

❧

Holyrood Palace was a dreary place, especially with
ice dripping from its roof. The snow that was pris-
tine white all around them had been ground into a
muddy bog outside the grand residence of the royal
court. A steady stream of horses and carts fought
their way through that bog to make it to the front
gate of the palace.

Not many of those made it through to the inside
of the palace yard. Quinton Cameron was one of
them. The royal guards stepped back as he and his
men approached, allowing them to ride into the inner
yard. Quinton continued on to the front steps, where
he dismounted and reached up to pull Brina off the
back of the horse she felt she had been clinging to for
an eternity.

Every muscle she had ached, and her feet were
truly numb now, but not from the chill. Instead they

had lost feeling from the pressure that she had used to clasp the horse between her thighs. Tingling shots of sensation began to return now that she was standing up, and along with them came pain.

Quinton grasped her hands and slid the rope off her wrists while his body kept the line of pages that stood ready to take the horses of those who were admitted into the yard from noticing the bindings.

"Ye'll mind me, Brina."

"Or what?"

She was being bold and perhaps foolish to bait the man, but she refused to bow to his will. His eyes were full of determination, and it gave her pause for a moment, because she had admired that same quality in Connor. She was suddenly confused and uncertain what to think.

"Ye do nae want to know the answer to that question, Brina. Be sure that I can be a dangerous bastard if I have to, but I'd prefer to leave yer handling to Connor."

He grunted and began to pull her along through corridors that seemed endless. Servants hustled by, but there was a lack of people dressed in finery as she might have expected to see. Instead she saw men wearing their kilts and wool doublets very much like her father did every day. It was common dress that served well as a buffer against the elements, and only the colors of their plaids were personal.

"These are my private chambers."

The double doors Quinton stopped in front of were guarded by four burly men. Each of them had a sword strapped to his back, but they also held boar spears that were the length of a full-grown man and topped with evil-looking metal spearheads that had one main point and two smaller ones designed to ensure any wound the weapon inflicted was a mortal one.

"Mistress Chattan is nae to leave without my permission, and that means hearing it from my lips."

The four of them reached up and tugged on their knit bonnets, but they looked at her, their gazes just as sharp as their spears. Brina could feel them memorizing her features and even her body size.

One of them reached out and pulled the door open. Quinton took her through it, and she heard it close behind her. The second it did, she struggled violently to escape his grip.

He released her, and she took a few more steps into the chamber to give herself enough space to feel as though she wasn't within his reach any longer. When she turned to look back at him, she decided she was only fooling herself, because the man was every bit as strong as those men guarding the door. He was larger too, the sort of stature the English feared from the Highlanders. There was something about her country that bred strength, and Quinton Cameron was a prime example of what an English army dreaded.

"Behave yerself, Brina Chattan. I didna steal ye to harm ye."

Brina bit back the first words that came to mind. The man held every bit of power over her at the moment. He watched her, his eyes narrowing with his consideration.

"I'll have a bath brought in for ye since I will nae have ye leaving these rooms."

He turned and left without another word.

Brina sighed and felt relief flowing through her until she turned and noticed the two maids watching. Both servants held their emotions behind stiff expressions, neither looking even a tiny bit shocked to hear that their laird had kidnapped her.

They lowered themselves when they realized she was looking at them. But once that courtesy was completed, they resumed tending to the fireplace. Gray ash filled it, and one swept it into a copper urn the second one held.

The chambers were quite nice, really. The one she stood in had windows that opened to overlook a long patch of snow-covered ground. But there were iron screens fitted over them. The iron was formed into delicate designs, but when she placed her fingers on it, she discovered it icy cold.

A beautiful prison, but set with iron bars, no matter the shape of them.

Two sets of doorways led out of the chamber; one faced a room that held a long table with a full dozen chairs. Brina stepped into the room, her curiosity drawn toward the table and chairs because they were carved with leaves and acorns to make for a lavish presentation. Against the wall stood a cupboard with silver plates all carefully displayed, and beneath those were goblets made from silver as well.

The amount of wealth made her tense once more. Quinton wasn't a man who had bragged to her without cause to support his words, he was a dangerous man, and the costly items gleaming in the afternoon sunlight gave credence to his position among the court. He could keep her his prisoner, and no one would question him, for fear that he would retaliate or refuse to do business with them.

She walked past the cupboard and into the next room, which was a kitchen. Her nose felt the difference in temperature immediately, and her toes enjoyed the fact that the stone floor was warm.

"Who are ye?"

A woman in an apron marked with several stains propped her hands on her ample hips and stared at Brina.

"The laird brought her and said she's no' to leave."

The two maids had entered behind her, and one of them answered the cook.

"Well now, that's an unkind fate, to be sure." The cook surveyed her from head to toe and frowned. "Ye look like the man tied ye to the back of a horse for the better part of several days."

Brina couldn't help but raise a hand to touch her head. Her fingertips discovered a fuzzy mess that had once been her neatly braided hair. Her veil had slipped down around her neck, and her cheeks felt chapped from the wind.

"The laird wants her bathed."

The cook snorted, obviously confident of her position. "I should think the lass would be wanting a bath herself. Sit down on that stool and take off yer shoes. They are likely caked with mud."

Brina shrugged. "I have no shoes."

The cook made another sound beneath her breath that was anything but submissive to the will of her laird.

"Well… fetch the tub and get some water heating. Her feet must be frozen."

The maids all scattered while the cook grabbed a wooden bowl and used a ladle to fill it with a steaming stew.

"Here. Eat while those girls see to getting ye a bath. If the laird took ye without yer shoes, I can imagine that he didna bother to feed ye either. Men are thick-headed at times; they cannae think past their duty."

Brina took the bowl of stew, and her belly rumbled in response to its aroma. The cook muttered before returning to whatever she was working at on the top of the kitchen table.

"What clan do ye come from?"

Brina had to swallow the food in her mouth in order to answer. "Chattan."

The cook raised one of her eyebrows. "And whose daughter are ye? That my laird would take such interest in ye?"

"I'm Laird Chattan's third daughter."

The kitchen went silent; every head turned toward her. The cook propped her hands back on her hips.

"My laird stole a bride of Christ?"

"Actually it was Laird Lindsey who stole me on the way to the abbey, and yer laird stole me from him. I do nae understand it myself."

The maids' eyes were wide now, and even the cook looked as though she was having a difficult time setting it all straight inside her head.

"Ah well, Lindsey is a good man. He's been here plenty of times, and the Lord knows that his family treated him unkindly for too many years to count. I suppose the man had his reasons for taking ye."

Brina returned to eating, even as disappointment went

through her. The maids would follow the cook and believe that their laird was innocent of wrongdoing. That meant that any of his friends were likewise innocent too.

It drew her back to the conversation she'd had with Connor. He'd been honest with her, and he knew how to survive in the politics of Scotland. She was just a pawn, but somehow she had never felt so much like a material possession until she had been taken away from him. The difference was in her heart. She felt something there, something that warmed her even as she tried to ignore the doubt beginning to attempt to smother that flame. It was a fact that Connor might have to allow Quinton to keep her.

It was possible Connor wouldn't want her back now that there would be questions about her virtue. His words about Deirdre rose from her memory to torment her.

There would be rumors about her now...

She shivered. That thought was too horrifying to maintain her calm composure over.

It was far too possible to ignore.

❧

"I do nae care about Connor Lindsey's bride."

Archibald Douglas, the fifth earl to hold that title, sniffed with disdain at Quinton Cameron. He leaned forward and pointed one of his thick fingers at him.

"If ye brought her here, she's yer problem. So fuck her if that's what's behind yer actions." He waved his hand. "I do nae care."

"Ye've been sitting in that chair long enough to start running to fat."

The earl roared and surged up out of the throne he'd been sitting in. It took him a moment to step off the raised platform before he got close enough to take a swing at Quinton's chin. They began to circle one another, their knees bent and their arms out wide. Archibald snarled.

"I should have ye tossed into the mud outside my gates for that!"

"Except that ye would be proving me right because ye need yer guards to deal with whatever unsettles yer stomach."

The earl snorted but straightened up, a dark frown marring his features. "Curse and rot ye, Cameron! Ye have a point. I'm stuck inside these walls too much, but I still say yer a fool to bring that lass here. Connor will no doubt be pissed."

"He'll most likely want my balls served up on a platter."

The lieutenant general chuckled, and it wasn't a nice sound. "Careful, laddie. I like the sound of that." He returned to his throne, sprawling out in it like a king. "Why did ye take her if ye knew he'd be angry? I thought ye valued the man's friendship."

"I value a united Highlands more, and so should you."

Archibald grunted. "Ye have a very annoying habit of telling me what I should do too often, man."

Quinton shrugged, unrepentant. "I'm right. Someone has to have the spine to tell ye that ye cannae afford to have the clans fighting among themselves over women while Scotland has a lad on the throne and England's king is making peace with France. What will the man do with his armies do ye think? What with his cousin being our sweet queen, someone I wager the English would like raising our king more than ye."

"England would like the clans fighting one another, I agree. Joan Beauford will nae be teaching her son to love the English while I'm alive." The earl growled low and deep, his hatred for the English clear. "What has the Chattan girl to do with it?"

"Yer cousin Melor blackened her sister's name to strike at Connor."

Archibald smirked. "So what? If he didna rape her, I do nae care. Chattan should have kept a shorter leash on his daughter."

Quinton stood silent, and the earl frowned.

"Fine, tell me why it matters that Melor had a woman?"

"What's important is that Connor took the third daughter so that he can pressure you to make Melor and his uncle release Vanora Lindsey once Connor's able to claim the Chattans as relatives by marriage."

"That girl is going to marry a Douglas even if it's one on the other side of my family. Connor managed to claim the lairdship against the odds but I won't let him build an empire through alliances." Archibald shrugged. "Maybe I'll let the man challenge ye, and ye can do me the service of killing him." The earl snickered. "Rather fitting, considering ye have stolen his woman."

"Which will leave ye with a clan that does nae want to be absorbed by the Douglas. Even if that man is wed to Connor's sister."

"So I'll hang the rebellious ones, and the rest will settle down."

Quinton chuckled, drawing a glare from the earl.

"They're Highlanders."

"I do nae care. They will become Douglas or die Lindsey."

Quinton snarled, "Well, ye should, but I wonder if I'm no' wasting my time to try and save ye from yerself."

He turned around to leave, disgusted with the man who couldn't see past his own clan colors.

"Hold."

Archibald Douglas really had been acting like a king, because his tone was one that only a monarch would use. Quinton turned back to face the man, and this time Archibald's expression was serious instead of taunting.

"The Lindsey will nae be so easy to absorb. I know that, man, but that doesna mean I'll be telling my Uncle to be giving up the Lindsey's sister."

"Of course nae. Ye crave an alliance with him, which is exactly why Connor stole a girl promised to the church instead of taking the one who Melor besmirched. He's making alliances too, and don't forget that Robert Chattan has his second daughter promised to the McLeod."

The earl grunted. "I see yer thinking; three clans standing against the Douglas will nae be a good thing for Scotland. Robert Chattan is too cunning by far. Why did the man have to have three daughters? One of them needs to go to the church for certain."

Archibald reached up to stroke his beard. "I'll think on it, for ye have made a fine argument. Keep the Chattan girl here. I may have to give Connor his sister back to keep the peace, but I'll demand that the

Chattan lass be taken to her abbey so that the Lindseys do nae come away with everything they want."

※⁓

Night fell and dawn broke again with no sign of Quinton Cameron. Brina knew every inch of the chambers by noon the next day, and the cook scolded her for putting so much wear on her shoes.

In all her days, she had never been one to squander the daylight hours with idleness, but she refused to clean anything that belonged to Quinton Cameron. Likewise, she would not cook for him.

The cook finally huffed her way toward a chest hidden in a back room and fit one of the keys hanging from her belt into the lock that secured it. She lifted the lid and began sorting through the items inside.

"Here. Put yer hands to work if ye know anything about using a needle. Yer wandering is going to give me nightmares of ghosts."

The cook laid a piece of folded fabric on the table and set a box next to it. Once Brina lifted the lid, she could see it contained everything for sewing. Needles were carefully stuck through a small square of wool with a full two dozen pins. A long pair of shears shone in the afternoon light, their edges sharp, without any burrs to ruin a delicate fabric.

"I could nae take fabric that does no' belong to me."

The cook shook her head. "Then ye'll keep wearing clothing that was paid for by Laird Cameron."

Brina felt her jaw drop. The cook was a wise woman, and she smiled in victory before returning to her kitchen. Of course, the woman had a good point.

Everything Brina wore had been paid for by Quinton. At least if she did the labor herself, it would be that much less that she owed. Reaching out, she ran her fingers along the fabric, smiling at the softness of the linen fibers.

Her lips suddenly rose into a smile that was full of mocking humor.

She unfolded the fabric and began contemplating it with a critical eye.

❧

"Ye do nae tolerate waiting very well, Connor Lindsey."

Connor jumped and turned to face the man who had sneaked up on him. Roan McLeod laughed at the expression on his face.

"Ye do nae take surprises well either."

Connor forced himself to swallow his snarl and offered the man his hand. Roan McLeod was only a few years younger than he, but his father was still laird, which gave him a carefree nature that often had Connor fighting the urge to hit him.

On second thought, it had nothing to do with the fact that his father was still alive. Roan did his share of handling the more difficult matters that faced the McLeods, and he was still a wiseass.

"I did nae expect to see you, Roan."

"Of course ye didna, but ye see, the thing is this, my father is beset by this idea that Robert Chattan is going to try to murder ye for taking his youngest daughter."

Roan took a mug of ale offered by Connor's staff. The small house was only a few blocks from Holyrood Palace, for he detested staying in the palace itself. A man couldn't belch there without it being reported to someone.

"Now mind ye, I think that Robert would only castrate ye, but I cannae go arguing with my sire."

"We'll see when he arrives."

Roan frowned, something flickering in his eyes that hinted at a very serious matter. "So ye sent for Robert Chattan? Good. I've words to have with the man."

Connor lifted an eyebrow.

"He sent my bride to me." Roan's tone left no doubt that he was displeased with Kaie Chattan.

"What's wrong with the girl?"

"Nothing. She's meek and obedient," Roan growled softly. "And I owe Quinton Cameron a large favor for telling me that the girl has a true calling to serve the church. I do nae need a brokenhearted nun in my bed."

"Ye didna wed her?"

"No." Roan spit out the single word. "I'm no Viking, nor do I favor having a bride whose heart is already taken. I sent her to the abbey."

"What of the alliance?"

Roan tilted his head to the side. "Aye, my father is no' pleased with me, but that girl kissed the hem of my kilt before she ran toward the gates like I was a demon."

Connor frowned, and Roan glared at him. "Now do nae you go fixing me with that look, Connor Lindsey. I know ye want an alliance with the McLeod through yer marriage, but I've got as much right as ye do to refuse the daughter Chattan set me. Besides, I still have one option to present to the man when he arrives."

"His bastard daughter?"

Roan grinned. "Aye. Since the man is a widower now, he can wed the mother and give me that daughter. But I'm here to stand beside ye against the Douglas; that much hasna changed."

"I thank ye for that."

Roan grunted. "Oh, be sure that ye will be thanking me. I do nae care for the way my father is looking at me, and I'm planning on having ye help me appease him."

"After I retrieve Brina."

Roan drew in a stiff breath. "I'm here to help ye try, Connor, but only a fool would fail to notice that the odds are nae in yer favor."

He knew it well.

Connor began pacing. He was a man of action and didn't care for having to deal with politics.

It wouldn't be simple, that much he could count on, which was why he was waiting for Robert Chattan. The alliance he had worked so long and even challenged the church to gain was going to be put to the test. The only difference was that he was going up against the Camerons instead of the Douglas. Quinton Cameron was more than a fellow laird, the man was a titled earl. In the Highlands, that might be dismissed but at court it set Quinton above the other lairds.

Robert Chattan didn't make him wait much longer. The Chattan retainers came up the street with enough speed to send the market venders scurrying out of their way. They pulled up in front of Connor's house, and he felt Robert glare at him.

"I've a score to settle with ye lad, laird or no laird."

Connor stood face-to-face with the man once he'd dismounted.

"We had an agreement, Chattan, and one that we both need if we do nae want to have the Douglas raiding both of us come spring."

Robert growled, as menacing as any man half his age.

"I hate to admit that ye have a valid argument, but ye had better be treating my Brina with gentle hands, or I'll break yer nose."

༄

"Ye're making the man a shirt?"

Brina stiffened and looked up from the cuff she was setting a sleeve into. Quinton Cameron stood in the doorway, watching her from half-closed eyes.

"So ye are alive. I was hoping maybe ye'd died in the last few days."

He laughed at her. "I thought ye were the one raised to serve the church."

"I was taught to adjust to any situation I might find myself in."

Quinton only nodded before walking farther into the room. He reached out to finger the sleeve that was lying on the tabletop.

"I think ye have done that better than Connor deserves. Are ye quite sure ye harbor affection for a man who stole ye?"

Brina didn't bother to answer. She drew the needle through the cuff in her hand in reply. A wife was expected to sew her husband's shirts as a service that said she accepted her position as his servant, but for an unwed woman to make a shirt for a man declared affection. It was an intimate thing.

"Return me to him, Cameron."

"I hope to."

Brina tightened her fingers on the thin needle to keep from dropping it. Her hands wanted to tremble with relief, but she didn't care to show Quinton her emotions so easily. Every hour of every day had dragged on so slowly, she wasn't sure if she was sane anymore.

"Is that a fact?"

Brina jumped, and the needle fell from her grasp. A second later she was lifted right out of the chair she sat in and deposited behind Connor Lindsey. She stared at his wide back a second before she was pulled even farther back by Shawe.

Quinton chuckled softly. "I wondered when ye'd show up, my friend."

"Friend? Are ye sure about that?" Connor snarled. "Ye bloody stole my woman."

Quinton straightened up and maintained his distance from Connor. That meant circling with him, because Connor was edging closer to him with his body tense and ready for battle.

"If I were set against ye, Connor, I'd have let ye toss away the only chance ye had to reclaim yer sister."

Connor stopped, standing in place while his men waited silently to see what would happen. "How does stealing my wife bring Vanora closer to being back on Lindsey land?"

"Brina isna yer wife, and once she is, the Douglas will never allow yer sister to step one foot outside the fortress she's living in until she is wed. The only thing that will force them to bring her out is the threat of ye marrying Brina."

Connor cursed. "Which is why ye brought her here."

"That's right."

"Oh, for Christ's sake!" Brina snarled from behind everyone. "Ye could have told me that. It wasna necessary to hit me on the head. I would have helped to bring Vanora home."

"No, you will nae, Brina." Connor turned so quickly, his kilt flared out, but he couldn't maintain his anger when their eyes met. His expression revealed just how happy he was to see her, and it blew heat over the flicker of warmth that had been slowly dying inside her chest. "It is a matter for men. I wish ye back in Birch Stone, where I know ye are safe."

"I am no' a child, and I am nae helpless."

Connor frowned at her, but Quinton raised one dark eyebrow behind him. Then a large hand appeared on Quinton's shoulder, and he turned to face Robert Chattan.

"Did ye hit me daughter?"

Robert didn't wait for a reply. He sent his fist toward Quinton's jaw, and the sound echoed throughout the chamber as Quinton staggered beneath the strength of it. Her father didn't follow his victim but stood in the opposite doorway while rubbing his hand.

"Brina, lass, come here."

She was already stepping forward when Connor stepped beside her and clamped his hand around her forearm to keep her next to him.

"No' yet, Chattan. I want yer word on the match. I'll have Brina for my wife."

"One of my daughters is going to the church. I've given me word on it." Robert Chattan was completely exasperated now, his voice making it clear that he was not going to be denied.

"One has."

Brina watched as a man wearing the McLeod tartan stepped up.

"It seems that yer middle daughter has a true calling to serve the church. It's a right unkind thing to send me a wife who has a true calling, Chattan."

Robert Chattan remained silent for a long moment while Roan McLeod glared at him.

"She never spoke to me about it until the trouble started." Her father looked toward her and Connor, studying them. "I'll admit that my pride was stung enough to make me deaf to anything Kaie said."

"If ye're ready to discuss alternatives, Robert, I'm ready to ask for yer blessing to wed Brina."

Brina bit back a gasp when Connor Lindsey, laird of the Lindsey, suddenly lowered himself to one knee in front of Robert Chattan. It was a custom older than anyone knew, but one that she was stunned to see him observing. Her father reached out and touched him gently on the head, bestowing his blessing. She stepped across the space between them and joined Connor, shivering when she felt her father's fingers on her head.

"Ye have my blessing, Lindsey. May yer marriage be a long one. Brina, be happy and know that I wish that for ye with all me heart."

"What do ye mean, woman?"

Connor was shaking with his frustration, but Brina refused to allow that to distract her from her purpose.

"I mean that Quinton Cameron was correct; once we marry, you shall never see yer sister. We must wait."

Connor was so quiet that conversation floated in from the outer room where everyone had withdrawn so that she and Connor might have a moment of privacy. It was still difficult to believe that he was there, so close that she could reach out and touch him. Brina didn't realize that she was in fact lifting her hand until Connor's gaze moved to see what she was doing. He closed the distance between them, then captured her hand in his larger one and carried it to his lips for a kiss that sent a shiver down her body.

"I swear I still want to beat Quinton Cameron near to death for taking ye away from the security of my land."

"But yer sister—"

He framed her face between his hands, his eyes a piercing blue. "Ye will leave that matter to me, Brina. I cannae bear the thought of ye risking yerself. I thought my heart would tear apart when I realized ye had been taken."

He smothered her next protest with a kiss that rejuvenated her soul. She hadn't realized how dry her lips had become until she felt his mouth against hers. She reached for him, wrapping her hands around his nape, and felt her fingers tremble as they touched his warm skin. She drew in a deep breath to once again fill her senses with the smell of his skin and pressed closer to him so that she might feel the beat of his heart.

A thump from the doorway broke the moment,

and she heard Connor smothering a word beneath his breath, which made her giggle.

"We'll have to wait to get to the buggering."

He growled and slid one hand down to rest on the curve of her bottom.

"Careful, lass. A husband has the right to spank his wife."

She broke away from his embrace because the conversation in the other room was becoming louder.

"Then I suppose it is a good thing that I do nae plan to wed ye just yet."

Connor glared at her. "Ye'll wed me before sunset."

"I agree." Her father spoke from the doorway. "Ye shall leave the matter of politics to the men, Brina."

"But what of Connor's sister?"

Robert Chattan drew a stiff breath. "I believe we should go and challenge the lieutenant general for her now."

"Agreed."

Brina followed the men, but Connor stopped her at the main entry doors to Quinton Cameron's rooms.

"Ye will stay here, Brina."

Her father turned and nodded in agreement.

She felt the yoke of the male-dominated society press down on her shoulders such as she never had before. They turned and continued on their way, and she couldn't help but admire seeing so many clan plaids together. Too often they fought, and she discovered herself agreeing with Quinton.

Scotland needed its Highlanders united.

❧

"Well now. I was told that there were four of ye out there waiting on me, but seeing it is still a bit of a shock."

Archibald Douglas sat wearing true velvet cloth while Connor, Roan, Quinton, and Robert all lowered their heads. His eyes were narrowed as he watched each laird show deference to his position of lieutenant general.

"I've come—"

"I know why ye're here, Lindsey." The earl snapped his fingers, and one of the tapestries hanging on the wall behind him moved. "And I assure ye that I do have what ye want, but it will nae be yers easily, on that ye may depend."

He gestured with his fingers, and a young girl stepped forward. She wore only a simple pair of robes, and her hair was braided and covered with a length of Douglas plaid.

"I think she looks very fetching in Douglas colors."

Connor had to suppress the urge to kill. He had never been a man given to murdering, but he understood now how it might happen in a flash of unexpected circumstances. The surprise of seeing his sister was enough to make his palm itch for the pommel of his sword.

"She is a Lindsey."

Vanora shifted her attention toward him, and her eyes were the same blue as his own, but he saw her worrying her lower lip, and she looked back toward the earl without saying a word.

"She is a female who knows her place, exactly the way the Douglas like their brides. Silent and dutiful."

"She's too young to wed."

Robert, Roan, and Quinton stepped up to support his position. The earl considered them for a long moment.

"Agreed. But I am not the one who took her. If the Lindsey are nae strong enough to hold on to their own, they will suffer losses."

"Yer kin rode in under a banner of peace. I thought that was only a ploy used by the English."

Connor's words earned him a snarl from the earl. Archibald sat forward, his face darkening with his rising temper.

"Careful, Lindsey. Ye stand to lose even more if I'm of the mind to take everything ye came here for. Ye rode through my gate this time, and I do nae have to allow ye to leave with anything if it does nae please me."

Connor shrugged. "True enough if ye want it to be known that the Douglas are intent on no' dealing fairly with the other clans."

It was a bold thing to say; one that might even cost him his life if the earl was in the mood to send him to the executioner. Connor walked across the room and stood in front of his sister. Her face still held the edge of childhood and a sprinkling of freckles. She smiled for him but raised a hand to cover her lips before any sound escaped.

"I am yer brother, Vanora, and ye were never promised to anyone."

Her eyes widened, and shock filled them. Connor turned back toward the earl.

"Very pretty, but it does nae change the fact that she is nae in yer control."

There was a calculating look in the earl's eyes that promised Connor a steep price for what he wanted.

Archibald turned to survey the other men in the room. It was clear that he wasn't pleased to see so many clans standing behind the Lindsey claim.

"Ye may have yer sister back if ye relinquish yer alliance with the Chattan."

Robert stepped forward. "That arrangement is set, and the banns read already."

"The banns were read on yer older daughter, who is nae the daughter Lindsey here wants to wed now." Archibald looked at Quinton. "Scotland needs its clans united beneath the crown, no' becoming too powerful by making alliances that do nae favor the king. So ye may have yer sister, because I know that ye shall arrange a match for her that will bring ye an alliance, or ye may have the Chattan bride Quinton stole from ye, but ye will no' have both."

"Vanora is my sister. She belongs on Lindsey land."

"She would no' be the only bride sent to live among her intended groom's kin in order to ensure that the wedding takes place and peace continues." The earl pointed at them all. "With Vanora wed to a Douglas, there will be an incentive for all of you to keep the peace. And if ye claim yer sister back, I'll have the Chattan girl taken and wed to my cousin for the same purpose."

The earl sat back against the padded chair and smiled smugly. "Ye shall no' have two alliances, Connor Lindsey. Choose one."

❧

"May that bastard rot in hell."

Connor was talking to the empty room. He paced

in a circle while he heard his friends conversing in the other chamber. But he stopped when he saw the sleeve still lying on the long table. It captured his attention because it seemed odd to have only part of a shirt lying about.

"I hope it fits."

Brina emerged from the kitchen, worrying her lower lip with her teeth.

Exactly as Vanora had done...

"Tell me what happened. This uncertainty is eating me alive."

Brina watched his lips twitch up, only for a moment before he nodded.

"Douglas plays as good a game as I do when it comes to forming alliances. He told me I could have one with yer father or one through having my sister returned so that I might direct where she weds."

It was almost too horrible to grasp, but Brina felt the truth of it burning into her. No clan would give up the advantage; that was as Scottish as heather.

"She's here, so close I can touch her and yet still too far away." He shook his head. "I've no' set eyes on Vanora since she was taken, and that was five years ago."

Brina sucked in a harsh breath because there was pain in his eyes, and it tore at her too much to ignore.

"Take her. I'll go to the abbey." Simple words, but they felt like dry wood chips as she forced them out. Tears stung the corners of her eyes, but she refused to allow them to fall. "Ye must reclaim yer blood."

"I cannae live without ye, Brina. Do nae ye know that yet?" He closed the distance between them and caught the tears that escaped from her eyes with his hands, smoothing them away while she shivered with the effort it had cost her to ask to be sent away.

"I would have ye happy, Connor, for I swear ye have given me such joy that I cannae bear to think of ye being discontented because of me." Brina could see water sparkling on her eyelashes as she looked up at his eyes. It might be her last moment with him forever, and she needed to memorize every detail to keep her heart from shriveling into dry nothingness. "I love ye, Connor, and I'm telling ye to choose yer sister."

"I didna kneel in front of yer father only to walk away from ye, Brina."

She whimpered, the sound escaping from her lips because dignity had long since been abandoned. All the customs and rules of behaviors had not prepared her for this moment when it felt like her very next breath hung on the decision that he would make.

"We are going to wed." He smoothed another tear aside. "And do nae be arguing with me any further, hellcat, for I've knelt in front of yer father now and received his blessing, when I'll tell ye straight that I never hit my knee in front of him for the match with yer sister."

A sob escaped from her chest, but it was somehow a happy sound, and his lips twitched up in response.

"The contract with yer sister was just a negotiation, lass. I knelt beside ye today because I love ye enough to crave yer happiness with our union."

Love—it was a word that many defined as a symptom of insanity or an unbalanced mind. Brina embraced it, reaching for the man who she couldn't face life without.

He kissed her, and she held him close, moving her mouth beneath his. Her clothing was too much separation to bear, and she eagerly shed it as he did the same. They didn't care where their clothing fell, only took time enough to make sure his plaid was tossed onto a table instead of allowed to puddle on the floor.

The bed was much smaller, but that allowed her to be closer to her lover. They touched and kissed and took solace in each other's embrace.

In each other's love.

&

Connor slept, but he was not resting like he had been the last time she had left him in bed. Brina could see the skin drawn tight around his lips, and dark circles beneath his eyes told her why he was sleeping at all.

She didn't have the luxury of fatigue to keep her mind from drifting off into blissful oblivion.

She's here, and yet she might as well be across the country, for all the good it does me...

"If ye cannae sleep, Brina, let us be on the road."

She turned her head to discover Connor watching her. He reached out and stroked her cheek. "It does me good to see ye still in bed beside me when I wake."

He smiled, but the expression did not quite make it all the way to his eyes. A sadness remained there that tore at her heart. In the distance, a church bell rang, and she suddenly thought of an idea.

"Where would the Douglas keep Vanora here at the palace?"

Connor frowned, every hint of sleep gone from his face. "Why do ye want to know?"

"Because maybe it is a matter for a woman after all."

"Brina—"

She sat up, and Connor followed her, shaking the bed with how fast he moved.

"Listen to me, Connor. Everyone will have heard how ye stole me away from the church by now." Her mind was whirling with ideas, and she felt as though she could not form them into words fast enough. Confidence was growing inside her, brighter and stronger with every breath.

"Aye..."

She clasped her hands together. "So if I were to go to where Vanora is, wearing an undyed robe of the church, they might allow her to leave with me, thinking that I am returning to the church. I doubt many have heard that we knelt for my father's blessing. Scandal always moves faster than joyous news."

"That's a fact." He shook his head. "I cannae have ye take such a risk, Brina."

She glared at him, frustration rising up inside her to a pitch impossible to ignore.

"And why nae? I do nae want to look back on the one moment that I was so close to her and did nothing."

He grabbed her hands and lifted them up to kiss each one. Pain showed on his face for the first time, and it sent tears into her eyes.

"I love ye for saying that, but I refuse to see ye risk yerself, Brina."

"Oh, *bugger ye*, Connor Lindsey." His eyes opened wide in shock. "I love ye too much to no' try."

She climbed out of the bed and tossed her hair over her shoulder. "After all, ye're the one who called me a hellcat. Well, I believe we should put it to the test. Get yer men, and I shall get a nun's robe from the church while dawn is still breaking. Everyone will think I've run away from ye. I am no' as helpless as other women. I know how to hunt and ride astride. More importantly, I have been raised to depend upon myself instead of being looked after by the men around me. If I fail, ye can blame the fact that I was raised to expect no' to have a husband to master me for my disobedient behavior."

"If ye fail, Douglas will have ye as well, Brina, and I will nae risk that."

She smiled, feeling victory within her grasp. "If he did that, he would upset the balance he is trying to say exists between the Douglas and the other clans. He cannae take us both without risking rebellion."

He suddenly stiffened. "It might work." He climbed from the bed, uncaring of the fact that he wasn't wearing a stitch. "I detest it, but I do believe it just might work."

Connor looked toward the window and the pink stain of dawn beginning to illuminate it.

"But only if we hurry, and even then we shall have to ride like the demons of hell are upon us."

"Or like the gates of Birch Stone are the golden ones that open into paradise."

Connor laughed, a low sound that she would have expected to hear him using with a man who had impressed him with his cunning. She grinned, enjoying the moment.

"Well then, my hellcat, let us see if ye can use yer temperament on the Douglas, for it's a truth that they consider themselves hard to humble."

※

Brina walked through the hallways of the palace without gaining a second look from anyone. She suddenly thought kindly of Newlyn, her father's head of house, and every switch that redoubtable head of house had applied to her ankles, for she knew how to move so that the skirts of her robe remained even with the floor. There wasn't a single motion from her hips, her walk smooth and practiced to make sure that she appeared like a statue until someone noticed that she was in fact moving.

The palace was full of Douglas retainers. They served as the royal guard and marched through the hallways, but for the moment it was too early for most of the inhabitants to be awake. It was the time of day that lovers left the beds they had shared for the night and returned to the places where they were expected to be.

It was also the time when those who served the church began to perform their duties so that sins might be absolved.

Discovering where Vanora was sleeping took silver pressed into the hands of the servants. Many of the nobles failed to recall that there was a quiet army of people serving them. The lieutenant general had grown so arrogant that he forgot to reward the boy who polished his fine drinking cup every morning or the maid who tended to his boots after he went to sleep. There were hundreds of servants who took pride in their duties, but that did not mean that they were content to be told it was their place.

"What are ye seeking, mistress?"

Brina kept her eyes veiled as she glided to a halt in front of a set of doors. The Douglas retainer wasn't really interested in what she was doing there; his gaze drifted to the two maids bringing fresh bedding down the hallway.

"I seek the Mistress Vanora and was told she is here."

The retainer shifted his eyes to her while he frowned. "Mistress Vanora is departing this morning."

"Yes, she is." Brina felt relief surge through her for the fact that she did not have to lie. "I am come to fetch her."

"The earl wants to see her before she goes? Aye, I can understand that."

He reached over and opened the door. Brina felt a trickle of sweat go down her back in spite of the winter weather. She moved into the chambers beyond the doors, and a maid looked up from where she was tending a fireplace.

"I seek the Mistress Vanora, please."

The maid studied her for a moment but dusted off her hands before quitting the room. It took every bit of self-discipline Brina had ever been forced to foster to maintain her position and not give in to the urge to pace.

There was a scamper on the hard floor, and a young girl came through the doorway. She had that spark of life that the young seemed to always have in their eyes, but it didn't go any further. Her lips were pressed into a firm line that didn't convey either happiness or unhappiness, only sedateness.

The maid appeared with a cloak and set it on Vanora's shoulders before she raised the hood and handed the girl a prayer book.

Brina felt her heart rate increasing, and she tried to force her breaths to come slowly and evenly, but for all her training to be meek and unnoticeable, she had never practiced how to deceive. The maid obviously thought she was taking Vanora to confession, and Brina forced herself to allow the deception to stand.

She turned and retraced her steps to the door, with Vanora following. The Douglas retainer didn't give them much of his attention, allowing them both to quietly walk down the hallway. Every step felt as though it took too long, but Brina forced herself to continue with her even pace. They turned the corner, and she drew a deep breath for having made it out of sight of the main doorway that led to the Douglas rooms. The palace was a huge complex with a labyrinth of hallways and wings.

But the calm did not last. Brina heard the raised voices before the Douglas retainer opened the door to allow the commotion to flood the hallway.

"Are ye insane? The master will hang ye if ye lose that girl!"

"Come on, Vanora!"

The girl looked shocked, her eyes as wide as saucers while she looked over her shoulder and then back to Brina. Her lips moved, but no sound came out.

"I am Brina Chattan. If ye want to return to yer brother's lands, come with me now."

"I do." Vanora squeaked out the pair of words even as they heard more coming from the chambers of the Douglas.

"Get after her, and ye'd better go quickly before she flees. She's no babe any longer to fear being on her own."

There was a pounding of boots while Brina searched their surroundings frantically for any place to take refuge. Two maids came out of a narrow door with their hands full of shirts that looked as though they had just been pressed.

"This way."

She tugged Vanora toward the door and opened it. The air on the other side was hot and moist with a heavy scent of smoke. It was a servants' entry to the laundry, and she pulled Vanora through it without any pity for the shock on the girl's face.

They needed all God's mercy to see them safely away, for the moment the door closed, she heard the heavy footfalls of the Douglas retainers passing by.

Nine

"The vestments are hanging over there." Brina looked up at a plump woman who was directing the dozen maids who were using flatirons. Small boys hunched over next to the huge hearths and worked billows to blow more air onto the fires. The flames flared up, making the room hot and heating the irons so that they sizzled when pressed against the fabric the girls were trying to press.

"And make sure yer hands are clean so that ye do nae smudge them."

Brina lowered herself, and Vanora followed her example. The woman waved them away before returning to ordering her staff about. Every maid kept her eyes on her work, obviously because their mistress was quick to notice when their attention wandered.

Brina heard Vanora gulp when they took the vestments, but the girl maintained her silence as they headed out the door. They could be locked in the stock for even touching something as valuable as the church robes without permission. They were made of the finest fabric and edged with purple velvet that was sewn with pearls and gold bangles.

But the vestments also made a good shield to hide their faces as they made their way through the back passageways. The windows there were large and already had their wooden shutters open so that the morning air could carry away some of the smoke.

That also allowed the scent of the stables to drift in. Holyrood had an immense stable structure built behind the main palace. The distance kept the foul smells from becoming too noxious.

All the main gates would be manned by Douglas retainers looking for them, but it was possible that they might slip out if they were willing to be humble.

"This way."

Brina hurried Vanora along, and they left the vestments on two hooks that were bare because the cloaks that had hung there were now being used. But the freshly pressed cream linen looked out of place in the back doorway of a kitchen and they would point the direction that they had traveled without a doubt.

"Hang yer cloak over them."

Vanora smiled and quickly unhooked her dark cloak. It was of finer fabric and lacked any rips or holes, but for the most part it was simply dark and nondescript. Once it was hung, it covered the vestments well.

Brina looked around the area and bent over to pick up a pail piled high with slop. Vanora sat her prayer book aside and picked up a second bucket. Stepping outside, Brina took a deep breath and said a short prayer. Brina felt the muscles running up and down her back tightening unbearably. Her heart was beating

too fast, and every sound seemed too loud as she
waited for someone to yell at them to halt.

Instead they carried their slop buckets across the
yard and into the stables. There, the sounds of horses
mingled with the conversation of boys working to
clean the stalls.

"What do we do now? Two women will never
make it past the gate, no' with you wearing that nun's
robe. It shall be very easy to spot."

Vanora had kept her voice low, but that didn't
prevent Brina from hearing the defeat in it. Brina
looked around the stable. There was a large hearth
with anvils near it, but there were no blacksmiths
working just yet. Instead there were many lengths of
plaid still lying on the benches and shelves, telling her
that the stable hands had risen to tend to the milking
and left their beds for folding after they took the milk
to the kitchens.

"I must change, and ye too."

Vanora looked at the clothing at hand. There were
shirts hanging from pegs and lengths of plaids too.

"But as boys? Do you nae fear the wrath of the
church? Look what became of Joan of Arc for wearing
men's clothing."

"I fear being caught by the Douglas more."

Vanora snapped her mouth shut and contemplated
that idea. "I agree."

Once the words were spoken, the girl flew into
action. She hastily pleated up two of the lengths of
plaid. Brina found herself staring at the ease with
which the girl performed what was largely considered
a male task.

"They made me practice a lot so that I might be a good wife, able to serve my husband in all tasks." She said it scornfully but didn't hesitate to pull her dress off and reach for a shirt. Brina gasped when she viewed the girl's back. Long purple bruises marred it, making the path of a switching.

Vanora shrugged into one of the shirts and turned suspicious eyes toward her.

"Show me yer back. I want to know what sort of man my brother is."

Brina pulled her underrobe up and over her head before turning around to allow Vanora to view her. She heard the girl sigh before she pulled a thick belt off a bench and used it to secure the pleated plaid about her waist. Brina did the same in spite of seeing Newlyn's disapproving face rise from her memory as she did so.

There were plenty who would tell them that dressing as boys argued against their place in life and therefore against God's choice to make them female. For the moment, Brina refused to allow that to keep her from escaping. Her future was twinkling with promise just on the other side of the walls. What did she care if the Douglas despised her for her actions? Court was not a place that she longed to be. Besides, in time their success would be admired, even if it was despised today.

That was Scottish humor.

"Yer brother is a good man, Vanora."

"He must be to have ye going to such trouble to fetch me." The girl handed her a bonnet, which sat on her head quite comfortably, but it failed to hide the length of her hair.

"Pull yer plaid up; it's still cold enough."

The length of plaid that was draped across their backs had several purposes, and one was to be lifted up and over the head to help keep boys warm. Dawn was now fully lighting the horizon. In spite of the frozen landscape, there were foot trails to mark where the servants had already been. Even at such an early hour, horses were being saddled and taken from the stables, while others arrived and needed tending. The back gate was where food came into the palace. There were carts being pulled in so that the cooks might impress the nobles within.

There was also a steady stream of empty carts and servants making their way out of the gate. Douglas retainers stood watch, stopping some carts to inspect them.

"The yokes will hide our hair." Vanora pointed to wooden yokes that were leaning against the stable wall. They were used to help a boy carry two buckets at once and shoulder the load more easily.

"Ye are clever."

Brina placed one across her shoulders and looked about for buckets to attach to each rope that hung from the ends. She didn't bother to worry that the buckets were empty, for it would appear that they had delivered their wares.

"Do ye think we'll make it?"

Vanora spoke in a tiny voice, but it increased in volume as she heard herself actually daring to speak.

"It's better than nae trying. We may be women, but that does no' mean we have no right to happiness."

"I've been told that." Vanora was no longer hesitant to voice her thoughts. She spoke them clearly and with venom. "But they could nae force me to believe such. I want to try."

There was a note in her voice that tugged at Brina's heart, but it also inspired her to begin walking toward the gate. Victory never went to the coward, but just possibly, today it might go to the meek.

They lowered their heads and fell into line with other merchants who had made their deliveries, each step feeling awkward because Brina tried to decide if she was moving too briskly or stiffly. Her heart was hammering so hard and fast inside her chest, Brina was certain that it would be heard by the Douglas retainers or that her face might be bright red from her distress.

Only fate knew if they would succeed or fail. But it was too late to turn back.

❧

Connor listened for his men, waiting for the owl screech. They hadn't all left together because that would have alerted someone to what they were about. The sun rose as more of his retainers joined him. Among the frozen branches of the forest, they concealed themselves and kept their horses quiet.

"Waiting is no' something ye do well, Connor."

Quinton Cameron slid up beside him and gained a calculated look from Connor.

"Now dinna be glaring at me like that, man. If I had nae brought fair Brina here, ye would no' have this opportunity to reclaim yer sister."

Connor continued to glare at Quinton. "If I forgive ye too soon, I'll never sleep peaceful again for thinking on what ye will do next."

Quinton smirked at him. "Well, yer sister is a pretty little thing."

"Do nae tempt me to return this by sinking it into yer shoulder." Connor pulled the dirk that was still in the top of his boot and offered it to Quinton.

"I might be tempting ye, but ye're wise enough to know that my method was the only one that would have made the lieutenant general bring yer sister out of the Highlands."

"A fact that has vexed me sorely, because I will find myself forgiving ye, Quinton Cameron."

He'd ridden the night more times than he could count in his quest to catch the Douglas moving his sister between their castles and holdings. He'd never been able to discover exactly where she was, and Quinton Cameron was more cunning than he had given the man credit for.

"I still want to knock yer jaw loose."

"I'll remember that, but for the moment let us fan out, for I believe the Douglas will have the notion that we are waiting for the women. They know full well that only Brina went to fetch Vanora."

Connor moved away, climbing through nearest the tree trunks where the snow had yet to reach. It made for a difficult journey; one that required skill if he didn't want to allow snapping limbs to announce his position.

But he was a Highlander, and he just hoped that Brina was enough of one too, because today would be the test of it.

Vanora was stronger than she appeared. Brina never heard a complaint from the girl as the day grew longer, and they still had not reached any of the clansmen they might feel safe with.

They'd left through the back gate of the palace, which set them in the opposite direction from where Connor would be waiting for them. Walking down the road was sure to see them found out, so she took Vanora deep into the thicket before they began to pick their way around the palace. It was a great distance; one that looked impossible to cover. They had had to lie down too many times to count, because pounding hooves announced the coming of mounted men. There was no way to tell before they were sighted just what colors those men would be wearing, so she had tugged Vanora down where they could not be seen. Every muscle ached before noon, and by sunset Vanora looked as though she were as cold as the snow.

"The darkness will make the going faster."

Vanora only nodded, but Brina could see the doubt in her young eyes. That same worry chewed at her, because once night fell, she would not be able to see any man's colors. The Douglas would be looking for them now; there was no doubt in her mind of that. But Vanora's hand hanging on to the plaid that was belted about Brina's waist kept her going. The sun sank slowly and disappeared, leaving them at the mercy of the elements.

Once the darkness surrounded them, her senses heightened. Every sound became louder, and the shadows suddenly looked alive. In that time before the moon rose, they sat still because there was no way to tell the direction to travel. More hooves approached, but these did not thunder past. Brina caught herself staring at the torch this party carried. That single point of light was like the scent of food to the starving; she was hypnotized by it, leaning forward just because she longed to feel the heat.

"There… in the trees."

Too late, she recalled how firelight shone off the eyes of animals.

She gasped and grabbed Vanora before plunging off into the darkness in the hope of finding a hiding place. They could hear the horses trampling the snow and brittle limbs of trees while the torches danced about. It was difficult to decide which way to go, and the horses sounded like they were closing in on them.

"Stay down. I'll draw them away." Brina pushed Vanora to the ground at the base of a tree, just inside of a snowbank. "Do nae look at the torches."

"I will nae."

Brina couldn't stay to hear more; she climbed through branches too quickly, and several snapped after scratching across her thighs beneath the kilt she wore. When she had covered enough distance, she turned and looked at the light.

"There… hurry up, ye fools!"

They began to ride her down, some of them coming up in front of her, while another pair remained behind her.

"I've got ye now, wench. No one evades the Douglas."

The horses crunched the snow all around her, while the men angled the torches down to illuminate her features.

"Which one is it?"

"I dinna know, but she's dressed as a boy."

There were grumbles about her that bordered on curses.

"Who are ye?"

Brina continued to move, slowly stepping back between two large tress that had limbs thick enough to make the horses refuse to follow her.

"Come out of there. Ye're caught now."

Brina took another step.

"Keep going back into the shadows, and I'll be happy to join ye, wench."

There was a chuckle from the man who spoke, but one of his comrades took issue with him.

"Twelve is too young, and the earl will want her back as a maiden."

The leader cursed at him. "That is no' Lindsey's sister. Look at her tits. They're too plump. That's Lindsey's bride, and sinking my cock between her thighs will be a good payment for this day's work that she's put us all to."

There were a few agreements. Brina suddenly gasped as the snow crunched directly behind her. It was the only warning she got that some of the men had dismounted and sneaked up on her. They laughed as she struggled, but twisted her arms behind her back brutally. Tears flooded her eyes as they forced her forward and into the light cast by the torches their comrades held.

"Well done, lads! Well done indeed."

"But where is the other one?"

The leader spit on the ground. "Who cares? Let her cower in a ditch for the time being. We have a pretty little treat to enjoy, and she'll stay where she is if she does nae want to get a taste of what a man takes from a woman who has led him on a chase."

The men behind her pushed her forward, and she went, grateful to be released. They laughed and rubbed their hands together while their eyes shone with growing lust. She turned in a circle and counted five of them, but there was not a single friendly face among them. It was suddenly clear why women chose to die in a keep rather than be taken alive by the enemy when a castle was overrun.

"Do ye have no honor?"

Their leader scoffed at her. "The same amount that ye displayed when ye walked up to my kinsmen in a bride of Christ's robe."

His horse danced around, fighting against his hold on the reins, because he wasn't paying attention to the angle of his torch. The fire terrified the animal, and it pranced in another circle, coming closer and closer to her. The men behind her jumped back away from the panicking animal.

Brina held her place, her eyes focused on the bow that hung off the back of the man's saddle. She must be mad to take the chance, but her eyes fell on that bow like a message sent straight from heaven. She reached up as the horse danced by and pulled it free along with the quiver, for they had only been looped over a button so that they might be hefted in a moment.

She stumbled backward, even as she fitted the bow into her hands by feel. The kilt made it very easy to climb the tree nearest her and gain an advantage over the group threatening her.

"Ye stupid wench, what do ye think ye will accomplish with that? The bow takes skill to use."

She had the skill, but lacked the experience of actually sending an arrow through a man's flesh, but she swore that she would not hesitate.

"Go on with ye. I'm warning ye, I know what I'm doing."

"The hell ye do, and the moment that I show ye how easy it is to rip that bow from yer grip, I am going to demonstrate the true purpose yer weak woman's flesh was created for."

He slid out of the saddle and sank his torch into the snow. Brina heard Bran's voice rise from her memory, instructing her on how to hold the bow just firmly enough to keep it steady. She pulled the string back and felt the arrow notch into the string perfectly while she looked down the shaft and across the sharpened head toward her target, her fingertips feeling the goose feathers set into the end of the arrow to help it fly true and straight to where she aimed it.

"I'm coming for ye, wench."

She let the arrow loose, and it cut through the air with a sharp sound.

"Ye bitch!" The Douglas retainer collapsed to the surface of the snow, his body crushing through the frozen layer on top while the arrow buried itself in the top of his thigh, exactly where she had aimed.

"Take him and go, or I swear my next arrow will bury itself in one of yer bellies."

"You cannae hit us all!" her first victim snarled. His face was a twisted mask of rage as he cursed at her.

"But I will strike at least two. Which of you is willing to die for the rape yer comrades will enjoy once yer blood is spilled onto the snow?"

Brina held another arrow ready, and this time she kept it higher, her attention on the men who had dismounted and were clustered around their fallen leader. The torch burned steadily where it was stuck into the snow, providing light. She watched the men look at one another before they hauled the first man off the snow and helped him back onto his horse. The arrow still protruded from his thigh because it would have to be removed when there was someone there to stem the bleeding once it was pulled.

His men all regained their saddles, and there was a sinister snicker from her victim when they positioned themselves alongside him and drew their own bows.

"Now who will die, witch?"

She bit her lip to contain the small sound of regret. She would not die a coward. Connor's face rose from her memory, and she focused on it and the love she was sure she felt for him. All the struggle suddenly seemed so foolish, for she had squandered precious time. Life truly was too short, and the last few moments of hers passed slower than any others.

But she smiled because love had made the lack of time worth it. She might have lived for decades at the abbey, but she would not trade those years for the time she had known with Connor Lindsey.

"Frightened now, aren't ye, wench?"

"No, I am content, and I shall no' hesitate to loose this arrow. One of ye shall fall along with me. I promise ye that."

"Stupid witch—"

Brina heard the swoosh of the arrows being let free, but she didn't feel them puncture her skin. Her own remained in her grip, in spite of her threat to send it into one of their bellies. Something held her back; maybe it was the joy that she cherished so much.

There was an odd gasping sound before the riders in front of her slumped forward, their hands going to their midsections before, one by one, they fell from their saddles. Their bodies hit the snow with a crunching sound, and they withered in the final moments of life before they all stilled.

"Brina Chattan, kindly do nae loose that arrow into any of my men."

The screech of an owl had her gasping and lowering the bow. She stared at the torch and watched as a form walked into the light. A huge man who came close enough for her to see his face.

She smothered a cry of joy with the back of her hand before putting the bow over her shoulder and jumping to the ground. Connor kicked the torch over, and it died in a sizzle against the snow, leaving them in darkness.

That did not keep her from finding him. He clasped her in his arms, pulling her tightly against his body as she smothered her cries against his chest.

"Ye told me she was a hellcat, but I'll admit that I thought ye were just bragging."

Brina lifted her face and snarled at the sound of Quinton Cameron's voice. He was only a shadow standing a few feet away from Connor.

Quinton laughed at her snarl, shaking his large

head. "And I never thought to see my good friend Connor here holding a lad against him, but I cannae argue with the evidence before me."

"We dressed as boys to escape the palace." She suddenly pushed away from Connor, but he resisted her efforts, keeping a firm arm around her waist.

"Vanora... I left her out in the darkness... over there, I think. Some of the others might find her. We've been hearing riders all day."

"As have we, lass, but we'll nae be defeated at this late stage of the game."

Quinton sent out a cry that sounded like a raven. He winked at her when she stared at him.

"I told ye that Connor and I were friends, lass, and that didna happen once we were men."

"Aye, that's a fact." Connor put out his hand, and Quinton clasped his wrist while he did the same. There was a wealth of meaning in the gesture, a unity between the two lairds that touched her heart because she had recently realized just how precious life was. She placed her own hand on top of their wrists before another raven's cry drew Quinton's attention.

Connor instantly took her toward the ground, his hand even coming up to push her face down so that no light might reflect off her eyes. The snow was bitterly cold, but she forced herself to remain still and not crack the icy surface.

The raven's cry came again, this time much closer and in a different rhythm—three cries together, a pause, and three more.

Quinton pushed himself up, and Connor did the same while pulling her off the ground.

"I found a lad who claims he's a Lindsey, even if he is wearing a Douglas plaid. But I don't think he trusts me a bit."

Quinton's second in command pulled a slight figure forward.

"Vanora?"

"Brina?"

The girl's voice trembled, but hearing it was too sweet to quibble over the details. Connor reached out and clasped her hand, his arm trembling just a tiny amount.

"Let's quit this demon-invested thicket, lads. I've a hunger for the Highlands."

❧

They rode through the night, using the moonlight to guide their way. There was still the danger of being confronted by Douglas retainers, but Connor hoped that speed might prove the deciding factor. They stopped only to allow the horses to drink, and the beasts didn't seem to mind being pushed so long. Once the sun rose, more Lindsey and Cameron riders joined them from where they had been sent farther up the road to disguise how many men Connor and Quinton were riding with.

"Archibald Douglas might be the lieutenant general, but while he's sitting in his palace, the Highlanders are nae waiting on his word to keep our own land safe." Connor's voice was smug with his pride, but Brina still felt a prickle of worry go down her back.

"Do nae ye worry that he'll retaliate?"

"I doubt he will, for once we reach Birch Stone, he'll know that he's been bested and will have to turn his attention on to no' being beaten by his own kind."

"A fate he so richly deserves."

Connor shot her a grin. "Careful, Brina. Cameron might just become jealous of me if ye continue to display that spirit of yers."

"What makes ye think I am not already, Lindsey?" Quinton pulled his stallion up, and it danced on its hind legs for a few steps. But the Cameron laird only smiled, enjoying the display of power from the animal. He reached down and gave it a pat on the side of its dark neck. Enjoyment sparkled in his eyes when he raised them to her.

"I wish ye luck... *hellcat*."

He let out a raven's cry, and his men followed him inland. Connor chuckled, and Brina turned her displeasure on to him.

"I am no' a hellcat."

One of his light-colored eyebrows rose.

"No, Brina Chattan, ye are my hellcat."

She huffed and glared at his smug expression. "I do nae understand why I love ye."

He leaned across the space between them and pressed a hard kiss against her pouting lips.

"I will be happy to remind ye just as soon as we reach Birch Stone."

She planted her hand against his chest to push him away. "Trust a man to think that is all there is to love."

Connor remained in place, her efforts gaining her no more than they had the first time he had ridden with her toward his home. But today his eyes were full of something else—a tenderness that stole her breath.

"I ken that there is more, lass, and I plan to spend a great number of years showing ye how much I ken that…"

❦

Quinton Cameron pulled his men up near dawn. Robert Chattan and his men met him in the middle of the land that led to Lindsey territory.

"It seems that ye have been busy, Cameron."

Quinton smirked, uncaring of the fact that Robert frowned. The Chattan laird pointed a thick finger at him.

"Ye did nae need to tell Roan McLeod about Kaie's change of heart. Women often have conflicting emotions before they wed. I had faith in Roan winning her affections."

"He had the right to know, Robert."

"Maybe so, but that ends my chance to form an alliance with him, for I'll have to send Deirdre to the church now."

Quinton shook his head. "Robert, ye are too smart a man to ignore the obvious. Get yerself off and catch that woman who ran away with yer fourth daughter."

Robert Chattan's face turned red. "Ruth swore she'd carve off me cock if she ever laid eyes on it again."

Quinton leaned down over the neck of his stallion. "I think the idea of seeing her daughter wed to Roan McLeod will temper her rage."

"Think again. Ruth refused the match her father made for her and refused me when I tried to wed her so that Erlina would nae be a bastard."

Quinton grinned, which caused Robert to raise one eyebrow. "What do ye know, man?"

Quinton nudged his horse forward, and stopped when he was alongside Robert.

"I know that Roan McLeod is nae content to have his father displeased with him. If I know Roan, and I assure ye that I do, he's most likely already off to deal with securing yer fourth daughter."

Quinton began to ride past.

"But she's a bastard."

"Something I suggest ye rectify before the McLeod take offense."

Robert Chattan cursed. He watched the Cameron ride across his land toward their own and spit out another few words of profanity.

But he suddenly grinned, because he felt more alive than he had in a long time.

"Well, lads, maybe it's time for me to take a wife again." He looked at the snow and nodded. Spring was going to be very interesting.

❧

Brina and Connor reached Birch Stone at sunset, and the bells rang along the walls while the retainers left behind to guard the castle leaned over the wall to wave to them. Connor rode through the front gate and on to the second one before stopping. Brina slid from the saddle, grateful to be on her own two feet once again. Her knees wobbled, but she was distracted from her own discomforts when Connor walked toward Vanora and lifted her off the horse that she looked frozen atop.

"This is my sister, Vanora, back on Lindsey land where she belongs. Well done, lads! Well done, indeed."

A cheer echoed throughout the yard, the bells ringing again, this time in celebration. Maura was sobbing, her face red but split with a smile. She snapped her fingers at her maids, but it wasn't necessary, for they all surged forward to cluster around Vanora and Brina while pulling them up the stairs and into the keep.

Brina smiled, because without a doubt, she was home.

Maura had begun the process of making baths ready for both girls, when she suddenly stopped and fixed Brina with a questioning look.

"Are ye married yet, mistress?"

"No, I am nae."

The head of house sighed. "Well, it seems as things are no' quite ready for celebrating, then."

Brina sighed, for she was going back to confession, and she looked down at herself, still wearing the male clothing that she'd used to escape in, and knew without a doubt that she was going to be barefoot for a much longer time.

Bugger it!

❧

Bathing had a way of soothing away tension. Brina stifled a yawn as she pulled a brush through her drying hair. It was floating in a soft cloud around her now, and the underrobe that she wore was soft enough to sleep in. The candles lighting the bathroom helped her slip further into sleepiness, and she stood up while Maura and her staff were still clustered around Vanora.

"Good night."

Vanora sent her a wide-eyed look, but the girl's cheeks were flushed with enjoyment too. Brina left her to the coddling she figured the girl was owed. She climbed the stairs toward the promise of the chamber that Connor had created to lavish attention upon her, but when she opened the inner door, she discovered that the ornate bed and plush accessories were missing. All that sat in the room now were chests and one table with several small boxes on its top. She walked into the room, feeling chilled when she had no true reason to be cold because of the heavy dressing gown that Maura had taken delight in draping over her shoulders. But at the same time her heart was filled with a sense of familiarity.

There was no light in the room, forcing her to take the candle lantern that hung in the back stairwell with her. Once she held it up to cast its speckles of light around the room, she noticed something else on the tabletop. It was light colored, and when she moved closer, she identified the sleeve that she had sewn.

"I couldn't leave it behind. Just do nae go telling Cameron that. The man doesn't believe in love."

Brina didn't jump. Maybe it was the fact that she felt his presence in the chamber, in spite of change in furnishings. She suddenly understood how ghosts might cling to a castle so long after their deaths. She felt the joy that she had experienced in the room so strongly that it didn't matter what filled it.

"Come, Brina. Quinton interrupted me giving ye a gift when he stole ye."

"A gift? But this chamber was a fine gift as it was."

Connor held out his hand for hers. "Trust me, lass."

She placed her hand into his, and he took her through the doorway again. He led her up another flight of stairs and then another, until they were at the top of the tower. He pulled the door open, and she walked past him.

Inside was everything that had been below. The fine bed with its goose-down coverlet and soft, creamy sheets. The table and chairs were there with candles flickered from where they were held in silver candelabras.

The difference was that the window shutters were open, and the windows were wider, with iron supports to keep the stone in place. The sound of the ocean filled the chamber, the scent of the salt water tickling her nose.

"Since ye seemed to like the ocean, I thought ye might enjoy this chamber instead."

"It's magical."

She walked to the windows and looked out over the water that glittered with silver moonlight. She could hear the sound of the waves crashing, and come daylight, there would no doubt be the sounds of sea birds.

"Which is exactly what I wish our lives to be."

Connor came up behind her, his arms encircling her waist. She turned toward him with the sea breeze chilling her cheek while she stretched up to meet his kiss.

Fate was kind indeed.

෧෩

"What do ye mean ye won't marry me, Brina Chattan?"

Connor growled at her as he shoved the bedding back and rose from it in nothing but what nature had gifted him with.

Which was plenty, in her opinion.

"I said I cannae marry you, no' that I will nae."

Connor stopped and propped his hands on his hips. "Make sense, woman, because I swear I'm getting ready to spank ye if ye do nae come down to the church and wed me before supper."

Brina shrugged into her underrobe and tried to keep her eyes from lowering to where his cock stood erect in spite of the cold ocean breeze blowing in through the open window shutters.

"That will be up to the priest. I have to go to confession again and complete my penance before I can marry ye."

"Ye already did that."

She turned on him as her fingers flew through the process of braiding her hair.

"And then I helped Vanora escape, and in the doing, I did many a thing that I fear the priest will nae be pleased with. But I did succeed in getting yer sister out of there, so ye may just wait while I satisfy the church, Connor Lindsey, or I will refuse to wed ye just to spite that temper of yers."

He suddenly chuckled. "I am no' the only one with a temper... hellcat."

"I dinna like being called that."

His lips lifted into a smug grin. "I know, but since ye are nae my wife, ye cannae be telling me what to call ye, lass. That is the privilege of the mistress of Birch Stone and no other."

She snarled at him but worked a lace through the eyelets of her overrobe before grabbing a veil and heading out of the chamber to seek the priest. She heard Connor laughing, low and deep, as she descended the first few steps.

Fate had a misplaced sense of humor, and that was for sure.

❧

The priest began fingering his robe before she made it past the third sentence in her confession. She watched the man's eyes widen as she continued and saw him swallow roughly when she came to the part about stealing the vestments.

"Ye stole Mother Church's property?" His voice was high-pitched and his lips bloodless.

"We moved it and left it safe and sound where it might be found."

He made a strangled sound beneath his breath.

"Shall I continue?" Brina asked.

The priest gulped. "Ye have more transgressions to confess?"

"Well, yes, ye see, in order to slip past the guards at the gates who were waiting to catch two women, we dressed as boys, and we did in fact steal the clothing, for it was all we had to wear; however, we left our clothing in place of what we took. Does that matter at all?"

"It does no'!"

Brina drew in a deep breath and savored the feel of her stockings and boots. She'd be losing them soon enough, it appeared.

"Well, we dressed as boys, and then after hiding all

day, I had to shoot a Douglas with an arrow in the thigh when the man threatened to rape me."

"How did ye know how to use the bow?" The priest's voice was loud enough to startle the two boys cleaning the altar. They turned their heads to look back at them, only to receive a furious look from their superior. Both boys snapped back around and remained that way.

"My father had me taught to hunt with the bow so that I might provide meat to the convent."

The priest began to mutter prayers, his voice shaky as he shook his head.

"How is my bride doing, Father? I do hope she manages to gain yer approval so that we might be wed at last."

Connor was turned out in the finest clothing she'd ever seen him wear. His kilt was a new one and pleated perfectly, with the back falling longer than the front. His boots were polished, and even his bonnet looked new. There was a brooch with an amber stone set into silver that she had never seen before, and he wore a doublet with silver buttons all neatly fashioned up to his throat.

"A husband is exactly what this woman needs!" The priest slapped his thigh and snorted. "Yes, I insist that ye marry immediately and take her in hand before her behavior inspires mass rebellion against God's order."

"Of course, Father." Connor walked down the center of the sanctuary as a flurry of footsteps came behind him. People poured in through the doorway the moment he cleared it, all of them scrambling to dip their fingers into the holy water and make the sign of the cross over themselves while they hurried into position to watch the nuptials of their laird.

Brina never rose off her knees but felt Connor join her. The priest began their wedding before she heard the people behind them finish surging through the doorway. The priest rushed through the prayers, barely taking time to draw breath in his hurry to pronounce them married. The moment he did, the priest gave a snort that drew a chuckle from her husband. He covered it with a cough as he tugged her down the aisle and out of the church.

"Do nae be so smug."

He chuckled again. "And why no'? Are ye nae pleased to be my wife?"

Brina cast him a slant-eyed look, enjoying the way he tried to guess what she was thinking. Flirting was definitely something she was going to have to learn about, but she did know a thing or two about teasing, and Connor Lindsey needed to be given back a measure of what he was serving up to her.

"Well... yes... I am pleased about being wed..."

She kept her voice even and dull before lifting her eyelids and fluttering them while her husband frowned at her lack of enthusiasm.

"And what?" he demanded.

"Well, I find myself right pleased to still have my shoes."

He growled, but it was in jest, because his blue eyes twinkled with merriment.

"We'll see about what ye have, madam!"

He leaned over and hoisted her over one broad shoulder, to the delight of his clan. They cheered him on as he carried her into the tower and up every single step until they reached their chamber. He tossed her onto the bed in a tangle of robes and braids, and she couldn't have been happier.

Fate had dropped her exactly where she needed to be.

THE END

About the Author

Mary Wine is a multipublished author in romantic suspense, fantasy, and Western romance; now her interest in historical reenactment and costuming has inspired her to turn her pen to historical romance. She lives with her husband and sons in Southern California, where the whole family enjoys participating in historical reenactments.

From

HIGHLAND HEAT

1439

SPRING WAS BLOWING ON THE BREEZE.

Deirdre lifted her face and inhaled, closing her eyes and smiling as she caught a hint of heather in the air.

A memory stirred in the dark corner of her mind where she had banished it. It rose up, reminding her of a spring two years ago when a man had courted her with pieces of heather and soft words of flattery.

False words.

The sound of approaching horses drew her attention. The nuns who had been down near the river running behind the church came hurrying up the hill. These were uncertain times, with a boy wearing the crown of Scotland. The undyed robes that the women wore flapped up, showing their ankles.

The sisters all clustered together, pushing their way towards the sanctuary of the church. Deirdre lifted a hand to shade her eyes so she might see the colors the men were wearing. They were Highlanders, with their knee-high boots laced tight over antler buttons. They rode their horses hard, but the animals were strong stock and took to the pace easily. A long sword was strapped to each man's back with the hilt secured at the left shoulder so he might draw his weapon in a single fluid motion. The folds of their plaids bounced with the motion of the horses but beneath the yellow, orange, and black wool she could see their thighs tightly clutching the backs of their stallions.

They were Camerons and she didn't need to wait for the dust to settle to know that their laird was among them. She felt the damned man's eyes on her even before she set her gaze upon him. Quinton Cameron was just as huge and arrogant as she remembered him. She felt her temper stir when the man set his blue eyes on her and grinned. The way he looked at her sent a shiver down her spine. It was indecent and, to her shame, exciting.

"I swear on all that's holy that I never expected to see ye here, Deirdre Chattan."

Quinton's stallion perked its ears and the man reached down to pat its sweaty neck with a soothing motion, never taking his eyes off her.

Deirdre frowned. "Well, ye are the one who suggested it to my father, so enjoy gloating."

Several of the nuns gasped from where they were peeking around the large arched doorway of the church. Quinton Cameron laughed at her audacity, tipping his head back and allowing the sound to fill the morning air. Behind him his retainers chuckled, sharing their laird's amusement, but they kept their eyes on her.

Quinton lowered his chin and considered her

from beneath his dark brows. The man was a dark Highlander. His hair was true black and his eyes the shade of coldest ice. Beyond being laird of the Cameron, the man also held the hereditary title of Earl of Liddell. Such noble peerage stations were becoming very rare in Scotland.

"Laird Cameron, what brings ye to our convent?"

Deirdre's sister Kaie stepped forward to greet the newcomers. She was training to become the mother superior and it would be her duty to welcome all who came to the doors of the church. Kaie tucked her hands into the wide sleeves of her over robe and faced the earl serenely.

Quinton Cameron dismounted out of respect for her position among the inhabitants of the holy order. The air filled with the sound of leather creaking as his men followed suit. The church was a unifying presence among the clans. Laird Cameron might be one of the highest ranking nobles in the land, but the church was set above earthly titles. Even the king knelt in church.

"Forgive me, sister, but I plan to search every inch of this Abbey."

Kaie drew in a harsh breath. "Men do not belong in this convent. It is a place for those women who have devoted their lives to God."

"It's also a place for anyone seeking sanctuary, sister. I know well that ye are bound to offer charity to those who appeal to ye for it." Quinton's gaze strayed to Deirdre.

"Of course that is true, but ye do not need to search the Abbey for my sister. She stands before you, Laird Cameron."

Deirdre felt a tingle race down her spine but her logic firmly argued against there being any reason for Quinton Cameron to seek her out. His face didn't give her any clue as to his mood. He hid behind an emotionless mask but something glittered in his eyes that irritated her. How arrogant the man was, she thought.

"Would ye be relieved to hear me say that I've come for yer sister?" Quinton aimed his attention back toward Kaie. "Is that yer way of telling me she has yet to take the veil? Or that ye would be gladly rid of her?"

Kaie stiffened. "Unkindness has no place here, nor does judgment."

Quinton's expression hardened. "Aye sister, I trust in yer devotion enough to know ye will nae tell me if the one I seek is here or not. Which is why I plan to send me men inside to search."

Her sister gasped, horrified by the idea of having the Abbey invaded by the Cameron retainers standing behind their laird. Quinton's face reflected his distaste but there was also hard determination shining in his eyes.

Kaie stepped back, as if she might prevent the invasion by blocking the door with her body. "Ye shall not." Her words were whispered and the men behind the earl didn't care to hear her displeasure.

The Cameron retainers surged forward but Quinton raised one hand and they froze instantly. Deirdre stepped up beside her sister. The Cameron laird considered her with a slight spark of amusement flickering in his eyes.

"My sister told ye no. Only English scum trespass

against the tradition of the church. Men do not enter the convent; do nae shame yer clan colors by acting like an invading army."

There was a soft murmur of agreement from the nuns hiding behind the doorway but only Kaie stood with her in the yard against the men whom they could only turn away with words.

The Camerons didn't look as though they were going to depart simply because Kaie had reminded them of church tradition. Several of them glared at her for comparing them to the English.

"My apologies, Kaie Chattan, but I will be searching this structure from the belfry to the privies."

There was no hint of weakness in his tone and he moved forward, all of his men doing the same. Deirdre refused to give way, standing her ground and tipping her chin up so that she could glare at him. Quinton Cameron didn't stop until his boots were touching the hem of her robes.

"I am nae impressed with ye, Laird Cameron. Tell me what ye seek and stop insisting on going where ye know men do nae belong. I am no' a liar."

"I seek the queen, Joan Beaufort, and if she is here, I intend to find her."

Deirdre felt her eyes widen but a moment later she let out a hiss that was full of anger. Quinton Cameron swept her right off her feet, cradling her like a child in his arms as her father had done when she was half grown.

"Put me down!"

He chuckled at her instead and carried her through the open doorway and into the first chamber of the Abbey.

"I warned ye, but I suppose I should nae be surprise
that ye did not heed me. I noticed when I first met ye
that ye are a true hellion." He lowered her to her feet.
Deirdre sent a vicious shove at him but the man didn't
budge even a step.

The man smirked at her as his men swarmed around
them and into the sanctuary. The nuns squealed and
fled toward the yard. There were too many bodies
trying to use the doorway and Deirdre was crushed up
against Quinton. He rocked slightly but his arms came
about her, protecting her from the surge of bodies.

"Take yer arms away." Deirdre didn't need to raise
her voice because she was pressed against the man
from her ankles to her head.

"Well now, hellion, there isna any place else to put
them, except between us."

He whispered against her ear, a hint of enjoyment
in his tone. She bristled but couldn't push herself
away from him with so many of the nuns trying to
get past them. His arms wrapped all the way around
her back and she felt his hand cup her nape. She
shivered, the contact jarring to her senses. She should
have felt only repulsion for his touch but her body
betrayed her as sensation rippled down her back, a
sense of enjoyment that was deeply rooted in her
flesh. He slid his hand up to grasp her thick braid
where it was looped up beneath the simple linen
hood she wore.

"So ye have nae taken vows of any sort."

There was a touch of heat in his voice that stroked
a memory she had tried hard to banish from her
mind. There had been a moment a year past when

they had been just this close and the arrogant man had stolen a kiss from her. Passion flickered inside her, refusing to obey her order never to rise again. She growled at the disobedience of her flesh and shoved away from Quinton.

Enough of the nuns had made it into the yard now, allowing her to step back from him, but he took the opportunity to stroke her back and sides as she moved, his hands open, the fingers sliding over her curves with unmistakable experience. There was a flicker of enjoyment in his eyes that irritated her because she liked knowing that he found her body pleasing.

Another betrayal from her flesh...

"What promises I make are none of yer concern, Laird Cameron. I live here, so ye'll be keeping yer hands off me."

"Is that a fact, Deirdre Chattan? Ye are nae a sister with that thick hair still long enough to cover a man's chest. Ye're a woman who is still searching for her place—maybe ye have found that today."

Close to him, his meaning was clear as daylight.

Available March 2011